Cowboys Don't Walk
A Tale of Two
by Anne Goddard Charter

Enjoy,

Anne Goddard Charter

December, 1999

**Western Organization
of Resource Councils
Billings, Montana**

Also by Anne Goddard Charter
Four Dollars and Sixty Cents Short...The Battle of the Bulls

ACKNOWLEDGMENTS

This book received the editing skills of Elizabeth Wood and Pat Dawson. Dennis Boyd designed the cover.

As my manuscript was in longhand, it had to be typed into a computer. Joe and grandson Boyd Charter instructed me on the use of their computer. Donna Charter, Sue Strosky, Marvel Strickland, and Janel Miller helped computerize it. Dale Tushman said "that is your title." And Kathleen Durham insisted I write a preface.

For reading the manuscript and making corrections and suggestions, credit to Louise Rodormer, Peggy Goddard and Pete Mikkelson. Wilbur Wood put the finishing touches on the final chapters, and Jeanne Charter helped herd us toward publication.

To all the above and others who encouraged me, many thanks.

DISCLAIMER

Because factual accuracy is neither my forte nor my goal; because people relate differently to the same or similar experiences; because memory does not record the way a camera does; and because even photographs, videos, and written history can distort, I am including some space in this book so you, the reader, can write your own version of events, comment when you disagree, or start your own story to hand on to descendants.

Printed on recycled paper.

Table of Contents

DEDICATION

To those who preceded me,
the deserved amount of respect due to each;
to those included in these pages,
apologies for any misrepresentation;
to those who follow,
God speed.

Courtesy of Terrence Moore

INTRODUCTION

This book is about Boyd Charter and Anne, your author. It started as an autobiography to preserve family history, both Boyd's and mine. It has become a family saga which spans the 20th Century, the transition period between the romance of the Old West and the emergence of the Modern West into the 21st Century.

It is about our family operating a ranch in south central Montana and what happened when everything we held dear was threatened by strip-mining. We took a stand.

"When we die, America dies." These are Boyd's words spoken in the 1970's, picked up, quoted, interpreted from coast to coast. What did they mean? Boyd explains:

> I said once that when we die America dies. I'm not trying to insinuate that if Anne and I or any of our neighbors die, America dies. We're not that important to America. But when it comes to people who have respect for the land and are trying to save the land from being destroyed, when people like us die, who will stand up here and fight for it. . . turn their money down and stand for what they think is right? When people like us die, America is dying.
>
> I'll die soon. I want to die with my self respect. I want to die knowing that I wasn't pushed aside or bought or scared to my groveling knees by the almighty dollar. This we couldn't stomach. We had to act.
>
> And so we became just one more example of the David and Goliath story in the sense that we took on the giant, industry, armed only with our passions and what we thought was right. We were fighting for the "Last Best Place" and the Western traditions that gave it its name. Freedom and independence, yes, but not exercised at the expense of others; old fashioned integrity, yes, where a handshake is your bond, and that ingrained love and respect for all of God's creation. Our strength comes from the land. Will this land be able to change the people who are now coming to Montana? Or will the people change the land?

Boyd felt this way:

> I say we have to stand and fight to preserve America. We have no choice at all. We have our backs against the wall. We are going to be the last generation of Western men if we lose. There is no place to pioneer anymore. Nowhere to go. Nowhere to hide. When we die, America dies."

COWBOYS DON'T WALK

We were married in the fall of 1942 just before Boyd was to leave for boot camp. The date for his induction into the Navy was drawing near. "Why the Navy, Boyd?" I asked. "Why didn't you wait to be drafted? You might have gotten a deferment because of the ranch." He replied, "I don't go for deferments, and of course I joined the Navy; cowboys don't walk!"

ROMANCE IN JACKSON HOLE

"You can't run a dude ranch without female help." With these words, I landed work for Frances Reyburn and myself on the Bar Double R Ranch in Jackson Hole, Wyoming, during the summer of 1942.

Our conversation took place at a kegger at the "Shack on the Mac," a small clubhouse on the Merrimac River in Missouri. Here I met Roy Nehr, who was taking over the McCormick guest ranch on the Gros Ventre River above Jackson Hole. Roy and a group of St. Louis businessmen had bought the ranch as a joint venture, but that hadn't worked out. He was planning to run it as a dude ranch.

For a long time, I had been consumed with the desire to go to Wyoming, lured by the romance of the West and macho cowboys. Having cornered Roy, I volunteered to run his kitchen for him, and Frances said she would manage the cabins. Roy was pleased and commented, "Hired for a free summer, and I'll even throw in a cowboy, Boyd Charter. His family owns one of the finest ranches in the valley."

A city girl, St. Louis born and bred, little did I dream that I would spend the next thirty-five years of my life with this cowboy. It was a union that most deemed ill-matched. The marriage would surely be short-lived. In the pioneer West, women from all walks of life had married cowboys and ranchers. They lived the hard rugged existence of the frontier. But these were modern times. What had the West to offer now?

Filled with excitement and hopes for adventure, Frances and I arrived by train at Gardiner, Montana, a week ahead of the guests. Roy met us and drove us through Yellowstone Park to Jackson, and then up the Gros Ventre River on the hazardous road that led to the ranch.

The first evening at the ranch, Frances and I were sitting on the gate looking down on the Gros Ventre River and across to spectacular Red Mountain where we hoped to see some mountain sheep. I asked Frances if she heard what I heard: the sound of music coming up the road.

As we listened, a herd of bulls came around a bend, lowing softly, with a cowboy herding them. He rode up and said "Pardon me, ma'am, can I bring my bulls through here?" My greenhorn reply was, "I don't know, you'll have to ask the owner, Roy Nehr." We finally caught on to what he meant: get the hell off the gate and out of the way. We moved swiftly! It dawned on us that this was the cowboy, Boyd Charter, and he was stopping at the ranch for the night.

6

This was just the first of many visits he made to the ranch, stopping either on his way up to his cattle, or on the way back to Jackson. Almost every Saturday night was a rendezvous of dudes and cowboys at the town bars. Most of the dudes stayed all summer, and many came back year after year, and were greeted by the local citizenry as old timers.

The highlight of the summer was a week-long pack trip into the alpine backcountry. Boyd was to provide the pack horses and mules, and be our experienced guide. We were to meet at the ranger station at 10 a.m. No Boyd; so we made sandwiches for lunch. The day wore on, still no Boyd; so we had to cook supper there. Roy offered, "I'll make my famous paprika fried potatoes and everyone will forget the delay. Anne, where is the paprika?" I had packed the supplies. A whole pannier had to be unpacked before we found the paprika on the very bottom. Boyd arrived in time for supper. He told us his horses and pack mules had left the country and it took him all day to find them. That night, he hobbled them.

I often said I married Boyd for his mules. They were beguiling, small pack mules, and one large white mule called Pinky. Pinky was not needed, but came anyway, nibbling the flowers like Ferdinand the Bull, and from time to time inspecting the line of riders to be sure everything was to his satisfaction. He was quite smug.

The scenery in the mountains was spectacular. At each change in elevation, there was a different variety of wild flower woven into mountain meadows, often making them a solid color.

On the way home, one of the pack mules went lame. Boyd set out to rope Pinky to take its place. Everyone was watching. Boyd would make his loop, cast it; Pinky would lay back his ears and lower his head. Boyd missed and missed again; everyone laughed and laughed. Finally, Pinky was caught, packed and joined to the pack train. A more dejected mule could not be found. He sulked all the way home.

Arriving back at the ranch in late afternoon, we found the ranch couple, cook and wrangler, had taken off. Luckily, there was chicken we could cook, and Boyd volunteered to make chicken and dumplings. He left a flour trail back and forth across the kitchen, but the results were delicious.

Mrs. Merine came in as replacement cook. She would consult the moon and stars and her geraniums for guidance in everything she did, including her cooking. One time when a roast beef dinner was slightly underdone, she claimed it was the phase of the moon. She proved quite a boon to me, however, explaining Boyd's past, his hang-ups and the girls who were in hot pursuit. She was rooting for me!

Boyd had quite a way with women, especially older women. He was great friends with many dudes who came back year after year. When he was about seventeen years old, Boyd had a job leading dudes on horseback rides. One rich Jewish lady arrived at the dude ranch, scared to death of horses. Boyd was assigned to her for the summer. He led her around on her horse for half the summer, and received her endless thanks and praise for the rest of it. At the end of summer, she wanted to take both her horse and Boyd back to Philadelphia. She wouldn't take no for an answer! Boyd had to flee the country a few days before her departure.

Finally, a very nice dude girl caught him and talked him into a formal wedding. Boyd liked her family, especially an uncle with whom he kept in contact. The marriage was never consummated. She had some sort of hang-up, and after three weeks the marriage was annulled. They parted ways. The girl subsequently had counseling and remarried. Boyd tried to withdraw from the world, so deep was his humiliation. When he finally resurfaced, he vowed he'd never get that involved with a woman again.

However, Mrs. Merine thought this aversion could be overcome. Dude season had merged into hunting season and I had offered to stay on to cook for the hunters. I hoped staying on would give Boyd and me a chance to see each other on a more intimate basis than was possible in the midst of dude ranch activities.

There was a strong bond drawing us together, but Boyd was full of doubts. His first attempt at marriage was a fiasco. Should he try it again? What did he have to offer me? His only possessions were his horses and cowboy gear; his future uncertain as the ranch would probably be sold. I implied that finding him was enough and that I liked what I found. I was willing to take the risks and to go wherever he was led to go.

In the peace and privacy that followed the dude season, Boyd shared his past, and his fear of commitment and an unknown future. He had volunteered for the Navy, rather than be drafted in the Army and have to walk, but he was not to be called until fall. It was possible the family ranch would be sold, as it couldn't be run without him.

Although we were galaxies apart in our background and upbringing, we sensed a common bond: we could trust each other. I was 29, he was 34. We had both done considerable "living," and were anxious to find a life-time mate and settle down. It wasn't exactly a proposal. It was more like a mutual decision to get married. Not a wildly romantic love affair, more a feeling that destiny had brought us together, that we were meant for each other, and we could meet whatever lay ahead.

Except for Mrs. Merine who cheered, his friends and family gave us six months. My St. Louis family was accepting and supportive, as they felt it was high time I got married, but I'm sure they too had their doubts. Our marriage lasted until death us did part: from October 25, 1942 to September 24, 1978, when Boyd died.

We were married in the lodge of the Bar Double R Ranch by a Baptist minister. My parents and my sister, Irene Elder, and Boyd's mother attended. From the ranch family came Roy Nehr and Ralph LeRoc, who was second in command. Ralph had driven us to town on Saturday nights and usually stopped a time or two on the way home for a short nap. Kay Folsam, a dude who had stayed over with me, decorated the lodge and generally took charge of the wedding plans.

We headed for Idaho Falls that afternoon, stopping on top of Teton Pass for Boyd to survey "his country" and to reminisce. Later, when we had a ranch of our own, while driving out to our mountain range, he would stop at the top of the rock cut, look out over 'the land of a thousand hills' and remark "How green is my valley." Little did we know then, this was an almost prophetic remark of the struggle that would ensue over the strip mining of coal on our ranch. Had the strip mining gone ahead as planned, he would have had to use the exact words of Richard D.

Llewellyn's book, *How Green Was My Valley,* which told of the devastating effects that coal mining had on the land and the people in Wales during the early years of this century.

After this warm pause, we continued on to Idaho Falls, where the charms proved to be few. We decided to return to Jackson, where we took a room on the ground floor of the Wort Hotel. It was Jackson's finest, and its charms were many. We were awakened about six the next morning by the sound of a band coming down the hall. Boyd leapt from bed fearing a shivaree, vowing he'd not be caught with his pants down. It turned out, the homecoming football game was that day, and the school band was mustering enthusiasm and support for the team.

That night we were sitting in the small Wort Hotel bar. This was before the hotel's famous Silver Dollar Bar was installed, and a year after the new hotel had opened. We were in a booth facing the door which led to the street, when in came Ivan, straight from a lone summer's vigil in a fire tower. He'd had numerous drinks along the way, and recognizing Boyd, reeled up and threw his arms around him. Boyd greeted him and slapped him on the back. But Jess Wort, who tending bar felt Ivan was imposing on us, ushered him out the door. Ivan promptly crossed the street to his pickup, got out his rifle, and opened fire on the hotel. Everyone dove under booths until the firing stopped. Then Ivan drove off. The only harm done was a few pock-marks around the door. That marked the end of our honeymoon. Boyd and I looked for those marks every time we returned to Jackson.

With the honeymoon over, it is time to look back to our separate beginnings. It was a gradual process, this learning about each other and the oh-such different lives we had led. It was many years later before I had the time or inclination to document any of our past. But the time did come when I began looking back over my life more often than wondering what was ahead. I began jotting down memoirs on miscellaneous bits of paper. I thought the time might come when I would organize them, at least to the extent of putting them in the same shoe box. From time to time I was the recipient of various gems of family and ancestral history which I planned to put in a shoe box labeled genealogy. If I gathered the material perhaps someone would discover it and write a family history. Children are seldom led to such tasks as they have an entirely different view of their growing up years, but grand and great grand children often wish they had asked more questions before it was too late. Perhaps one of them would take on the task.

However, as I became enamored with my past, I was reluctant to turn the telling of it over to another. I had to show how, in spite of our incredibly different backgrounds, a union was formed which defied the odds and produced some surprising results.

RELATIVES GALORE

My life encompassed the best of two worlds: the amenities of an urban social life in St. Louis, Missouri, and the fulfillment of a life on a ranch in Montana. "All Gaul is divided into three parts," as is my life fairly equally divided: birth to marriage, 1913 to 1942; marriage, 1942 to 1978; life after Boyd's death, 1978 until who knows. I shall start with those who preceded me.

George W. Augustine, Jr.

The story of my great grandfather's death would be a fitting story for the television show "Unsolved Mysteries." Articles in the *Summit Beacon* of Akron, Ohio, June 15 and 16, 1853 give the following account:

> The Coroner's Jury were unable to agree on a verdict in regard to Mr. Augustine's death: four believing that death had been occasioned by strangulation; and two that he had accidentally fallen into the canal, death being occasioned by drowning.

The article gave an account of all who had seen him on the fatal day. It continued:

> Some small change, a silver pencil case and other articles were found on his person; but a memorandum book and *porte monie*, both of which is known he carried, and both of which he had been seen to use within 2-4 hours of the time of his disappearance, were missing and have not been found. This, perhaps more than all the other facts, goes to justify a suspicion of violence; and when taken in connection with the fact that he was known to handle a large amount of money and that he engaged extensively in buying wheat at several points on the canal, makes a strong case. It is not supposed, however, that he had much money in his possession. He paid out a large sum in the bank in the afternoon, but not in currency.

It stated that, although his death occurred in a populated area, no cries for help were heard; but, being a feeble man, he could have been easily overcome. Although a recent resident of Akron, according to the paper, he was known as "a man of the strictest integrity and business habits and generous impulses."

The day after he disappeared, toward evening, ". . . the lock tender at lock 15, about a quarter of a mile below the business portion of town, had discovered a dead body; on examining for an obstruction which prevented the gate from opening. It proved to be the body of Mr. Augustine. The face was bruised, there were several liver spots, the eyes were both livid and much swollen, as were the lips, but the body contained little or no water. The appearance of the face indicated in the estimation of many, death by violence; most probably strangulation; as if the hand had been placed over the mouth and nostrils. Yet medical authorities seemed to justify the conclusion that the appearance of the face might be occasioned by accidental drowning, if he had fallen into the lock when it was nearly empty, a distance of 15 or 16 feet."

One wonders why the case was so casually handled. My Aunt Anne, granddaughter of George W. Augustine, Jr., provided me with the newspaper articles, as well as family stories and notes from her journals.

She wrote: "We were told that Grandfather George W. Augustine, Jr.'s ancestors came from Alsace-Lorraine, at the time of political troubles in 1848." This does not fit in with his given age in the articles, however. It seems more likely for his forbearers to have left during the political unrest in 1789, the time of the French Revolution, when Alsace-Lorraine once again came under French rule. The population was a mix of German and French people; Augustine is a German name, but the women have French features and Augustine descendants show characteristics of both races.

George Jr. was thirty years old at the time of his death. He had married Amanda Melvirne Conkey on February 20, 1844, in Tuscaramas, Ohio, at age 21. They had three children. George Hershey Augustine was born in Massilon, Ohio, on August 24, 1848. He was just nine years old when his widowed mother married D.D. Giles, and he went to live with his Uncle Charles in Mendota, Illinois. When Charles left to serve in the Civil War, young George was moved to another uncle, Jacob, where he earned his board and keep while attending Mendota Lutheran College, the equivalent of a high school education.

After one year working in the Mendota Post Office, George went to Eastman Commercial College and completed an eight-month course in just four months. He then went to work in Chicago at the Carson Pierce House of Dry Goods for $200 a year.

Following the trend of many ambitious young men after the notorious fire of 1871, supposedly caused by Mrs. O'Leary's cow kicking over the lantern in the milking barn, George left Chicago. He was 23 years old when he headed for St. Louis, where he found work as a cashier. After several years, he became a cashier at Dodd Brothers & Co. for $2500 a year. By 1879 he was head of the credit department, and in 1883 became a junior partner.

From Aunt Anne's journal:

> Father told me once he would like to have gone into banking, but when this job was offered him in the credit department, he accepted it, as it was nearly like banking. He was hard working, an early riser, but always home by seven o'clock dinner. Once in a while there were parties when parents and grandparents went out, or evenings at the opera or theater. Plays came to St. Louis for one or two-weeks stays. There was no rushing out to dinner every night such as overtook us in the 1920's.

Father was always kind and gentle. I cannot remember his losing his temper with his children, and he was interested in all our activities. He became interested in mining and invested in a property at Ajo, Arizona, where there was a mountain of low-grade ore. Two different attempts were made to process the ore into copper, both failed. Those were our poorer years.

The property became the New Cornelia Copper Co., later bought by Luther Greenway for Calumet and Arizona Copper Co. and developed by Phelps Dodge into a large and profitable producer. The mountain is now a deep hole.

In 1904, father bought Fairlawn near Kirkwood, Missouri, a property of about ten acres with a small lake, an ice house, a tennis court, a large vegetable garden, stables, corn barn and pig pen; a smoke house where hams and bacon were cured, an orchard and beautiful old trees on a sloping lawn. It was real country then.

Father's mother, Grandma Giles, came to visit us from time to time, but never stayed long. I loved her. She was a tiny, little wiry woman, a widow for the second time. She lived in Mendola, a small town in Illinois. Father's father had been held up and killed when he was driving with the payroll for workers on the Erie Canal. Father was quite young at the time and he began early to earn his living and help his mother.

It was at Fairlawn that my sister Louise married Warren Goddard on a beautiful April day in 1910 when the lilacs were in full bloom. There was a snowstorm the next day.

I married Nelson Dean Jay, June 23rd that same year. Roses were for decorations. We left St. Louis for Milwaukee, Wisconsin. Mother sold Fairlawn after Father died, Sept. 1919.

Both my mother's and my grandmother's wedding dresses are in the Museum in Roundup, Montana.

The journal continues:

We were grateful for having had a saintly mother. Florence Brush Augustine (1860-1937) was an ardent worker for her Second Presbyterian Church in St. Louis. Her prayers must have prevented many misdemeanors by her family. As children we never went to sleep without hearing her read a chapter from the Bible.

(Mother)...was always occupied. When we were young, clothes were made at home. A seamstress was often at the house, but mother supervised and we worked with her. No 'ready-mades' then. Not only dresses which were much more elaborate than now (1963), but one or two petticoats were worn, fancy panties, many hand tucks and lace trimmings on long full skirts. Evenings, mother often sewed by hand, sitting beside a long library table lighted by a 'student lamp', which was shaded by a green glass globe. It was oil burning until electrified. Nana (Grandmother Brush) sat opposite reading aloud, *Pickwick Papers*, *Mr. Dooley*, *Eugene Field* or from her favorite magazine, *The Outlook*. Mother's was *Ladies Home Journal*.

Mother was famous for her grape juice made from Concord grapes grown at Fairlawn. I thought the grapes were delicious, but to this day cannot bear the taste or smell of the preserved product. My sister Louise tells me, 'The reason you hate grape juice is that Nana made us take Castor Oil in it.'

When sewing, (Mother)... would sing or hum. She joined the choral society which gave her great pleasure, as she had a rich true voice. A cabinet in our dining room was filled with china which she painted when young. Anne Goddard Charter has it now.

After we moved to Fairlawn she decided to keep chickens, white ones, and take care of them herself from the incubator to the frying or roasting pan. She knew each one and its habits and enjoyed having them swarm around—a pleasure I did not share. She could do anything she decided she wanted to do.

She was always busy, even after we children grew up. She joined the Wednesday Club (culture and social) and, after father died, traveled extensively. She was in one of the first groups allowed into Russia after the Communist regime came to power.

THE BRUSH FAMILY

Aunt Anne also wrote about her maternal grandfather, George Whitfield Brush. Born in Brooklyn, New York in the early 1830s, he married Anne Elizabeth Westerfield Carter (Nana to us) in 1855. They started their family in New York, but moved to New Orleans around 1863 when their second child, Florence (Aunt Anne's mother) was three years old.

Aunt Anne writes:

The panic of 1873 had wiped out grandfather Brush's business in New Orleans where they had lived for ten years before coming to St. Louis. Their daughter, Florence (my mother) was then thirteen. Why they left Brooklyn where he was born, I do not know, nor do we know anything of grandfather's background. Nana talked so often of hers that he never mentioned his!

Aunt Anne left this charming account of our Brush ancestor:

Grandfather Brush was the fairy grandfather of a child's dreams. We used to wait on the front steps for him to come home, often there would be a large paper bag in his arms, maybe popcorn balls (delicious). Once I was told to put my hand down to the bottom of the bag where I touched something so warm and soft I was frightened, but not for long, a ball of white fluff with a black spot over one eye, became our great joy and companion. Mac, was named after McKinley, who had just been elected President of the United States.

But even if grandpa had nothing in his arms, we could fill them and pull on his long white whiskers dropping down each side of his face.

He was not a good businessman, but he enjoyed gardening, our dad's yard was a show place, both on Delmar Ave. and Westminster Place. Flowers, vines and trees covered the wooden fence which closed it in. Perhaps it was to keep us from digging up his plants that he reserved a patch each for my sister Louie and me. Floyd was rather small then, but he inherited the green thumb. My sister, Louise remembers him bringing home pear and peach saplings from Texas and planting them in the backyard.

Grandfather Brush died when we were living on Westminster Place. He had a chill which developed into pneumonia. I was awakened in the night by mother asking me to find a mandolin string. The doctor wanted it to use to stop a hemorrhage. Grandfather lived only a short time after that.

Continuing her "Early Impressions" written in 1963, my Aunt Anne says this about Nana, her grandmother:

From as far back as my subconscious days, before memory, Nana stands out as the dominant figure in our family. To this day her voice rings in my ears. We used to refer to its carrying qualities. She and our grandfather, George Whitfield Brush, lived with us for the sake of economy.

My mother, Louise Augustine Goddard's version of why the Brush grandparents lived with them, I quote from a letter; 'Not a matter of economy, as Grandpa had a good position with Ely Walker but he had to travel so much and Nana refused to be left alone. After you were born we moved. Grandpa divided the cost of the house with father and that is why they always had the best and biggest front room.'

Aunt Anne continues:

As a result of their sojourn in New Orleans, Nana was frequently to be found reading either her French New Testament or her French cookbook. We all benefited from the latter, as some delectable dish was likely to emerge to regale us at the next meal. We were brought up to relish calves brains a la this or that, fried pigs feet, which when properly cooked can hardly be surpassed, and ragouts of fish from Southern waters.

It was a treat to be taken by Nana to the big French market in St. Louis on Thursday afternoon to pick out a red snapper whose eyes shone brighter on Thursday than when sold on Friday morning in the local market. Stuffed and baked, the memory is still mouth-watering.

My sister, Louise, adds this to Nana's personality sketch:

Nana was the one who gave us our standards of gracious living and keeping up with the Jones's as it were. Also all the niceties and superficialities of life which meant so little to mother, who always stressed what was inside you and not what covered up your inner workings. Then her musicianship was truly remarkable, all our friends were always impressed by the facility with which she ran up and down the piano keys.

Nana lived to a ripe old age, and as I was only four when she died, I have no real memory of her. She was the matriarch, having inherited the qualities that made her ancestors good soldiers and civic leaders, but being a woman living in the end of the 19th and beginning of the 20th century, she had no one to boss except her family. My sister Louise remembers her sitting in an upstairs window at Fairlawn when we came to visit, watching us children play. If we did anything she disapproved of, she would tap on the window with her thimble.

Aunt Anne resumes her story:

In those days we lived on Delmar Avenue between Grand Avenue and Vandeventer Place, almost city limits then. A horse drawn street car passed the house, but one Sunday afternoon we were taken to Grand Avenue to see a new invention and watch the first electric street car go by. The trolley was overhead and the sparks were terrifying, causing mother to announce that she would never ride in such cars. Of course, she did until the day she was driving her own automobile.

One evening our parents were invited next door to see a surprise. The next morning they told us of an amazing event. Our neighbors had their house wired with electricity. They could press a button at the foot of the stairs and light a light on the second floor, and when they went to bed another button at the top of the stairs put out the light below. We were living with gas jets which had to be put out by hand or with the aid of a long pole made for the purpose. It had a small wax taper used to light the gas jets.

My earliest memories of Aunt Anne and other relatives are as we sat around our dining room table in our house at 21 Brentmoor Park in St. Louis.

If you looked in on one of our family gatherings you would find on my paternal side Goddards, Chamberlains and the Goddard children; and on my maternal side, Augustines and Jays.

"Baldy," my father, would be whetting his knife in preparation for carving the turkey, or rib roast, or Mallard ducks, whichever dominated that particular

15

feast. He served each plate individually—light or dark? well done or rare? thigh, drumstick or breast? A maid would then pass potatoes, vegetables, and rolls.

Table conversation was kept lively by Uncle Fred Chamberlain's recital of poetry and older sister Irene's original doggerel about individual members of the family. We younger children added to the merriment by giggling at unexpected moments, sometimes uncontrollably, and when necessary, we buried our faces in our napkins.

After clearing the plates, the maid would come round with a little tray and scraper to brush crumbs off the damask tablecloth. The children made this last task worthwhile.

Next came the finger bowls, where we wiggled our fingers while anticipating dessert. Its arrival was prefaced by my father asking, "What's for dessert... stewed prunes?"

Coffee was served later in the living room, as the men smoked cigars, and the children collected the colorful cigar bands.

I will introduce my family members, and tell you what impressed me about them as a child, and some of the stories I heard.

Beginning with the Goddards, I have to admit neither my grandfather, Joseph Warren Goddard, nor his wife, Maria Pearson Goddard, came to the family dinners at home. Grandfather must have died before we moved to Brentmoor Park, and I can't remember grandmother Goddard ever being at any of the festivities. She had asthma attacks, and probably stayed close to home where I picture her in my mind. However, I do remember driving down Wydown with her in her electric car. Cousin Sam remembers the "electric" parked by her door on a slope when the brake failed. It rolled down the slope of lawn, across the street, up the slope of the Chamberlain's house and back into the street. I regret that I have so few memories of her more active life, but one does get a glimpse of her early life through letters and news clips handed down.

Joseph Warren Goddard moved to St. Louis from Brookline, Massachusetts, and went into the wholesale grocery business with a Mr. Nave, according to the heading on stationery dated 1874. Their warehouse at 522-524 N. 2nd Street, was just a block from the levee, and most of their wares probably came by riverboat. Later, according to another letterhead dated 1886, the business was moved to 109-111 N. 2nd St. and became the Goddard Grocery Company. This area now is a baseball park. All three grandfathers, Brush, Augustine, and Goddard moved to St. Louis within four years of each other.

At some point in Joseph Warren's later life, he was involved in a horse drawn trolley-car accident and was confined to a wheelchair.

There are early letters from his wife, Maria Pearson, (Grandma Goddard to us) to her sister Mary, and her mother (great grandma Pearson to me) about "Odie," her son Warren. Later he was called "Baldy" by his friends, but my mother always called him Warren. My parents had a special whistle, and when she wanted him to come in from the garden, she would whistle and call out "Waaarren!"

My father, Warren, and my Aunt Abby Chamberlain were twins, but all the letters kept from their childhood are about Odie. At age two, Odie fell out of an attic window onto a porch roof. He broke his upper thigh, but it healed well. Later, at some point, his mother put the wrong drops in his right eye and he was blinded in that eye. Only a close observer, however, would be aware of it and it didn't seem to affect any of his activities. My father liked driving, poker, duck hunting, deep sea fishing and gardening.

The first letter from Odie to his aunt and grandma tells that he was in the First Reader, and that a new stable for Washington Avenue cars was being built. It was probably one of those horse-drawn cars that caused the accident his father was in.

At age 8, in messy writing, he tells of a snow in November. And on January 20, 1884, at age 12, from Alton, Illinois, he writes "Papa and Abby, Sam and I went across the river today and it looked like a week day because they were cutting ice and building a new ice house." He mentions, "I have to go three miles in the horse car to school." In another letter written in beautiful script, at age 14, (September 5, 1886) he tells of the Exposition to open in St. Louis, that he has learned to swim, and that he is writing for his mother, as she was busy getting ready to go to Godfrey for a wedding. However, when his mother saw how short his letter was, she couldn't help filling up the empty pages with mostly idle gossip. She mentions Eliza coming back from Falmouth, and that "Aunt Abby is talking about coming out here with Mr. G? Don't you think that will be a visit and a half! She is evidently bound he shan't come alone, she must be afraid to trust him."

Some twenty years later, in 1906, son Warren receives a letter from his father saying the children (Jane and Irene, my half sisters) were fine and enjoyed going to the Shirley Hill picnic. He wished him health and happiness on his 34th birthday. The Goddard family owned a cottage at Shirley Hill, N.H., where they spent their summers.

An undated newspaper article, headed "Square Meal for the Boys" tells of one of the family civic activities:

> The youths of the Newsboys' Home, No. 705 Pine St., were yesterday treated by Mr. and Mrs. Joseph W. Goddard to a square Thanksgiving dinner. Nineteen boys were present and four remained at the Home. These latter, however, were provided for by the same philanthropic hearts and hands. It is reported that the boys were so full of turkey, oysters, plum pudding and other accessories of the meal that they were obliged to pocket the oranges, apples, nuts, raisins, etc., this being done by consent. Mr. Bacon marshaled the Young Americans. Three cheers were given for the host and each member of the family, songs were sung and a good time experienced.

It is interesting to note a present day movie (1992) called "The Newsies," which depicts conditions news boys lived under, and the triumphant fight for their rights against the newspaper giants.

We went to Grandmother Goddard's house every Thanksgiving. Grandma was always dressed in black with a high collar or neck band, always sitting in the

*George Whitfield Brush (TOP),
George W. Augustine, Jr.
(BOTTOM, LEFT), and George
Hershey Augustine (BOTTOM,
RIGHT)*

Louise Augustine Goddard (TOP, LEFT), Florence Brush Augustine (TOP, CENTER), Anne Elizabeth Carter Brush (RIGHT), and baby Louise Goddard (CENTER)

Abby Goddard

Warren Goddard

19

same chair by the front window on McPherson Avenue. There were toys on shelves by the entryway for us children to play with, after we had said our greetings and were waiting for dinner.

Celia was my grandmother's maid, housekeeper, cook, nurse and companion. She was a pleasant, white haired, ruddy, comely Irish woman who, according to novels about Irish immigrants, probably came to this country as a young girl and became a servant. We loved her. In addition to a wonderful dinner, she always created a fantastic pyramid of fruit with a turkey on top. Every Thanksgiving, I try to emulate that tower, but never succeed.

After my grandmother died, we would go to Aunt Abby and Uncle Fred Chamberlain's house for Thanksgiving. It was on the south side of the street directly across from my grandmother's.

In the late 1920's a tornado struck that section of St. Louis. My father was at work downtown when he heard it had hit McPherson Avenue. He drove west on McPherson until the traffic was stopped, then from there he kept going on foot. The fronts of all the houses on both sides of the street were sucked out, making the whole area look like a series of fully furnished doll houses. But when he reached the corner, he saw his mother's house standing unharmed, as were the other houses on her block.

I was at John Burrough's school at the time, which was in the country. Some of the chimneys and cornices on the school roof were demolished and the electricity was cut off, but otherwise it was fine. Anxious parents came to rescue their children, as the trolley was out of commission.

My Uncle Fred was in the bird seed business, which prospered until somehow salt got into the seed and killed some pet canaries. He diversified his business, however, and it survived.

To the very young, the charm of Aunt Abby's house was the magical music box on her front table. It was played for us as soon as we came in. I was especially fascinated by her cut glass, displayed in a beautiful hutch, probably an antique even then. When she died, cut glass was not an "in thing" and nobody wanted it, except me. It was packed in barrels along with most of my wedding presents, until 1958-59 when we bought a house in Billings, Montana. I also inherited my grandmother's sterling silver tableware, engraved with the Augustine "A".

Sam was my father's brother. He and his wife, Florence, had two children, Sally and Sam, Jr. Sally, my sister's age, died at age twelve of a strep infection. Penicillin had not yet been discovered. I remember we were told she probably got it by using someone else's towel or washcloth at summer camp, and I've had a thing about the interchange of towels, sheets, toothbrushes, food and drink receptacles, etc., ever since. Sanitation and Victorian ethics entered into my early training! I was not only protected, but unbelievably naive!

Sam, Jr. was my brother's age. He later became the first Democratic Governor of Arizona. At first, my family, dyed-in-the-wool Republicans, were loathe to acknowledge this as an honor. Husband Boyd was also brought up a Republican in the rancher tradition, but when we became the "little guys," in need of protection from "corporate giants," it was the Democrats we turned to for help. Terry Goddard,

Sam and Judy's son, is carrying on the political tradition. He was mayor of Phoenix, and almost became the governor twice. Hopefully, he will run again or find a position where he can use his talents.

Aunt Florence was the intellectual. She wrote poetry, and belonged to the same literary club as Grandma Augustine. The Christmas Eve playlets that we children participated in were under her tutelage.

On my mother's side were the five Jays: Uncle Dean, Aunt Anne, and sons Nelson, George and later Bobby. On rare occasions they were in St. Louis and joined our festivities. Dean Jay, small-town boy from Peoria, IL became the first millionaire we knew personally. He was in banking. He worked for Morgan & Co. in New York until he became head of Morgan & Cie. in Paris, France. They lived in an exquisite apartment in Paris, and had a walled-in country house near Fontainbleau where they spent their summers. His life in Paris spanned the time between the two world wars. He and his trusted chauffeur Emil, who had been with him since day one, fled France just ahead of the German occupation. When he left, the country home was in the hands of Henri and Ferdinand. This faithful French couple had also been with him from the beginning, and seemed old when I visited there as a girl.

When Dean Jay returned after the Nazi defeat, he found all the furniture labeled with Nazi officers' home addresses. His famous wine cellar was intact however, as Henri had skillfully camouflaged the cellar entrance. Henri and Ferdinand welcomed them home with tears and thanksgiving.

I have always been proud to have been named after Aunt Anne. She was everything a real lady should be: quiet and reserved, gracious, loving, and, if more could be needed, artistic. Sister Louise also inherited Aunt Anne's gifts for flower growing and arranging, needlework and decorating. Louise once did eight dining room chair seats in needlepoint, as well as eight other chairs in crewel, each with a different bird and flower motif. She also has done a needlepoint seat cover that is in a restored Irish Castle.

Aunt Anne, instead of keeping a travel journal, kept notebooks filled with her watercolor sketches of the places she visited.

I don't remember Floyd Augustine, my mother's younger brother, being at family gatherings before his marriage to Mildred McDonnell, or of their presence after Mary and John were born, but I do remember making presents for Aunt Mildred; so they must have graced some of these occasions. Floyd served in World War I. He was not only quite handsome and dashing, but was a very sweet and loving person. We have a priceless photograph of him at about five years old and typical of the day. Dressed in a *Little Lord Fauntleroy* suit, he had long golden curls and was seated in a goat cart! His hair later turned dark. Floyd was ten years younger than his sisters. But he was not a late-in-life baby, as his mother, Grammy Aug, was married very young in contrast to my mother and myself who were almost thirty.

Grandfather Augustine saw to it that his wife could live comfortably after his death. Her son, Floyd, was a stockbroker and managed her affairs, doing very well until the stock market crash of 1929. Like so many others from tycoons to the little guys, everything was lost in the crash. As a teenager, I was only partially aware of the agony that this produced, but I did know that my Aunt Mildred went to work and became highly successful as a fashion buyer. That was when Grandma Aug came to live with us for a time. Of course, I was not privy to all that went on, but I never heard her lay blame or complain. The only thing she insisted on was getting to church every Sunday. My brother George remembers well, since he had to take her. On returning from church, while waiting for Sunday dinner, she would sit down at the piano and belt out the "Battle Hymn of the Republic" in a most lively manner.

Then there was the day she found "the missing document." It was of prime importance and its loss had been the subject of conversation for days. One morning she came downstairs with a grin on her face. "I've found it," she said triumphantly. "I worried all last night and couldn't sleep, so when I got up this morning, I just got down on my knees and asked the Lord to help me; then I walked directly to where I had hidden it!" This impressed me greatly. I knew then that my grandmother and the Lord were on very good terms! Later, thanks to her influence on my early life, I too felt the same closeness to the Lord.

MY STORYBOOK CHILDHOOD

Once upon a time a baby girl was born in St. Louis, Missouri, the fourth girl in the family. I was that baby, named Anne after my mother's sister. Fortunately a little over a year later a boy was born who could carry on the family name, Joseph Warren. We called him Joe. A bonus brother was born eight years later and named after my mother's father, George Augustine.

Being born in the early years of a new century, I was constantly swept from one wave of change to the next, barely aware of what was happening around me. Memories of horse-drawn ice wagons, gas street lamps and the lamp lighter who came every dusk are hard to reconcile with science fiction stories which have become a reality. The pony express was replaced by fax machines. Robot brains are programmed into computers.

Two big moments of history stand out for me: as an Eagle Scout welcoming Admiral Byrd to St. Louis after his historic trip to the North Pole, and watching from my window (because I had the measles) Charles Lindbergh's triumphal St. Louis parade celebrating his solo flight to Paris. This didn't prevent me from falling in love with "Lucky Lindy," as did every female at the time. It was exciting when he married Anne Morrow, whose parents were good friends of my Aunt Anne and Uncle Dean Jay. I felt it a personal tragedy when the Lindbergh's first baby was kidnapped and killed.

From my earliest memories, mine was a storybook childhood, as were my adolescent years. We had nurses who gave us the constant attention we needed, a mother who loved us, was always there and who sang us to sleep. We also had a loving father. When we pounced on him in bed he would proceed to carve us up like chickens which caused much tickling and giggling.

At this point, I will mention my newest granddaughter, Annika Charter, born September 21, 1987, because I can see myself at her age in many of her actions, and because she was a "late in life surprise" as was her father, Steve, my brother George and cousin Bobby Jay.

From almost day one we knew she had a mind of her own and facial expressions mighty similar to those of her grandma at that age. Somewhat self-satisfied and just a mite defiant, with a whole lot of, "I can do it myself!" I can remember at about three being punished for something by having my hands tied with a towel and being shut in the bathroom. I tore the towel to shreds with my teeth, opened the door and marched out triumphantly. At a somewhat older age, I was made to sit in a chair and stare at the front door knob that I persistently turned the wrong way, screwing up the faulty mechanism. This was so demeaning to me that I couldn't forgive my mother for it until I had children of my own!

I was the one who was always smarting off for the camera; who at age six rode on the back of an ostrich, my sister and brother being too scared to try. We were in California at the time to be near my grandfather Augustine who was dying of TB. I had my sixth birthday there at a seaside hotel in Delmar. I received my first Brownie camera and tried clicking the shutter as I held it against my mother's purple corduroy bathrobe. She said it wouldn't hurt the film if no light got in. Later that morning we found an orange crate on the beach. The older children took turns standing on it, as the surf pound up around them then swirled away. I wanted a turn too. I could do it if they could, after all, I was six now! But when the surf sucked back out into the sea, I was terrified. I thought I would be carried out to sea. Scared as I was, it didn't spoil my love of the ocean.

My earliest school memories started with learning about Eskimos and igloos in the first grade and "reading" books by flipping the pages and looking at the pictures. When I did begin to read, I had a lot of trouble with the word 'wheat' in *The Little Red Hen.*

When I was eight years old, I remember walking home from school with one of my best friends, both of us so proud we could hardly stand it. We'd had to repeat kindergarten but were now skipping second grade and were promoted to our own age group in third grade.

The only drawback with third grade was that we had to write a story. My story read, "On Monday this happened"... and so on through the week. I still have trouble with plots.

I went to Community School, a new, small experimental school. My mother was on the founding board. Now it is a large school, leading in quality grade-school education. Anne Leschen, daughter of brother George and Peg Goddard was one of its outstanding teachers, who became assistant to the principal in charge of the Middle School. She is now teaching 7th and 8th grades at John Burroughs where she had also been a student. She loves working with that age, which by many is regarded as difficult to say the least.

I was still in Community School, fifth grade probably, when I decided to win a pony by selling subscriptions to *People's Popular Monthly*, a magazine that sold for a dollar a year. The twelve ponies pictured all looked so wonderful I couldn't decide which one I wanted most. I hit friends, neighbors and strangers for miles around, seldom missing an afternoon after school and making the most of weekends. People forfeited their dollars willingly. Everybody was reading the *People's Popular Monthly*. How could I not win? The fateful day of decision came, but I was not among the winners. My family was so incensed that my mother called the contest headquarters, only to be told I had come in 13th.

So much for my faith in contests. I took the loss in my stride however and learned that it paid to be a good loser. Soon afterward my dad, Warren Goddard, who had many contacts in the Missouri countryside from his early days as salesman for the Goddard Grocery Company, found a farm family whose son wanted to sell his pony and buy a bicycle. He made the trade and I became the proud owner of Redtop. The tool shed of the garage became a pony stall. It was up to me to transfer straw and manure daily from the stall to my Dad's compost pile. So for several years Redtop helped fertilize my Dad's garden and mow the lawn (all two acres of it). It was a proud day when I drove a two wheel wicker pony cart to school accompanied by my sister and brother. I tied Redtop to a post in the lot behind the school until recess, when I took my friends for rides. (I did mention it was a progressive school didn't I?)

One day, when walking home from Community School, I caught up with a man who was leading a magnificent St. Bernard. I fell into conversation with him and found she could be bought for $25, the exact amount I had hoarded in Christmas and birthday gold pieces! While he waited out of sight behind the garage, I crept up to my room, got out my hoard and paid in gold. My astonished family accepted the fait accompli as best they could. They thought the dog was probably stolen and put an ad in the paper to find her owner. But, as there was no response, I remained the proud owner of Lady throughout the school year.

Faced with a long hot summer when the family would be away and with Lady already panting from the heat, my father miraculously found a dog breeder who would buy her. I could either have my $25 back or a puppy out of her first litter. I chose the puppy, of course. Unfortunately Lady died without puppies. Again I learned the advantage of accepting disappointment without undue fuss, and once again my father rose to the occasion.

A friend who raised Airedales had a new litter of puppies, and I was given the runt when barely weaned. He was named "Pucky" by my baby brother trying to say puppy. I loved that puppy so much I would get teased. Someone would ask, "What will you sell your dog for, I want one just like him". My firm reply was, "Not for a *million* dollars." Years later, when the Consolidation Coal Co. (Consol) was trying to coerce us into selling our land so they could strip-mine our ranch in the Bull Mountains, this same sentiment was restated by my husband, Boyd, as they were pressuring him to name a price. His reply, "There are some things your money can't buy. I am one of them, my land is another."

Pucky and I were constant companions in those early years. I used to carry matches with me on our walks. Airedales are aggressive and I had read that to separate two dogs clenched in battle, you hold a lighted match under their noses. This lore came from stacks of literature I would gather up at dog shows. While away in the summer at Camp Kineowatha in Wilton, Maine, I wrote weekly letters to my dog, a roundabout way of informing my parents that all was well.

Before the summer camp years, my mother would take us children to spend the summer somewhere on Cape Cod. Woods Hole, Martha's Vineyard, and Wiano are some of the names that come to me. Our Grandmother Augustine was often with us, and my father would come the last two weeks in August. I remember boiling lobsters in great pots on the beach for his birthday celebration August 29.

The earliest trip east I remember was during the flu epidemic of World War One in 1918 when I was five years old. We were dressed for bed before leaving home, as the train left at night. Travelers had to have their temperature taken under their arm before boarding the train because of the influenza epidemic. We children would chant, "We opened the window and in flew Enza."

Although we were supposed to go right to bed, we first had to swing like monkeys from the bar of the upper bunk in our compartment. The train was a child's delight: the crossing from car to car over the scary, shifting connecting plates; visiting the lounge car with its outdoor platform; flushing the toilet and seeing the tracks beneath speeding by; and, of course, the dining car, with its linen tablecloths and impressive waiters. Our favorite for breakfast was figs with cream, and for dinner, lamb chops. To this day, these foods bring back those early memories.

The summer I was seven, we sojourned in Wood's Hole. To everyone's great surprise my brother George was born shortly after our arrival, June 27, 1920. He was a six month preemie, born in the Gloucester Fisherman's Hospital. My mother not only had a successful birth, but also had her first taste of eel, which she liked, until she found out what she was eating.

Miss Sibly, RN, was *the* baby nurse of St. Louis and had taken care of all of us for the first few weeks of our lives. We had all been born at home with the family doctor in attendance. Miss Sibly was sent for to take care of baby George. His incubator was a basket lined with newspaper and hot bricks.

Under Miss Sibly's care, George thrived. At least today he looks as though he must have thrived. I have been told that when my father and his twin sister Abby were born, each could be held in the palm of your hand. My father grew to over six feet tall and weighed around 200 pounds, as did George.

Those days we spent at the seashore are precious memories. Our grandmother took us to the beach most often. She was always trying to improve the landscape. If a hole needed filling, we all rigorously dropped stones into it. She also saw to our religious training, taking us to church every Sunday.

Several years later, two grandmothers dominated the summer we spent in Shirley Hill, New Hampshire, near the town of Manchester, home of the textile mills. Our Goddard grandmother provided the cottage and our Augustine grandmother took charge of us, while our mother and father were on a Scandinavian cruise. They even ventured into Russia. My father said the men wore out their pockets, feeling to see if their passports were safe.

This was a different sort of summer from those on the Cape. It was strange to be landlocked, not to be able to go swimming, and to eat our meals in the hotel. We played a lot of croquet, took walks to the tipping rock, and made imaginary homesteads out of moss, rocks and twigs while playing in the woods. We also stripped the loose bark off the birch trees to take back to St. Louis.

That summer ended in tragedy. On Labor Day, after picking up my sister at her summer camp, we side-swiped another car. The impact threw my grandmother out of the car (no seat belts then). No one else was injured, but she was in a coma for a long time and in the hospital for three months. She had severe headaches for years after. I was told the driver of our rented car leaned down to pick something off the floor boards, taking his eyes off the road for a split second, making him veer over the middle line and clip an oncoming car.

It is no wonder I have never enjoyed touring. I am always ill at ease driving with my children or with any of their generation at the wheel. They think nothing of looking over their shoulder to talk to someone in the back seat, gazing at the far horizon or at a nearby grass crop. And now a new hazard has appeared—cellular phones. This obsession of mine, no doubt goes back to my childhood experience.

We somehow managed to get back home to St. Louis and a normal life, taking our birch bark with us. This we turned into spectacular Christmas gifts for all the relatives: boxes, trays, wastebaskets, anything that imagination and willing fingers could create.

The largest and most spirited of our family gatherings was on Christmas. We children were not allowed into the living room until after dinner. When the doors to the living room were opened, we saw for the first time the magnificently decorated tree that reached to the ceiling. Holding down its lower branches were gleaming balls the size of small balloons. They were heavy and had come from Germany with many other priceless ornaments. I still have one large ball and a few of the old fashioned ornaments. Under the tree lay all the gifts exchanged between family members.

Our Christmas ritual started the evening before when we hung our stockings over the fireplace in our parents' room. Christmas morning we made the mad dash to see if Santa had come. Stockings always bulging with an orange, a gold piece in the toe and many other wondrous toys. Under each stocking was a pile of gifts — dolls, games, books, coloring sets, paper dolls, etc.

One Christmas we got walking dolls almost as big as we were. They could wear our outgrown clothes. Their legs, knees and feet were jointed so you could hold them and make them walk. They were interesting but not particularly lovable. Another Christmas Louise and I were entrusted with the China dolls that had belonged to my mother and her sister. My doll now belongs to granddaughter, Kasey Anne Nilson, a fourth generation doll. With the doll is a photograph of the little Augustine girls taken about 1886-87 with those same two dolls.

I remember another Christmas when I was nine or ten, when the family present outshone all the others. It was a crystal radio set. We spent all day moving the little needle around the crystal trying to hear some talking or music through the static. Always after the initial excitement had worn off, we'd each take our loot to our rooms. I would arrange mine, oh so carefully, admiring and re-admiring. I was sure there had to be a Santa, for no family could possibly be rich enough to provide so many wonderful things. To have all the relative's gifts in addition to Santa's made the day almost unbearably exciting.

My two half-sisters, Jane and Irene, were much older. My father's first wife, Irene Wallace, died when baby Irene was born. After her death, my father and the two little girls moved in with Grandma Wallace who was called "Dearie."

Jane, Irene and Mildred (mother's brother Floyd's wife) were young marrieds at the same time, a confusing mix of generations. Jane's husband, Watts Smyth, taught us to dance. He and Jane were the fast set of the jazz era; he the playboy and she the flapper. They continued to learn every new dance which came along until they were threatened with heart attacks at an advanced age. My sister and I spent a summer with them at Ocean City, Maryland, when I was 16, Louise 18. I managed to keep my naive outlook on life in spite of that summer!

I was a pain in the neck for Irene when she was of the age to be courted. She had a variety of beaus who came calling and I would either greet them at the door or be hiding behind the couch where they would sit. They finally decided the only way to get rid of me was a bribe. After receiving treats of candy I would leave them alone. After she married Ted Elder, I fell in love with his brother Jock. He

Floyd Augustine dressed as Little Lord Fauntleroy (TOP, LEFT); Anne and Louise Augustine (TOP, RIGHT); Anne Goddard (Charter) celebrates her sixth birthday with a ride on an ostrich (BOTTOM, RIGHT); Anne, Louise, and Joe play outside the Brentmoor home; and the Goddard family's coat of arms.

*Warren Goddard (LEFT);
George Augustine Jay
(BELOW); photographs of 21
Brentmoor in 1916 and 1989
(BOTTOM, RIGHT); and left
to right, Joseph 'Joe' Warren
Goddard, friend T. Peck, and
Louise Goddard (BOTTOM,
LEFT).*

had a wooden leg, but managed to play tennis and dance. When he was a young boy, he tried to jump on the back of a wagon to hitch a ride. His leg caught in the spokes of the wheel. The first thing he said was "Don't tell Dad," as riding on the backs of wagons was strictly forbidden!

He also played the ukulele, so I had to have one. He taught me to play "Anybody seen my kitty" and "Barney Google." I was 11 or 12 years old at the time.

Irene was a wonderful sister. As we grew up and her children came along, we had some wonderful times together. This relationship continued throughout our lives.

I was not anxious to grow up and relinquish the recreations of my youth. A bit of a tomboy, I was an active Girl Scout into high school, getting the Golden Eagle award. I also received several best citizen and athletic awards in high school, an outstanding student citizen award in the Swiss-French School, Les Fougeres, as well as being senior class president at Wells College. I was also chosen to be the exchange student from Wells College to Frankfurt University, Frankfurt Am-Main, Germany. I was not a "goody-goody" or anyone special, though. I was a normal teenager during a time when teenagers had it easier. We too drove too fast, took risks, stayed up all night, necked, but few exceeded the limits. Of course we defied Prohibition, perhaps following the example of our elders but more likely just for the excitement.

The recognition I received for "cooperating with the powers that be" was due to my gift of an easy-going disposition and an ability to get along with people. My zest for life and enjoyment was tempered with an ability to resist authority, without defying it.

There were two major tragedies in my young life and I kept them so wrapped up and hidden, they rarely surfaced.

My cousin George Jay and I were the same age; my brother Joe was a year younger. The three of us were soul mates and we did not have to be together often to maintain that special relationship. Aunt Anne and her boys occasionally lived in St. Louis, and I believe even stayed with us following World War One, when Uncle Dean first went to Paris to head the French branch of Morgan & Cie.

The summer I was fifteen, it was my turn to go with grandmother Augustine to visit the Jays at their country home in Fontainbleau about 40 miles south of Paris. The Jay children were Nelson, my sister's age, Bobby, my little brother's age, and George. I shared that summer with George.

It was George who made me feel good after my first perm when he said, "You sure look a lot better!" I hated my hair and had complained to the male French hair dresser about my straight, baby fine hair. He replied, "Mais Mademoiselle, it ees the hair one loves to touch." His remark made me feel more like the young lady I was supposed to be!

To help me achieve that role I had my Aunt Mildred. She was the family "fashion plate" and made it her chief mission in life to see that I did not forget to wear my white gloves. I sometimes felt like the White Rabbit in "Alice in Wonderland," but I loved her dearly, and when I wrote to her, I always mentioned that I hadn't forgotten to wear my gloves.

George and I had many interests in common, but perhaps our favorite was riding in the enchanted forest of Fontainbleau. Then came that fateful day when Uncle Dean, George and I were cantering along one of the forest trails. George's horse stepped in a hole and fell. George was thrown on his head and broke his neck. I raced to the house for help, but must have been in a state of shock. I felt only horror and isolation. I could not share my grief. I retired to my room and into myself.

Shortly after that, my grandmother and I left France with Nelson who had to return to school. I felt my Uncle was so devastated, he couldn't bear to have me around. I can remember no sharing of grief.

That following winter my brother Joe was killed in an automobile accident while being driven to school. Again I cannot remember openly grieving or crying or being able to share my feelings with the rest of the family. We never talked about how we felt. I believe that fifteen year old girl died that year with her two best friends. It has been therapeutic to be able to write about it.

I found a letter from Joe written the year he died to my sister who was attending the French School in New York City. Joe identified it as the year the St. Louis Cardinals won the World Series in baseball against the New York Yankees, 1928:

> *Dearest Darling Lovely Sister Louise:*
> *At this time I happened to be sitting in the Den after supper (you know the half hour before the toil of studying begins). In front of me appears my other Dearest, Darling Lovely, Sister Anne, who is attempting to dance. A dance taught to her by one of her darling friends. Her graceful figure goes sweeping around the room, knocking over every lamp and chair. Ouch! right on my sore toe. There she goes down to the floor. What a fool-she thinks she is on the stage and is trying to sing. Now she is the audience and claps.*

The den was where we spent many a winter evening in front of the fire. One time after Joe's death, I had fallen asleep on the couch. Half awakening from a dream I asked my mother who had just come in where Joe was. She said, "Why, Anne, you know Joe is dead." This not only embarrassed me but further froze my feelings.

The den was our most informal room and would probably be called a family room today. It was in the only home I remember, 21 West Brentmoor Park. We moved there when I was about two. The "Park" consisted of a large circle with houses on the inside and outside of the drive. The streetlights were gas and the lots were two acres in size, some even larger. Our next door neighbor had a pond on the low side of his property where we were allowed to play and skate in winter. A small bridge over a ravine was perfect for playing Billy Goat Gruff. A family on the far side of the circle had a milk cow that we visited often. When we were very small, we would walk through the woods on the far side of the park with our nurse. One day I felt a soft spot under my foot and pressed down as a child would, only to unleash a swarm of hornets nested in the ground. As I grew older it was around this circle and through these woods that I walked my dog, rode my pony and learned where every bird's nest was and how many and what color eggs were in each. The quail's nests were hardest to find.

A series of these residential parks were built. Brentmoor and West Brentmoor being the first are listed in the National Register of Historic Places. Technically in Clayton, they are just one mile from the St. Louis city limits.

When we moved to West Brentmoor we were surrounded by countryside. There was a farm across Wydown that I barely remember, but I do know they had chickens and guinea hens and a rooster that crowed at dawn. I was told an old lady lived there who was dying. I still associate the cock's crow with death or imminent death.

In the biblical story, Jesus tells Peter just before he is crucified that Peter will deny him three times before the cock crows. Perhaps this story reinforces my feelings.

Although the back of the Park was wooded, our two acres with the house in the middle had only one tree, an oak. The tree, middle sized and growing conveniently near the house, was the center of our play area, providing shade, acorns and branches to climb on. It grew to tower over the house.

My father, a gardener at heart as were most of the early Goddards, transformed this bare acreage into a place of beauty. He planted the broad sweep of lawn in front of the house with bushes and shrubs following the curve of the road to screen the house. The elms he planted grew rapidly. At the back of the house, French doors opened onto a terrace, with brick steps leading down to an expanse of lawn encompassed by two rose gardens. Farther on was a small orchard of fruit trees and the grape arbor.

Behind the garage were my father's hot beds where he started his plants, the compost piles, his very productive asparagus bed and an extensive vegetable garden. The lower end of the property had thick hedges shielding it from Wydown and the streetcar tracks. It was the '04' Trolley that took us to school, music lessons and out into the world. My sister disapproved of my picking green onions and eating them on the way to catch the '04' to school.

Although my father hired a gardener, he did a great deal of the gardening himself. He would don his old clothes as soon as he got home from work as President of Goddard Grocery Company. Because of his appearance, he was often mistaken for the gardener. All of his children, each in their own way, carried on his love for the land and of gardening.

Farming and merchandising were in the blood of my forefathers and have been passed along to subsequent generations.

My father must have been a very good business man with a calculator embedded in his head. We visited his office one time on the second floor of the Warehouse. There were no partitions and lots of activity. We found him, cigar in mouth, hat on the back of his head, giving instructions to a salesman as he added a column of figures.

The Goddard Grocery Co. was a profitable business for many years, and functioned well until chain grocery stores came in. It was through investments, however, that my father made enough money to build his dream house. A man's house reflected his success in life and though my father was a down-to-earth man, with no pretenses, the house he built mirrored the trends of the day and was far from modest.

Built of red brick with a slate roof, the house had a full basement and was three stories tall. In the basement was a large laundry room, an incinerator for garbage and a mushroom cellar. Next to that was an open area and at the far end was the furnace room with the coal bin and chute. Coal trucks unloaded into the chute to fill the bin. Coal dust was the norm, as was persistent coughing. Windowsills and furniture had to be dusted daily. One time I showed my mother how I could draw in the coal dust on my wallpaper using an eraser. Shortly after that new wallpaper appeared in several rooms. It was a great day when we were able to convert the coal furnace to natural gas.

From the vestibule, you entered a long hall with closets flanking the inside door. At one end of the hall was the formal dining room with a breakfast room extending out onto the back terrace. The kitchen, pantry, a bathroom, back hall and maid's dining room were all at that end of the house. There were stairs going down to the basement, and back stairs up to the second and third floor. A clothes chute went from the second floor down to the basement. We would gaze down it, wondering if we dared to jump onto the pile of dirty clothes at the bottom. Fortunately, we never dared!

Directly across the hall from the front door was the living room, with folding French doors. French doors opened onto the terrace as well. Adjoining the living room, which had a fireplace and could easily accommodate the grand piano and several couches was the music room with our wind-up gramophone. Opening up onto the terrace, the sun room housed a rubber tree and other huge plants. The sun room and the breakfast room mirrored each other at opposite ends of the house. Above these rooms were the summer sleeping porches. We nailed sardine tins to long poles and filled them with kerosene to kill the mosquitoes that covered the ceiling in summer. When the weather was hottest, we put wet sheets over us. When it was cold, we would pile on the blankets and see how long we could sleep out on the porch without freezing.

Downstairs, across the hall from the music room, was my father's den where a cozy fire always burned during the winter months. The dining room also had a fireplace, and there were two more in the upstairs bedrooms. The fireplace in the living room was only lit for special occasions, and the others never to my knowledge. They must have been built just to hang up our Christmas stockings.

Upstairs were six bedrooms, each pair with a bathroom between. The third floor had three maid's rooms, a bath and storage rooms at each end under the eves. It took a full-time cook, a maid and a nurse to keep the household running smoothly. In addition there was a part-time gardener, a laundress and a seamstress, who constantly updated our clothes. Being the fourth girl, I had lots of "made over" hand-me-downs. The only thing that bothered me about this was having to stand still for the fittings.

We were fascinated with the attic and loved to explore under the eaves. This space was filled with several generations of family possessions, old furniture and antiques. We had a prefab playhouse that we could put together ourselves. We were allowed to construct it in the third floor hall, which became a fine playroom.

The stairs were another source of entertainment. We had read stories and poems of children playing on stairs, even being confined to stairs as punishment. These stories whetted our imagination and were the basis for many games.

The broad front stairs went up half a flight to a hall which crossed the front of house, and had a built-in bench, to rest on in case you couldn't make it to the top. The second flight went up from the end of that hall. There was a railing all along the upstairs hall and curving down the stairs to the bottom, with a narrow ledge all along the outside of the banister. We did dare to climb over the railing and walk along this ledge from top to bottom when no one watching. We'd also slide down the railing, but as it was neither long nor steep, it lacked the excitement of stair railings in older houses.

The house was sold after my father died and my mother moved to a smaller place on Polo Drive in Clayton.

BASIC EDUCATION

From Community School I went to John Burroughs School, which like Community was another first in St. Louis. The first private, progressive co-educational school. There were well established private schools for both boys and girls, the Country Day School and Mary Institute. So, of course, there was great rivalry between us, and in the early years we learned to be good losers in many sports. Although my mother had gone to Mary Institute and had taught Latin there, she was as enthusiastically involved in starting this new, progressive school as she had been in helping to start Community school. John Burroughs has been an outstanding leader in education through the years.

Although my grades were acceptable, I did not pass French in my college boards. I had applied for Wells College as it was my mother's college. It was agreed that if I went to a French school for a year and still wanted to go to college, I would be admitted to Wells. The French schools were the popular finishing schools of the day. They were to prepare a young lady for the career of marriage. I was sent to Les Fougeres in Lausanne, Switzerland, where I learned to ski and speak bad French with other English-speaking girls who spoke bad French. The highlight of the year was when my friend, Ruth Ferris, and I were invited to spend the Christmas holidays at St. Moritz with my Aunt and Uncle Jay. The romantic feeling that I remember, skiing through the village streets at dusk, from the slopes back to our hotel, still gives me goose bumps.

I did attend Wells College. Years later, my husband quite often asked me what good my education did me living with him out on the ranch. I would carefully explain that a liberal arts education was supposed to prepare you for living. And so it had; it prepared me for living with him. Then he'd try another tactic, "Anne, aren't you sorry you married me?" My reply, "No way, there has never been a dull moment."

I did make one concession to my family. Maybe I should explain first why I was so determined to go to college. Their plans were for me to "come out," to be a debutante launched properly into society. Hopefully this would lead to a suitable marriage. My Dad did maintain his sense of humor about this though, always reminding me to marry someone rich so we could take care of him in his old age. I was then expected to live happily ever after bringing up my children in the way I had been brought up.

In spite of enjoying all my growing up years, I was beginning to sense the difference between the haves and the have-nots. I felt ill at ease when I considered what seemed a highly superficial social life. College was to be my escape. The concession I made was to make my debut during the summer and first semester of my sophomore year. I kept up my courses by going to summer school, and in the fall took courses at Washington University in St. Louis.

The official opening of the debutante season was the Veiled Prophet Ball. This was a Chamber of Commerce type organization made up of successful business men of the city. No one was supposed to know the identity of the Veiled Prophet who reigned over his Court for one year. Each year a Queen and four Special Maids of

Honor were chosen to represent the social elite. The remaining Debutantes were Maids of Honor. My sister had been a Special Maid of Honor, so I had to settle for being one of many escorted around the auditorium by an eligible bachelor. I would have settled for skipping the whole performance, but once launched into the mad whirl of luncheons, teas and balls, I did have a rather fantastic time. Of course I already knew all the eligible bachelors, and although there were several who would have had me, and though I thought highly of some of them, I just couldn't see getting married and settling down in St. Louis.

This was all going on in the midst of the great Depression. Regardless of the economy, many gowns were bought in Paris and the Country Clubs were turned into elaborate fantasy lands for the balls. Those who spent most extravagantly felt they were providing local jobs, thus helping the local economy. (The trickle-down economy of the 1930's is now called Reaganomics.)

My coming out ball was comparatively modest. It was held in our house. By moving most of the furniture out we were able to accommodate an orchestra and about 200 guests. I am ashamed to admit that this *was not* the greatest day of my life, and when it was over, I breathed a great sigh of relief! As a debutante, I did make some new friends however, and I have kept contact with many of them throughout the years.

When I returned to college the second semester, I was greeted with my friends singing an old song with the last two lines altered to go, "We don't come out, but we go to college."

For our 40th Reunion in 1975, I wrote this view of my college years:

Prohibition, Bobby Socks And Zippers
In the early 1930s we traveled by train, which was simple, efficient and sometimes high adventure. Homeward bound one Christmas vacation, we discovered Guy Lombardo and Orchestra in the Pullman car next to ours. We became so well acquainted that he kissed us all fondly good night. We would arrive in Aurora on the Auburn-Ithaca train, and could always depend on Larry being there in his red truck to greet us and haul our baggage (including steamer trunks) to the dorms.

No one had cars (Nancy as head of Collegiate sported one her senior year), so it was important to know men who did, which wasn't easy because it was not until our senior year that Ithaca men were allowed on campus on Sundays. Because of Prohibition, it was a daring decision, fraught with imagined dangers, when a speakeasy in Skaneateles or Syracuse was the destination for a date. Dartmouth house parties were known for serving "Dragon's Blood"— a grim concoction that was rumored to have killed numerous imbibers. We always felt heroic when we returned safely from the close encounters.

In 1933, 3.2 beer was legalized (except at Wells). This coincided with a League of Nations Assembly jointly sponsored by Wells and Lehigh University at Lehigh. Our "Ethiopian representative" still wonders how she managed to pass out on 3.2 beer.

As the Depression was with us during our Wells years, and the majority of our class was on scholarship, some had to drop out because of finances. Others spent a year or two at less expensive schools but came back to graduate. All did not suffer equally.

Vacations were important times and though Florida was not yet "the place to go" we did have favored vacation spots: Lake Placid for winter, Bermuda for spring break. A telegram is known to have been sent from Lake Placid to Dean Roys asking for a refund of tuition money so that vacationing Wells girls could become ski bums (this term was not in use at the time). Her response in effect was that the College staff unanimously granted the request in the best interests of the College. Her signature: "That Sardine."

Bermuda vacation usually consisted of living on the cruise ship, but it was not unusual to take an all night shore leave. Riding bicycles in long evening dresses was a common sight, and bedraggled whoopee makers were sometimes sighted climbing the ship's ladder just before the breakfast bell sounded. Although a compromising situation, few improprieties were committed.

All extracurricular activities weren't off campus. For the most part we provided our own entertainment. Radios were a novelty and drew crowds to the rooms they occupied. Sophomore hazing included mowing the lawns with fingernail scissors, and banner fights that involved hiding the banners in places that threatened the foundation of the old gym as well as the upper structure of Main Building.

Our meals were served by elderly waitresses in uniform, which didn't improve the fare, but maintained the tradition of our being young ladies. After dinner activities included a trip to the Main basement for a smoke (the only place it was allowed) and some bridge or dancing in the "Ass" (Association) room to 78 rpm records or Suzie Jennings Cleavland's piano renditions.

We were known to go skiing in bathing suits after a spring snow, to roller-skate on the highway, and to clothe ourselves in leaves after skinny-dipping. Our attire, when being worn, included Brooks Brothers sweaters worn backwards to button up the back with a string of pearls and, of course, our saddle shoes and bobby socks. Zippers came in about 1934 and provided more entertainment than utility at first, especially the rumors about those on men's "flies."

There were frequent trips to the Jam Kitchen and to the Averys'. Jean was a member of our class; we became members of her family. Uncle Bud and Auntie Jean were a special part of our Wells years. They did a lot of parenting for many of us.

As a class we eliminated a lot of antiquated rules and probably created new ones to become antiquated. Our class song, "Gainst Henry Wells" expressed our sentiments very well, and we have since created the tradition of updating it for our reunion banquets. There is great promise for subsequent updates.

For our 50th Reunion I wore my black Dior evening dress that I had worn as a debutante. I still have it. We had heart shaped name tags that hung around our necks. Our final act was to gather at the willow tree in the ravine and hang our hearts on it, as we sang "So we'll hang our hearts on a weeping willow tree, and bid a last farewell to thee."

Anne's debutante photograph

Students take a break from their studies by skiing around campus at Wells College (LEFT). After skinny-dipping, the proper attire consisted of leaves (CENTER). As part of her job with the American Youth Hostel, Anne demonstrated bad bicycling habits as part of a bicycle educational safety campaign (BOTTOM).

Anne Goddard Charter

On our 60th reunion, eight of us repeated this ceremony.

During our freshman year we had to take among other courses, French or German, Greek or Latin. Not wanting to show how little French I had learned the previous year or how little Latin I remembered, I chose Greek and German. I almost flunked Greek, but decided on German as my major. The reason was Herr Fleischner, the German professor, a fascinating and challenging poet, philosopher and teacher. So instead of studying the English and American classics, I studied German classics. Later, when I returned from Germany, I brought with me a complete set of leather-bound classics by German authors. These volumes were confiscated, no doubt, from Jewish homes and libraries and sold to me through secondhand book stores. At the time I saw it as a bargain. It was only later that I came to realize the cost in human lives.

Both Prohibition and the great Depression were in full swing during my college years, as well as the rise of Nazi Germany. But being college students, so wrapped in our own lives, we saw little with historic perspective.

Wells gave language students the opportunity to spend their junior year at a University in France or Germany. Luckily, my father vetoed my request to go abroad. Luckily, I say, because I probably wouldn't have been able to learn enough to pass my exams. He said it was too dangerous with this Nazi upstart, Hitler, who had come into power in 1930. If the situation stabilized however, and I had another chance, I could go later.

My second chance came after my senior year, when I was chosen as the exchange student to go to the University of Frankfurt-Am-Main for the 1935-36 terms. Although by this time Germany had been completely militarized and had made no secret of its expansion plans, the United States had taken an isolationist position. Like an ostrich with its head in the sand, we thought we were safe.

Most of the German exchange students were sailing on the same ship, so as you can imagine we had a ball. Once in Germany though, we went our separate ways. That first night alone in a hotel room in a strange country was the most lonesome feeling I had ever had. The feeling didn't last long however, for I found my way to Frau Hagen's, a boarding house for foreign students. There were two Dutch businessmen and one Dutch girl living there to perfect their German. I was soon introduced to the foreign students club and throughout the year participated in every imaginable excursion and vacation trip. We took several skiing trips into the Bavarian Alps, one taking us right past Hitler's Berchtesgarten retreat. As there were no ski lifts at that time, we would go by train to some village high in the Alps and then ski all the way to the bottom. Uphill climbs preceded downhill runs, with plenty of cross country thrown in. We would bind seal skins to our skis for the uphill to keep from slipping backwards.

I also bought a "faltboat" a kayak-type boat that could be folded up and carried in a case similar to a golf bag. We paddled down the Main River, usually camping overnight somewhere along the river bank. And when we had gone far enough, we could always find a train to take us back. In fact, any free weekend I could find friends to go hiking. We would take a train to a village, follow the hiking trails to the next train stop and then return home after a stein of beer and generous helpings

40

of peasant bread and cheese. These excursions culminated in a walking trip from one end of the Black Forest to the other.

Six of us planned the trip, two American men, two Englishmen, one Scottish girl and me. At the last minute the other girl dropped out, but I went anyway. We walked about ten miles a day along the beautiful forest trails, staying in Youth Hostels for 25 cents a night, as we did on all overnight trips. It was about a 100-mile trek and I completely wore out my shoes. One night in a small village while having our evening "brot and beer," we met a young woodcarver. I asked him if he had ever carved a nativity scene. He said no, but he would like to try. I gave him the twelve dollars he thought it would be worth, and he agreed to carve one, and have it finished before I had to return home. I gave him my address and the date I was leaving.

My father had predicted that I would fall in love with a German, and of course I scoffed at the idea. But I did. I fell in love with a medical student, in spite of the fact that any future for us was hard to visualize. I was completely enthralled with Bavarian-flavored Germany, but the thought of living there, and raising a family was unthinkable, even if Hitler was out of the picture. Many of the German students my age or older, who had grown up under a different regime, were far from supportive of their new dictator; for one thing, Hitler had outlawed their dueling clubs. Of course, they had to keep their feelings to themselves. Younger students were in the Hitler Youth clubs and there was no way to even hold a conversation with them. You listened, but said nothing. We thought little of the future, and were deaf and blind to the atrocities that were going on, blithely enjoying the beauties of Bavaria.

All outside activities were extra, of course. My father had given me a letter of credit for $500 to cover extras or emergencies. Because I am by nature quite frugal and cut corners whenever possible, and because of the inexpensive hostels and student rates, I had credit left after the University-year was over. My sister Louise planned to join me for a trip into Austria. My beau, Hans, and Bob Smith, a lifetime friend and shirt-tail relative from St. Louis, would go with us. When I went to meet my sister at the train station, I discovered the train had come and gone; no sister. I was ready to panic, but went outside to look around and saw a taxi parked in front of the station. I asked if he had perchance taken an American who couldn't speak German to a hotel? He had and he delivered me to the same hotel. Louise was safe and sound and so glad to see me she forgot to be angry. We returned to my lodgings where we left everything we didn't need for our Austrian trip. I assured her she could leave her letter of credit too, as I had enough left on mine. All was fine until we arrived in Austria and I tried to get Austrian money. My letter of credit had expired! I had expected to be in Germany for only the eight months of the university term. It was now just over a year and my letter of credit was valid for one year only. We waited in Vienna while Louise took the train back to Germany to get her money! By this time we felt like seasoned travelers! Sister Louise and I had another memorable adventure in the picturesque town of Garmish-Partenkchen. We were intrigued by the houses with paintings on their outside walls, the *gemutligkeit* and the quaintness of the village. A fall storm had dropped two feet of fresh snow, so we thought it would be a kick to rent skis and try our luck at cross-country skiing. We left the trails for a short cut back to town, and our luck ran out. We bogged down in waist deep snow and for a while thought we'd never see civilization again.

The climax to this unbelievable year came when I set out for the designated Post Office to pick up the nativity set I had ordered. My sister had gone directly to Paris, where we were staying with the Jays until we set sail from Cherbourg. When I went to pick up the nativity set, it had not yet arrived. I was a few days early, however, and was determined to wait despite the fact that I had only a few German marks left. It arrived the next day. Though I had not a cent in my pockets, it was worth the wait! The nativity set carved by the young woodcarver is one of my most cherished possessions. The set includes the traditional kings, one with his camel, three shepherds, one the simple one, often found in small remote villages, their sheep, and of course, Mary in her blue gown, Joseph, and the babe in the manger. These pieces have mellowed beautifully with time, and have helped me celebrate the birth of our savior for more than fifty years.

Fortunately, when I arrived penniless in Paris, I was met by Emil, the Jay's chauffeur, and was able to borrow enough money from him to tip the porter!

LIVING ON MY OWN

When I got back to the states, I learned there was an organization in Northfield, Massachusetts, called the American Youth Hostels. Its founders, Monroe and Isabel Smith, had studied the hostel movement in Germany under its founder Richard Schirrmann, and were adapting his methods to the United States. I was intrigued. I had benefited by staying in Youth Hostels all over Germany and I was eager to see them established here. I joined this young movement by going to work for them. There were about eight of us at first and we all lived in a big old house across the street from Monroe and Isabel Smith and their family. We were not quite volunteers. We made enough for room and board and travel expenses while on the road, which usually meant bicycling. We took turns preparing meals. What stands out most vividly in my memory were the stacks of bread, the ever-present peanut butter and the breakfasts. Our breakfast cereal consisted of raw oatmeal covered with various fruits, brown sugar and milk. The theory being, if you ate oatmeal raw, it would expand in your stomach and you wouldn't get hungry.

We were jacks of all trades learning to do whatever was necessary. One of the office jobs was publishing the American Youth Hostel (AYH) magazine, illustrated by our in-house artist Isabel. It was filled with articles and advise, written by whomever, enhanced with photographs taken, developed and artistically displayed by the staff. We experimented with "bleeding" the pictures, a new technique at the time. We solicited ads through the mail and from canvassing sport and bicycle shops in Boston. We set up walking and biking routes with a Hostel at fifteen-mile intervals. And we lead bicycle trips through the countryside.

Connie, a co-worker, and I talked ourselves into a summer abroad to further study the youth hostel system. We wanted to take movies, make a "documentary," and it gave me an excuse to see Hans again.

That summer we bicycled through parts of Germany, Holland and Belgium, consulting with hostel leaders, and finishing the summer in England. We planned to board a German ship to return to the USA. A crisis occurred however when Hitler "absorbed" Austria and demanded control of the German Sudentenland, territory incorporated into Czechoslovakia after Germany's defeat in World War One. War seemed inevitable. All German ships were being recalled. We were stuck in England, war imminent with Germany and no way home.

Fortunately a compromise between England and Germany was reached in September 1938 by persuading Czechoslovakia to give up their acquired territory. We sailed for home on board a German ship. But the peace was short-lived, and England declared war on Germany the following year, September 8, 1939.

My reunion with Hans was also short-lived. Germany declared war on Poland the following year, and Hans, a medical student, was conscripted into the army and sent to Poland.

I heard from him once after I was married, but could not find it in my heart to say I had given up on us. I suppose he never knew whether I had received his letter or not.

After returning to the U.S., I went to Pennsylvania to follow up on contacts there and start a youth hostel chain in the picturesque Pennsylvania-Dutch countryside. I was so fascinated with the barns decorated with the hex signs, I thought of touring the country taking pictures of barns and writing a book about their history. Many years later this type of illustrated book became very popular.

Generally, when setting up a hostel chain, we would map out a route that would make an interesting bicycle trip, then go into a town and set up meetings with whomever we could get to listen. We'd show movies, distribute literature, give talks about the purpose of hosteling, and join up new members. Those who became interested would help us find a usable house or barn that could be fixed up by the community. The ideal situation was to have the hostel on property where a couple would be willing to be the house parents. The accommodations at first were very simple. There was a boy's and a girl's dormitory, each equipped with some kind of bunks and mattresses, including even straw mattresses. Blankets were provided, but the hostelers carried their own sheet sleeping bags. The sleeping bags we know had not been invented. There was also an area where the hostelers could prepare their own meals.

After a few years I was drawn back to St. Louis. I was sent by AYH to set up a chain in the Missouri Ozark Country. I lived with my family again and found some office space and sponsors to cover my expenses.

We started with a hostel in DeSoto, Missouri, about 40 miles south of St. Louis. It was at Cedar Brow Farm run by our good friends Tee Peck and Anne Fisher. From there the chain ran south into Ozark country. Once the chain was fairly well established, I turned it over to competent hands and began to think about the rest of my life.

I had dreamed of living in the country, either on a farm or ranch. I decided I should know how country folk made their living! With these lofty thoughts in mind, I enrolled in a course of animal husbandry at the University of Missouri in Columbia. The only other girl in my class was Jean Pore. Jean and I have kept up with each other all these years, and she has come to visit us on our ranch.

That year I learned about pedigrees for cattle and hog breeds. I became "hog queen" for winning the hog judging contest. I also exhibited my expertise as a hog caller. I learned about crop rotation and other good farming practices, but I hadn't solved the pestering question, what next? To my surprise I was offered a job that summer on a Wyoming dude ranch where I would meet a real cowboy. I jumped at the chance, met the cowboy and my life was changed forever.

It was at this time that I first heard the name of Boyd Charter at that party on the Merrimac River. It was the decision to head west for a summer adventure that changed my life so completely.

But first, who was this cowboy I was about to meet?

PART II: BOYD'S BIOGRAPHY

BOYD'S RELATIVES

Boyd's life encompassed the tail end of "when the West was young," a whole era when cowboys were still cowboys, a transition period of war and post-war, when East merged with West; and finally ranching in the Bull Mountains, where he took a stand to save the land. Though Boyd's life span is ended, no one knows how far the ripple effects will go.

Oral history of the decades before Boyd was born was passed on to him by his father, Bert Charter. He told tales of his exploits with the Butch Cassidy gang and Boyd retold these stories and others he remembered from his childhood with great relish at home. It was not until after his mother died however that he made them public.

After an article was published in *True West* magazine, "Dad rode with the Wild Bunch," by feature writer Kathryn Wright, Boyd's brother-in-law Olin Emery wrote a rebuttal insisting that "Bert was friendly with all outlaws, and lawmen alike," but that he had no part in any of the robberies. He ended his article by saying, "My greatest interest in this matter is to redeem the loving memory of a fine, honest, hardworking man for the sake of my late wife, Bernice Charter Emery, two daughters, grandchildren and great grandchildren."

In the July-August 1979 issue, an old friend of the family also wrote a letter to *True West* in response to the article:

> I read with a great deal of interest "Dad Rode with the Wild Bunch" in the February issue. It brought back pleasant memories of over half a century ago when my father owned a ranch near Dubois, Wyoming. The summer range for this ranch was along the continental divide and joining it on the west was the cattle outfit from Jackson Hole. The principal ranchers were Pete Hansen and Bert Charter.
>
> My older brother, Manley and I rode on fall roundups with these ranchers several times. At this period of Charter's life he was a very respected rancher. I didn't know he had been a member of Cassidy's bunch. On more than one occasion I heard one cowboy say to another something like 'Say did you know old Bert was a wild one in his youth? Mixed up with a bunch of outlaws, I hear.'
>
> My brother Manley and Bert's son Boyd were good friends and they used to wrestle and rough-house around in the evenings on these roundups and nearly wrecked what little homemade furniture was in the old Fish Creek cow camp.

It seems strange that no one in the Jackson Community seemed aware of Bert's past, except of course Will Simpson. However, in those days no one asked about a newcomer's past, and if they knew something, they kept their mouths shut.

It is easier to remember stories than names. In pursuing memory search I rediscovered Boyd's cousin, Bert Charter, who visited us on the ranch on numerous occasions when Boyd was still alive. He is 89 years old (in 1995) sharp and witty as ever, but alas, suffers from instant name recall, as I and many of my peers do. Cousin Bert did, however, reveal some stories about Albert (Boyd's grandfather) and others of the time.

The following is what I have been able to unearth about Boyd's father's history. As time is forgiving, as all participants must be dead by now, and as the way a man ends his life must be the important part, I feel he will forgive me if I reveal some other aspects of his past.

Robert Henry Charter, Boyd's father, was better known as Bert, or when associated with the Butch Cassidy gang as "Kid" or "Kid Madden." He was born in Delhi, Iowa, June 14, 1873, six years after Robert Leroy Parker (alias Butch Cassidy) was born in the Utah farming community of Circleville in 1867.

We surmise Bert's grandfather, Albert Charter's father was the one who emigrated from England, as Albert and his brother fought on opposite sides of the civil war. Albert was wounded by a saber, and carried a scar from his right shoulder to his left hip. We know nothing more about Albert's brother, but Albert must have ventured westward after the war.

Albert made his living as a carpenter. He married Mary Hughes, daughter of Judge Hughes. Unfortunately, I cannot come up with a first name for Judge Hughes, Boyd's maternal grandfather, as everyone seems to have called him "Judge." His story as passed down to me is that he was the first Circuit Judge in Wyoming. He homesteaded on Cherry Creek, Colorado, which is now in the center of Denver, during the 1858 gold rush.

Cousin Bert tells a story about Judge Hughes' brother, who carried the mail between Wyoming and Colorado. On one trip he was caught in a blizzard. His horse got away from him, leaving him stranded with only his pack mule. As it was impossible to have any sense of direction, he decided the only way to survive the storm was to kill his mule, use the hide as shelter, and the flesh for nourishment until the blizzard abated, which could be several days. When he took out his knife to slash the mules throat, it let out a loud bray and jerked loose. He took off after his mule and kept following that mule, until it lead him into Laramie and to safety.

Judge Hughes was married to a Cherokee and although they may have had other children, we know only of Mary born in 1853.

Albert and Mary made their home in Delhi, Iowa, where their five children were born: Mamie, the oldest died when she was 11. Bert (Robert Henry) was the first boy, then came Ernest (the father of Boyd's cousin, Bert), Wade and Arl.

Albert deserted his family and disappeared when son Bert was about 12. Albert turned up on various occasions at his son Ernest's house over the years, and cousin Bert recalls hearing tales of Albert's part in the Civil War, and remembers seeing the saber wound scar from shoulder to thigh. Cousin Bert said on his last visit, when Albert was 76 years old, he departed in pursuit of a widow woman.

A portrait of Mary Hughes Charter shows a strong woman, as well as a proud and handsome one. Mary eventually remarried a Colonel and had another son, Babe.

Bert kept in contact with his brothers or they with him. They often turned up at his ranch in Jackson and were known as "the Uncles." He was never reconciled with his father however. He left home at the age of 12 or 14, riding the rails to Rawlins, Wyoming, where perhaps he hoped to find his Grandfather Hughes.

ALIAS "KID MADDEN"

In Rawlins, Bert's first jobs undoubtedly were cleaning out stables and tending horses. This led to his job tending horses at the Bitter Creek Stage Station. It was a favorite gathering place for cowboys, many of whom were members of outlaw gangs. At about this time, Jeff Dunbar, the famous outlaw leader began his career. Rebel gangs began showing up from all over the West. Bert not only hobnobbed with these cowboys, but he became one of them while riding for some of the biggest ranches in Wyoming.

One of his earliest friends was Harry Longabough, alias Harry Alonzo, the "Sundance Kid." Bert said that Harry was an extra good cowboy with a wonderful personality. It may have been through Harry that Bert met Cassidy, as they all rode for Ora Haley's 2 Bar // cattle ranches at various times.

Glimpses of Bert's early life are revealed through newspaper clippings from the Craig Colorado *The Pantagraph:*

> After spending a few months among the gay and lovely belles of eastern society, Mr. Bert Charter has returned to this city. While in the effete Iowa civilization Mr. Charter dropped his sobriquet of 'Colorado' with a dun sickening thud, and rejoiced in the title 'Mr.' However, a few days in the wild and woolly west will take the shine off his shirt bosom and the memory of many fair eastern damsels out of his head.

Bert was 20 years old when this story appeared.

An article written by U.S. Fitzpatrick, titled "Home on the Range," also about this period of Wyoming history was published in *The Last Frontier* volume I. Mr. Fitzpatrick describes his family's move to Lay, Wyoming, and how his sister Eva attracted cowboys "like bees to honey." He wrote:

> Eva was to be postmistress, mother would operate the road house which meant providing lodging and meals for the few who might come wanting such accommodations, and Dad would operate the ranch as well as our own ranch five and a half miles up Lay Creek.

In telling of the cowboys who had come with the trail herd, he wrote:

> When Ora Haley brought his herds from Wyoming into Northwest Colorado, the men who came with them were these same seasoned cattle-wise riders.
>
> Naturally, with a pretty eighteen year old post mistress now handing out the mail, the cow punchers had a ready-made excuse to come to the post office. Waddies who received anything more than an advertisement for Mueller saddles or Cubine boots, maybe once in six months, came regularly when in the vicinity.

Among the mounted 'bees' who were attracted by the 'honey' was Jens Maddsen, the tall handsome Swede who believed himself to be somewhat a lady's man. He had good clothing and even owned an overcoat. Jens must have believed he was making some progress.

One day Jens, Ed Sizer (Miles), Jim Norvell, Bert Charter and Joe Martin (Blansit) came for mail. Windy Brown the mail carrier had just come and Eva was busy sorting the mail. So the cow punchers bunched up across the road and waited, talking.

It was probably Jens who suggested a little fancy riding, no doubt to impress the postmistress. At any rate, the first we noticed, Jens was on one of the horses, trying to make it buck. The pony had been dozing in the warm sunshine and didn't have any interest in bucking matches or postmistresses. He wouldn't accommodate. Finally Jens told Bert Charter, "Give me a handful of that prairie sand and I bet I'll make him uncork."

Bert handed up a handful of sand and Jens leaned forward and poured it from his hand into the horses ear. The pony came "uncorked." all right. Jens didn't have time to get leaned back and sittin' the saddle, He turned a complete somersault in the air and landed flat on his back. He didn't move. Only his toes twitched. Presently he spoke in a thin, hoarse voice: "Oh my God, I'm dying. I'm dying. Bring Eva."

As the others leaned close, he repeated, "Bring Eva. Bring Eva. I'm dying."

He might have had the others convinced, but not Bert Charter. Bert gave him a nudge in the ribs with the toe of his boot. "Get up you dang faker," Bert told him. "Y' ain't no more dyin' than I am."

"I am too," insisted Jens, "I'm hurt bad. You saw me get throwed."

After a little while a couple of the men went and caught Jens' horse and brought him back. Jens sat up, put on his hat, and got up and got on the pony and they all headed for the Horse Camp. For many a day when the crew was in town, all they had to do to get Jens to buy a round was to whisper "Pour a handful of prairie sand in his ear," or "I'm dyin'. Bring Eva."

Butch was in the penitentiary from 1894-96, so things were probably relatively calm then. The *Craig Courier*, Saturday, January 9, 1897 reported: "Harry Alonzo and Bert Charter went to lower Snake River last Monday to establish a winter camp and look after the cattle of the Reader Company 'till Spring."

In the same paper it mentions that "John Wilkes foremen for J.G. Massey. spent the New Years in Dixon with his family."

Come spring, we find in the *Craig Courier*, March 20, 1897, "It is reported that Bert Charter has bought 100 head of cattle from John Wilkes."

And further on in the same paper this item appears:

It is reported that 'Kid' Charter does not seem to want the title of 'bad man' to pass him lightly by. Last Tuesday he stood in front of Wm.

49

Dunbar's place of business and fired three shots from a Winchester up the street in the direction of D.C. Jones' residence, whereupon, he was summarily dealt with by the constable, John Baker. Uncle John is the right man in the right place. Having no justice of the Peace in this precinct, Charter was taken before Justice Groshart of the savory.

On August 10, 1898 in *The Steamboat* of Steamboat Springs, Colorado, is an account of the death of Jeff Dunbar, who was referred to as a famous outlaw leader. The article describes the events of his life and death in the highly exaggerated prose of the times. The article claimed Dunbar was the leader of some 400 men, listing eight of them, including Butch Cassidy and Bert Charter, "and a score of other less prominent, but none the less desperate characters." The article goes on to surmise that Butch Cassidy might take over the leadership, "but it is generally believed that there is not a single man in all the league possessed of sufficient ability to hold the gang in line and keep them subject to the dictatorship of any one man."

My impression has been that the gangs were independent of each other, working around a small core of men who did the planning. Butch Cassidy became a legend before he became history, and it continues to be difficult to sort the facts from myths.

The popularity of the legend can be attributed to the "Robin Hood" nature of Cassidy's personality, his bravado in thinking he could outwit as well as outrun, and his ability to turn from cowboy into bandit, and back again, without the law catching up or catching on. When it got too hot, they got out of the kitchen, or tried to. Many returned to their respectable lives. Fortunately for them, they were not in the position of those who run for public office today, who have the foibles of their youth held against them. Many of Cassidy's men prospered without their past ever coming to light. There was honor among these thieves; they kept their oath of silence.

One of the Hole in the Wall Gang's favorite hangouts was Baggs, Wyoming, a town friendly to them and where the citizens put up with their escapades. Other attractions were its location on the Colorado-Wyoming border and the three belles of Baggs; Maude and Jannette (Jano) Magor and Mary Calvert.

Maude and Jano's parents were Thomas and Eliza Magor. The first we know about Thomas comes from a newspaper article in the *Galena Daily Gazette*, Galena, Illinois 1876. Titled the "Hazel Green Horror," it tells of a whirlwind that ravaged the town killing several people. From the article:

> Johnson Richards, the son of the dead lady, at the time the whirlwind struck the premises was in the hay loft of a barn on the lot and was instantly killed, while Thomas Magor, a young man who was on the first floor of the barn, received a frightful cut about the face, which, though not dangerous, will disfigure him for life. The barn on the premises of Mrs. Richards was demolished, and a fine trotting horse owned by Thomas Magor instantly killed.

The couple lived in Corwith, Iowa where the girls were born and moved to Baggs in 1888 when Maude was six years old. They ran a wholesale-retail store and the town's hotel. Bert liked to tell the story about how his father-in-law Thomas landed in a tree. The story goes that Thomas was returning with a wagon load of supplies, including some dynamite, when his team spooked. The dynamite exploded, possibly from leaking out onto the wheels, and Thomas landed in a tree unhurt.

Baggs was a busy town, a crossroads of pioneer travel. The country between Baggs and Rawlins was wide-open and uninhabited. In addition to the store and hotel Baggs had its own doctor. Dr. White delivered both Boyd and Boyd's sister Bernice. Dr. White's wife was almost 100 and living in a nursing home when we visited Baggs in the early 1970s.

Boyd tells this story of the pranks his dad said he and the boys used to pull in their younger days:

> They would ride to Baggs, get drunk and shoot things up. One time they shot the heads off of twelve chickens. They took them into the hotel and gave my grandmother a five dollar gold piece for each chicken and told her to cook them for supper. All twelve of them. At the table Eliza told the gang—'You boys better behave! Think of what you, sitting around my table, are worth in rewards!'
>
> Another time their damn shots didn't just go up in the air, but they hit the damn hotel, putting quite a few holes in it. They carefully counted the holes and paid a dollar for every damn one.

Mary Calvert, the third "belle," was the best friend of the Magor sisters. According to Boyd, "Her dad owned quite a big cow outfit there. In that day and age the Calverts was one of the most prominent families in southern Wyoming, or northern Colorado. But this Mary Calvert married that Elzie Lay."

All three girls married members of the gang. Maude married Bert Charter, Jano married George Musgrove who had been a member of the infamous Black Jack gang, and Mary married Elzie Lay. According to Boyd, "Elzie was the brains of the whole outfit. Cassidy was the guy with the guts and Lay was the guy with the brains. There was a hell of a lot of money moving around them days. Nine times out of ten it was gold! They'd be making a shipment from one bank to another, you see, 'course in them days the only way they had of shipping it was on the railroad where they had them safes in them baggage cars. 'Course they couldn't afford to rob that goddamn train every day, 'less they knew something was on it. And Lay's job, by god, Lay was well educated, Lay's job was to get in with all those different railroad people and he knew damn well there was a shipment of gold on that train when they hit it, or a shipment of money."

From what I've read, Butch was arrested only once, in 1894, for supposed horse stealing. He had a scar that allegedly resulted from resisting arrest. Butch spent a short time in the penitentiary, but when the Judge released him for good behavior, he warned Butch not to do anymore robbing in Wyoming. The prosecuting attorney at his trial was Will Simpson, a lawyer who later moved to Jackson Hole, Wyoming.

Bert didn't talk much about his past, and Maude never mentioned it to my knowledge. But Boyd had early memories of his own. When he was five or six, he remembered a member of the gang (Billy Sautelle) stopped by their ranch in Pinedale, Wyoming. Billy was the meanest member of the Cassidy gang and the only one who had killed anyone. Boyd said Billy never sat with his back to a window and always kept his eye on the door. During his stay with Charters, he offered to help out by milking the cow. Now, most ranchers hate to be tied down, so they'd keep the cow's calf near so it could milk for them if they had to be away. They'd let the calf suck two tits, while they milked the other two.

In Boyd's words: "This guy's name was Billy Sautelle. He was more or less a lonely bird and a little bit trigger happy. Anyway, he came along there at our place and was staying there. My Dad had two or three milk cows, we had our own milk and butter. He's out there in the corral milking this old cow and this old calf kept butting the cow. Now this old calf I'd made a pet out of. I used to lead this calf around and ride him and everything else, and he's my pet. Well, that calf kept butting the old cow, and the cow would move around. So this old Sautelle picked up a rope and tied this old calf to the corral fence and give him a good old kick in the belly. And there's a big old bunch of cow manure laying there, and hell, I couldn't just watch him abuse my calf, so I reached down and I grabbed a whole handful of that fresh cow shit and hit him in the face with it."

In telling the story Boyd would conclude, "Sautelle didn't do anything but cuss a lot. I don't think he wanted to tackle my Dad. They were friends."

When Boyd was nine, just before leaving Pinedale, he remembers his Dad being gone for a week or more. When he got back, they packed up and left, having sold their little ranch and freight outfit. Later some old timers said they saw old Bert on a trail that hadn't been used for years. It ended in the Robber's Roost country in Utah, a cave-pocked area attractive to outlaws, and a good place to hide loot. Bert later said his $8,000 helped pay for the Jackson Hole Ranch. After his mother died, Boyd came into $55,000 as his inheritance from that ranch. He used it to buy our Bull Mountain Ranch. So, when the railroad came and tried to get our ranch in the Bulls so they could strip-mine the coal under it, Boyd allowed as how it must be divine retribution: that the railroad was just trying to get its money back.

He also remembered as a teenager two men who drove into the ranch in a Model T and camped in the meadow. He said, "My folks gave them groceries, and they stayed a spell. They talked a lot with my dad, but one of them liked to shoot grouse, so I'd go with him up into the aspen grove on the ridge behind our house and shoot grouse. That man was one of the best shots I'd ever seen. Later, I heard my dad say that Cassidy was the best grouse hunter he'd ever known."

Shortly after this, Will Simpson came to visit Bert. Evidence that Cassidy was friendly with many local lawmen comes from Larry Pointer's book, *In Search of Butch Cassidy*.

Will Simpson had been prosecuting attorney in Lander between 1892 and 1896 when he followed his family to the Jackson Hole valley. Butch was arrested and tried for stealing horses in 1894. Simpson was well acquainted with Butch and his trial. Some writers paint Simpson as an enemy of Cassidy, representing the righteous arm of the law. But Bert knew better.

The Phillips manuscript, "Bandit Invincible, The Story of Butch Cassidy" may throw some light on this relationship:

> The sheriff was a friend of Butch along with many others and Butch went willingly without chains along with Sheriff (sic) Orson. The sheriff treated Butch as a companion traveler and no one suspected him of being the Hole in the Wall leader of the Wild Bunch, who had been captured and sentenced to prison as they had nothing in the papers. Orson recommended Butch very highly to the Warden at the pen.

This manuscript, along with a revolver which had Cassidy's brand, reverse E, box E carved into the grip was saved by the Lundstroms, some of Cassidy's few close friends with whom he discussed his past.

After a night on the town, Will Simpson and Bert decided to top it off with a bottle of whiskey while they reminisced sitting in the front room. It just so happened that Boyd slept in a room that opened into it, and he was awakened by their rather boisterous arrival. That night, with his ear to the door, Boyd heard just about everything he ever knew about his dad and the Wild Bunch. Cassidy had visited Simpson, too, and this is what set them off matching stories.

This is the account Boyd gives as he describes his Dad's first job with the gang:

> Dad's first job with the gang was holding the getaway horses. When they'd rob one of them trains, you see, or a bank, either one, well they didn't go off and leave their horses. Maybe there'd only be actually two guys who actually rode into the bank but they didn't just go in there and tie their horses up to a post, 'cause Christ, they just might pull back and break loose, or somebody might get between them and their horses, so they always got somebody to hold their horses. Well, you see, that was when my Dad was pretty darn young, his first job was holding the getaway horses.

And that is the part Bert played in the famous heist of the coal mine payroll in Telluride, Colorado, 1889. Boyd's version:

> If you've ever been to Telluride, Telluride's built right in a canyon, fact is most of the buildings there are on a steep side hill. And going out of there you had to go right straight up over a goddamn mountain to get outta there, or else go right down the creek and the damn railroad was right there too, you know. So they didn't dare go down the creek 'cause they could come up to them on the railroad. So there was a trail up out of there that ran right up that steep goddamn mountain, with switch backs, you see. So Cassidy and Elzie Lay, they're the ones that went

down there and robbed it, and got the payroll. My dad stayed up on top of this mountain with a string of fresh horses up there. When they started out of there, there was this train, in fact the train that had the payroll, so they had to go down this creek for a ways, right down this canyon and so some of them guys grabbed rifles and shotguns and hopped on this goddamn train and they had, why they had a pretty good gun battle for a ways, 'til they could finally get out of the canyon and start up this trail. By this time they had a posse on horseback to take out after them. So my dad was on top of this mountain where he could look down and see the whole show down there. So, while he had these fresh horses tied to some trees there, why this big old colt came in there, kind of a big old gentle horse, just getting in there and smelling noses with these saddle horses they had tied up there. So dad was thinking he might cause one of the horses to break loose, so he caught him and tied him up to a tree. He looked down there and here comes Cassidy and Lay up those switch backs and the posse right behind them. So he waits 'till he sees that Cassidy's over here and the posse's down there and he ties a big old piece of dead tree to this old colts tail and then gives that colt a boot out over that mountain, and the funniest part of the story he told me—that old colt, the tree dragging along you know, 'course he spooked and Jesus he went down through there, down on this trail where the posse was and he whupped right through the goddamn posse and their horses spooked all over the goddamn mountain.

So in this way, Bert became part of the gang, joined with them in their escapades, and cowboyed with them on some of the biggest spreads. They were all top hands and knew the country.

In those days cowboys would come out and work for them big outfits like the Middlesex Land and Livestock, and the Two Bars. Those outfits ran thousands of cattle. Well, some of the cowboys would take up a little piece of land and decide they was goin' to start into the cattle business themselves, maybe get 50 to 75 or 100 head of cattle and then here comes the goddamn Two Bar and they'd throw about 10,000 head of cattle right in on top of them, and of course naturally, his cattle would mix with the Two Bars and then when they'd get ready to move they'd just take the whole goddamn outfit and go. 'Course that's what you'd call a range war. Some guy would come in there and take up a homestead on a spring. Then maybe he'd fence off a little bit of hay for his saddle horses. Well, fact is, they'd come along and knock the goddamn fence down and go on in and graze him out. In other words, them big outfits were just like big coal outfits now. They wouldn't give them little outfits a chance. So about that time along came Butch Cassidy and the Sundance Kid, Bob Musgrove and oh hell, all the others. They couldn't get a chance to get outfits of their own so they started robbing banks and trains. My dad was in that outfit, they done all that just in protest of all them big outfits. That's how it all started.

The outlaws were friendly with most of the small ranchers, and Boyd tells how these ranchers made it possible for the outlaws to survive:

> The outlaw gang 'd come along and leave five or six head of horses at this ranch. They'd probably tell them now, hey listen, keep these horses in there so if we come here in a hurry, we're not going to have to go out and hunt them horses. The ranchers would take care of the horses and feed and water them, whatever it took to keep them in shape. So there was a little old couple who were some of those we were talking about. They had a little old ranch out there on Bitter Creek, and they borrowed five hundred dollars from the old banker there. So they couldn't pay back the five hundred and the banker was going to foreclose. Well, the gang could always stay there, so they came along and this old guy said this banker was going to foreclose on him. Cassidy said—'What do you owe him?' She said, 'Five hundred dollars.' Well, they usually kept this money right on them, you know, so Cassidy gave this old guy five hundred dollars and said, 'When that guy (the banker) comes by, pay him off. Just give it to him, and be damn sure you get a paper signed that you paid him.' So Cassidy went down, Cassidy and Lay was together, and laid along the trail, and here comes this old banker riding up the trail, and course, they was out of sight. So this guy he rode on up to this ranch, they just stayed there, and in a few hours he came back down the trail so they just stepped out and took the goddamn money away from him. Here the debt was paid off and they had their money back.

Another story Boyd liked to tell was about Butch and his little dog Sunday. Sunday, though small, was a bona fide member of the Wild Bunch and went with them on the trails. One hot summer day they were making a fast getaway with Sunday running alongside, a posse hot on their heels. Sunday was tiring and lagging behind and the posse passed him. When Cassidy saw this, he told his men to ride up on the ridge and play some Winchester music to distract them while he slipped back to get Sunday. They played the music, Butch picked up Sunday, carrying him in front on his saddle, and they all got away.

Close encounters were probably as important as the "gold" and lasted a lot longer in the recounting.

In the 1960's Boyd and I went to see Jano Magor (Musgrove), hoping to get some information or stories from her. She had recently recovered from a stroke and must have been close to ninety, but she was still a handsome vibrant woman, able to live alone in her small apartment. She told us that when she came out of the stroke she was cussing and talking Spanish, her subconscious asserting itself, no doubt, for although she had been exposed to rough language all her life, "ladies did not cuss." She had become fluent in Spanish during her South America

Mary Charter

Albert Charter

Bert Charter

Maude Charter

Butch Cassidy (LEFT), unknown (CENTER), and Bert Charter (RIGHT). This tintype photograph was taken in New York City in 1902. Courtesy of Gail Garrett, National Unit Gallery.

sojourn with George Musgrove after the gangs broke up, but hadn't spoken it for years.

When we brought up involvement with the Cassidy bunch, she told us of having been offered a considerable sum to tell her story to the producers of the movie "Butch Cassidy and the Sun Dance Kid." "I could have used the money," she said, "as you can see I'm practically living on welfare, but we girls took an oath when we took up with the gang, never to talk about their affairs, even among ourselves." Her resolve to keep silent was still relevant, as many members of the gang went "respectable" after it broke up, and some of the families never knew of the past.

In a series of articles in Hearst-Magazine-Cosmopolitan, Matt Werner commented that "their wives often knew nothing of the nature of their work. Mrs. Lay is the widow of Elzie Lay (Leigh). Mrs. Lay is a woman of superior intelligence and for many years shielded her early association with the gang." So, Jano offered little new information to Boyd and me, but would talk of things we already knew about. What she was most eager to talk about, however, were her adventures with George Musgrove.

Shortly after the gang broke up, Musgrove went to Brazil and got a job running an English-owned ranch up the Amazon River. He sent Jano money to come and join him at the mouth of the river, where he would meet her, and they could board a boat going up stream. It turned out he couldn't make it, but he sent a friend who saw that she got on the riverboat and who stood guard at her cabin door until their arrival at the ranch. Jano told us of the primitive conditions and the jungle surrounding them inhabited by native Indians. She said she always had the feeling there were eyes peering out at her, and that she had no privacy at all, even when answering the call of nature in the bushes. One time when the highfalutin' owners from England were visiting, a native man came running into the compound stark-naked. She was so embarrassed she grabbed a pair of George's pants for him to put on. From then on, she said, whenever the natives wanted some clothing, they came visiting—naked.

Soon, through devious means, George Musgrove was able to start an outfit of his own and apparently made plenty of money. The Musgrove's made numerous trips between Mexico and the U.S., and Boyd as a young boy on the ranch in Jackson remembered her visits. He was especially impressed with her ring-covered hands, and the expensive jewelry she wore.

The Musgrove's ranching career began at the same time that Butch Cassidy was in South America, and they met on several occasions. One of those meetings, according to Larry Pointer, was in Mexico.

The Mexican Revolution was being led by Francisco Madero, aided and abetted by folk hero Pancho Villa. Butch knew Pancho Villa and because of this connection, Jano and her husband were able to travel through Mexico on one of their early trips back to the states. She told us that in spite of being under the protection of the revolutionaries, they had to cross a field littered with dead bodies in order to reach the border.

She concluded her South American sagas by saying "George got so mean I had to leave him." Her last trip to South America was in 1912 with Sarah Jabens, a friend from Baggs days. According to Boyd, Jano continued to live a colorful life until old age caught up with her. She died a few years after our visit.

With the heat on in 1898, the gang broke up. Some of the members headed for Mexico and South America, including Cassidy and the Sundance Kid. Bert Charter and Bill Blackmoor, however, headed north for the Yukon gold rush.

The trip proved high adventure if not lucrative. He and Blackmoor built a boat with which they were able to shoot the infamous White Horse Rapids. After two years searching for gold, they mushed 1,000 miles with dog teams to return to the U.S. The final leg of the journey Bert made by once again riding the rails. His loot for all this was a watch, held by a watch fob made of gold nuggets. This is in the possession of the Boyd Charter family, as is the watch that was allegedly given to Maude by Etta Place. It is not Etta Place's gold watch, but maybe one from a robbery. There are no discernible markings on it. The ivory-handled single-action Colt .45 is in the possession of Joe Charter.

On returning to Baggs, Bert bar tended in Jack Ryan's saloon. He still was not tied to home, however, as a tintype sent to us by Gail Garrett indicates he was in New York with Cassidy in February 1902. The tintype she purchased was called "The Wild Bunch" and was taken at the DeYoung studio, 826 Broadway, near Grace Cathedral in New York. Butch Cassidy is on the left, an unknown is in the middle, and Bert Charter is on the right, wearing the identical suit, cravat and tie pin that he wore in an earlier photo that we have.

Butch had returned from South America in 1902 to go to Buffalo, New York, to be treated at the Pierce Medical Institute for an old case of gonorrhea. While in New York, Butch and Etta and pals lived high on the town. He and Etta had a now famous picture taken at the same studio, as above. Etta was dressed in a velvet gown, Butch in tails. The photographer thought them distinguished, mistaking them for "Western society," according to an article *The Wild West Magazine* reported about their visit.

From New York, Butch returned to South America, and Bert to Baggs to marry his sweetheart. He and Maude Magor were married in Rawlins in 1903, and lived in Baggs until 1912.

Apparently it took some time for Bert to settle down completely, for although living in Baggs, he owned a share in Jack Ryan's saloon in Rawlins. It was a gathering place for any gang member who happened by. The story goes that one time Bert and Billy Sautelle ran a bunch of Mexicans out of town, considering them too "knife-happy." Later on the Mexicans returned, and Bert said that even later as a rancher he never got off the train in Rawlins while shipping cattle from his ranch to Omaha.

In a letter written to Boyd in 1966 at the time of his sister Bernice's death, Talbot Bailey says "I wrote Olin that I had not seen much of the Charter family since 1912. I remember well the morning your family drove away—six horses and a flat rack with a lumber wagon trailer, all possessions loaded and people headed for a new life. I also remember the old tom cat returning to Baggs after eluding all the coyotes on the prairie. The only time we saw any of you before 1930 was at Pinedale in 1916 just before you sold out and went to Jackson."

In this letter he mentions some other Bailey relatives. During Navy days, Boyd and I visited Ruth and Bayard Bailey in California, and in summer 1977, Magor and Dorothy came to visit us.

But I never did get the Bailey relatives sorted out. Jack Bailey, who visited the ranch after Boyd's death tried to help me as follows: Thomas and Eliza Magor's children were Maude, Lizzie, Victoria, Harley, Harvey, Neil and Jano. Maude married Bert Charter. Lizzie married Ed Bailey, and their son Magor and his wife Hazel had a son Jack who was the one who visited us and whose son Jim Bailey we also got to know.

Now for the confusion. A Magor cousin married William Bailey (no relation to Ed, although they were both teamsters and both from the vicinity of Baggs). Their children were Talbot, Bayard, Fritz and Magor.

And with that partially resolved, back to their departure from Baggs in 1912. Bert had started freighting and made enough to buy a small ranch near Pinedale. Boyd describes it thus:

It wasn't a big outfit. He had about 300 acres and there was that old log and dirt roofed house there and he was running freight for a living, trying to make enough to eat off of and build himself up a herd of cattle, course he eventually did after a period of time. But anyway, he bought 12 head of cows, there was a creek came right down to the house, oh, it was a pretty good sized creek and a lot of big old woods. I can still remember it, big, old high woods. The beaver came in there and built a dam on this creek, a great big beaver pond right down over the bench from our house. We moved there in the fall of the year and then them goddamn beaver moved in. This beaver dam froze over, anyway these cows, the whole damned outfit of 'em, walked out on that ice and broke through and drowned. The whole damn herd of 'em. I can remember my dad came into the house and told my mother. I remember I was just four or five, he said, the cows was all down in the pond dead. We walked over there to the edge of this pond and looked down there and looked at those cows. And my mother cried, and my sister and I cried. That was the first herd of cattle.

Well, he had his freight outfit and kept on freighting. He started up a freight outfit with a string team." Pointing to a picture on the wall of the cabin in the Bull Mountains, "This isn't a picture of his outfit, it's a Huffman photograph. I got ahold of this picture and saved it. When you tell people about string teams, it's likely they won't believe you. See, here he's got twelve head of horses, twelve head in two lanes. He never pulled one of these, it's a water wagon. When they had to make dry camps, they had to water them horses so they had a water wagon. Well, the wagons like dad had, pulled coosters behind them and the string team was controlled with a jerk line. They didn't have lines to hang on to, they just had one line, a rope that went from the wagon to the lead horse. He was the jerk line horse. My dad turned an outfit like that around in the street of Rock Springs, Wyoming. The saloon keeper there bet him a hundred dollars he couldn't turn an outfit like that around in that street and he turned it. That was a lot of money in those days.

A jerkline horse, a good one, was worth his weight in gold. When they jerk that line, you see what the line was really for was to get the horses attention, then 'gee' was right and 'haw' was left. They'd jerk this line here and get this old pony's attention, then they'd holler 'gee! gee!' and he'd turn right. And you just keep jerkin' him and hollerin' 'gee!' at him and you can just bring him clear around. He hauled between Pinedale and Rock Springs, winter and summer across that desert.

Usually two freight outfits drove together. On one trip he was hauling with Ralph Tailor, who on a later trip froze to death on that same desert. On this trip they were hitching up in the morning for the home stretch into Pinedale. Bert was breaking in a raw horse for wheel horse. As he was hitching him up, the horse bolted, throwing Bert under the wagon, which ran over him. Ralph managed to get him into one of the wagons, hitched the two twelve horse teams together and with the aid of a shot whip, drove the 24 horses with two wagons and two coosters. Going down the long hill into Pinedale, the brake flipped out of the ratchet and the horses had to outrun the wagons into town. Not a horse had gotten out of the stretchers. By the time they got stopped the whole town was out watching. A rough trip for Bert who had a broken pelvis. There were no doctors in the county, so they took Bert home in a buggy, and he lay in bed until his pelvis grew back together.

While Bert was on the road with his freight wagons and during his recovery, Maude cared for the children, irrigated the ranch and fed the cattle. In the fall of 1916 they headed out again for new horizons and opportunities, thinking to head for Oregon. All their family possessions were loaded into a wagon, pulled by six horses. Bernice and Boyd, eleven and nine, herded the loose horses. The trail, covered with ice and snow in places, led through the Hoback Canyon, some of it in the river bed. Crossing over the Hoback rim, the wagon turned over, spilling all their possessions down the hill. They had to set the wagon upright, then gather up all their belongings and repack them. When they arrived in Jackson, Bert needed hay for his horses, and found he could buy some from Bill Redmond, whose Spring Gulch Ranch (the S & R), he discovered, was for sale. He had found the perfect ranch and wouldn't have to travel any further. It became one of Jackson's finest cattle ranches, and Bert Charter became one of its most respected citizens. He died of cancer in the Mayo Clinic in 1939.

Donald Haugh, a genial alcoholic who made his living by writing, wrote two books about Jackson, *Snow Above Town* and *The Cocktail Hour in Jackson's Hole*. In his book *Snow Above Town,* he gives the following version of Bert's funeral:

A rancher, one of the veterans of these mountains, has died. He died out on his ranch the day before yesterday, a fellow well liked throughout the valley. He was old, a pioneer, one who knew how to run a ranch and make a success of it; he was one of the last of his kind, and he made no bows in the direction of the dudes and tourists, you can bet on that.

He was peaceful and inoffensive, and it is to be regretted that in his death he had become an *issue*.

The issue is this:

The cemetery is on a knoll at the foot of the hill that rises behind the town. The road that goes out to it follows the side of the hill for about a quarter of a mile. On this hill is the community ski slide. The Forest Service cut a swath in the forest, and a committee appointed by the Commercial Club smoothed off the snow, and built it up where this was necessary.

One place where a lot of smoothing off was necessary was the road. The road is notched into the hill, and since there was no place for the slide to go but over the road, the notch had to be filled in. This took a lot of snow and a lot of work. The idea was that when it was necessary to use the road to the cemetery, this snow would be removed: quite a job, since on the up hill side of the road the snow is packed ten feet deep.

Well, tomorrow being New Year's Day, a grand ski meet is arranged, in which skiers from all over the valley are to compete. It is the biggest sports event of the winter, and already the contestants from remote corners of the valley are in town with their skis.

The *issue* is that either the ski meet will have to be given up, or the funeral postponed. Experts have declared that there is no hope of both opening up and then filling in again, within the space of a single day, the section of the road over which the ski slide is built. The reason is that the snow would have to settle for a couple of days, and be repacked several times, before it could be used. Otherwise it would be just soft spots in the slide that would send the skiers flying in all directions.

On the other side, there is the law. This specifies that burial must be accomplished within specified number of hours after death. Also on this side is the sentiment of the old ranchers friends, contemporaries of his, old-timers, who look upon all this skiing and playing around in the snow as a lot of nonsense.

So it is a delicate situation.

The town as usual has taken sides. Proponents of the ski meet, other than those directly interested, point out that old Bert would want the fun to go on; that he would certainly vote for the ski meet if he were in a position to do so; that in his younger days he would have stood guard over the slide with a rifle, if necessary. Never a kill-joy, old Bert.

Advocates of the funeral, while granting this, point to law, declaring that the idea of breaking an important law on his last day above ground would not sit well with Bert.

The man between the two forces, and in a manner of speaking on top of them, is the head of the furniture department in the hardware store. He is a coffin salesman, undertaker, assistant coroner, and master of ceremonies for funerals. He is taciturn, humorless sort of individual who takes no part in the social life of the town other than that which comes his way in the line of duty. At such times, though, he is the social life of the town.

The current situation is the biggest break he has ever had. Here it is the day before New Year's, half the valley is in town, and he is the final authority in an *issue* of the first water. He has emerged from the dim light and linoleum aroma of the furniture department and is moving from bar to bar, stepping often into the post office, pausing to address small knots of citizens who gather around him when ever he pauses in his movements, and he is taking it mighty big and living the high spot of his career and he is not making his decision until the last moment in order to stretch it out.

There is no question about how Bert would want this part done. He's resting easy, the only one in town who is, and he would want the head of the furniture department to take it big and make it last, which was the way Bert did it, as long as he could.

The problem was finally resolved. The ski event took place, so the funeral was either a day early or a day late, there's no one who remembers for sure. Bert's obituary merely stated:

Services were held in the American Legion hall, Wednesday with the Reverend Joseph Hill Coultes of Ashton, Idaho officiating. Interment was in the Jackson cemetery. Many floral offerings and a host of friends paid tribute to a pioneer who loved the west.

GROWING UP WESTERN STYLE

The substance of Boyd's biography evolved from the things he told me that remain in my memory, and my interpretation of them. If Boyd were telling the story it would be more earthy, humorous, far-fetched and tongue-in-cheek. He could lie outrageously with the deadpan expression to go with his fabrications. He was brought up in the days when lying was expected on certain occasions, the obvious being during horse trading and telling tall tales. You were supposed to be able to judge the true merits of the horse or the tale and to respond accordingly. If you didn't, you were never told otherwise.

As was the practice in his growing up years, Boyd used cuss words freely but never vulgar ones. If in the presence of women, he would ask for them to forgive or excuse him. Cuss words were used as filler or for emphasis or flavor; salt and pepper being preferred to sugar.

One could take offense at his use of "goddamn" or "Christ," but for him they had no more relation to the deity than "son-of-a-bitch" has to someone's mother. There wasn't an irreverent bone in his body. He had the same deep reverence for the Creator and His Creation as was proclaimed by some of the great Indian chiefs and medicine men who perhaps lurked somewhere in his genes. He was proud to have Indian heritage; both his maternal and paternal great-grandmothers were Indians.

I will continue to use excerpts from Mike Wardell's taped interviews to give Boyd a chance to tell some of his own story.

Boyd was nine when they moved to their Jackson ranch. The Charter Ranch and the Hanson Ranch adjoined and the ranch children went to school together in winter riding in a sleigh.

Boyd went to school through the tenth grade. After that he either worked for his dad, the Wyoming Game and Fish Department or the U.S. Forest Service. The Charter Ranch was located in Spring Gulch just out of the town of Jackson — only a butte separated it from the town. Their spring range was shared by other valley ranches, on the flats along the Snake River and towered over by the Tetons. This land was condemned and bought by the Rockefellers to become a national monument. It was almost a mortal wound to the ranchers who fought it desperately. But later, much later, Boyd said it was a good thing, as that act saved at least that much land from the developers.

The Charter summer range was high up in the Gros Ventre Mountains—the grazing borders marked only by drift fences. The cattle were trailed up every summer, and when quite a young boy Boyd was sent up with old time cowboys to keep the cattle off "poison" (larkspur) and to keep them on their allotted range. He resented at times being with the "old coots," but realized later that during these summers he got to know some of the last of the old-timers, some of them still clinging to the ways of the legendary mountain men. The Gros Ventre Range harbored some of the West's real characters and Boyd could regale his audiences with stories about them for hours on end.

There were three small ranches and numerous trapper cabins way back in the mountains, and of course Boyd and anyone else passing by would stop in for a visit. Brothers Butch and Eddie Robinson were the subject of many of his stories. Once he stopped by when no one was home. As was customary he headed for the coffee pot. Finding it filled almost to the top with grounds, he figured it would be a good time to clean it out for them. As you may know, the old time wood stoves had a shelf on which sundry articles were kept. Boyd swore that he found some of these sundry items among the grounds, including an alarm clock and an old glove. Of course, when Butch and Eddie came in and discovered what he had done they were furious for cleaning out grounds plum ruins a coffee pot. They *had* wondered what had become of the alarm clock, however.

Guy Kyle and his wife lived up the Gros Ventre on the Lafferty Place. Boyd spent many nights and shared many a meal with them, and from time to time would lend a hand when needed. One time Guy's wife asked him to put on a dress she was making as Boyd was about her height and she wanted to see what it looked like and to adjust the hem. He obliged, boots and Levi's sticking below the hem. One day as he and his old-timer friend rode into the yard they passed by the doorless outhouse where the missus happened to be sitting. He called to his wife, "Shitting, honey?" Her reply, "Hell no. I'm shitting shit! What do you think I am-a damn beehive?"

In the mountains Boyd always had his dog with him, and one time riding back to one of the mountain cabins, his cruising dog encountered a bear which proceeded to chase him. The dog ran to his master for protection; the master on his trusty steed with dog and bear close on his heels raced for his cabin at top speed. Boyd vowed they'd beaten any horse racing record ever set, and that it was the only time he arrived at camp with a bear behind.

One of the jobs Boyd had with the Game and Fish Department was to track killer bears. If a rancher reported cows being killed by bears on his mountain range, all the bears in the vicinity would not immediately come under the death penalty even if more than one had been seen feasting on the carcasses. There were bears that would kill their prey, but most would only eat meat if they came upon a carcass. So Boyd's job was to seek out the killer and shoot it. He did not consider the job particularly dangerous, but he did like to regale us with one close encounter with a grizzly. "If you're going to kill a grizzly you'd better do it with one shot," he liked to say. Well, there was this grizzly on the mountainside above him, that he had previously spotted as a killer. He figured he was within range so he leveled off and shot, whereupon the grizzly stood up on its hind legs, let out a roar and started down the mountain. Boyd swore he could feel the hot breath of that monster as he pulled the trigger for the fatal shot. "I had to dodge to keep him from falling on me," he vowed, "and that was too damn close for comfort." He kept that huge pelt a long time.

When he worked for the ranch his mountain sojourns were in the summers. His growing up years seemed to be divided between working for his father, the Game and Fish Department, the Forest Service and one summer for a dude ranch. My theory is every time he had a fight with his dad, he sought employment elsewhere. One summer while in his teens, he and his pal, Albert Nelson got jobs for the Forest Service building drift fence. But I'll let Fern Nelson tell about this summer in her story called "The Necktie Party:"

This is not about a hanging, although it could have been just as final for the victim, and these two kids I'm telling about could have had an unpleasant life of jail and suspicion instead of a long and useful career of ranching and other pursuits.

The two were ranch boys raised along the Gros Ventre River. They knew all they needed to know about horses, fencing, packing and batching, so they got a job with the Forest Service to build drift fence for the cattle range on the headwater streams up the river. This was as near as they could get to their ideal life of pioneering.

Between them they gathered up quite a string of horses—twelve or fourteen head. They had their own gear, of course, and outfitted a pack string from the Forest Service stores.

The job they were to do was a drift fence on Togwatee Pass, to be built of treated posts and wire. The posts they could cut on the site, but the wire and cans of arsenic paste to treat the posts had to be brought in by pack horse.

All supplies and equipment could be hauled thirty miles up the river to the end of the road by truck, so the boys saddled up a couple of horses, drove the rest of them and set out for the summer job.

They arranged to arrive at the Red Rock ranch on Crystal Creek at the right time to stay all night. Bill Redmond, owner of the ranch, was a family friend of both boys and knew them like his own kids. Bert Charter, the father of the older boy, Boyd, had bought a ranch down in the valley from Redmond.

Albert Nelson, the father of the taller boy, had been friend and neighbor even before young Albert was born. They knew they were welcome so they just turned their loose horses into the lower field and rode on to the house. They were welcomed indeed and had a good visit, two good meals and a lot of good advice about how to take care of themselves over the summer.

When the boys were getting their horses out of the lower field next morning, one of Redmonds horses got itself into the middle of their string and was pretty hard to cut out. After they had chased him around some, and he still caught up with them before they got out the gate, Boyd yelled to Albert, "Hey wait. If he wants to go so damn bad just let him. Old Bill won't know where he is and if he should come up to our camp and finds we got him, we'll just tell him the horse came into camp and we were holding him there until we could bring him down. We can use him better than Bill can. Hell, he don't need half these horses he's got till fall anyway."

So they didn't actually drive off the horse. They just let him come along. He was a good camp horse, a good pack horse, even a good saddle horse. They used him all summer.

The boys were workers and didn't need much supervision. Once in awhile a district ranger would check on them to see how the work was going. They camped on the head of Squaw Basin pretty near the Wind River cow camp. The drift fence they were building ran along the divide between the Wind and the upper reaches of the Buffalo and the Grovont (sic) rivers, from Pilot Knob to Lava Mountain. It was supposed to keep cattle from the two counties mixing.

The boys felt pretty big, fencing along the top of the nation, the Continental Divide. They could spit on one snow bank and may have it go to two different oceans.

The work was hard and handling the arsenic paste somewhat dangerous but they treated everything as fun and it was fun, even cooking and digging post holes. Cowboys and other mounted visitors stopped by quite often and on weekends the boys would go visiting themselves. Being on top of the world and about as far from home as they were from Dubois, they often rode down the Wind River instead of the Grovont (sic). Saturday nights in Dubois could be pretty hairy.

One of those Saturday nights in Dubois they were making the rounds. It was Prohibition time and nothing was called a bar much less a saloon, but the liquid goods could be had in the pool hall like the Rustic Pine Tavern, the Smoke House or the Branding Iron. Even though the boys were very young, Albert was no more than 16, Boyd maybe 18, they had been doing men's work and were treated like men. They were getting as liquefied as the rest of the guys 'up town.'

As the night wore on they wandered in and out of all the spots in town, not wanting to miss anything. While they were in the Smoke House milling and gabbing, some native of the Wind River side got drunk enough to take a swing at Albert because he was a "Damn S.O.B. Jackson Holer."

Boyd jumped into the fray immediately and so did everyone else in the bar. It was a good thing for our Jackson boys that most of the patrons didn't care a bit who they hit. In fact hardly anyone knew who or what started the fight. It was a happy-go-lucky free-for-all.

The Jackson boys were holding their own, getting in some good licks, when upon turning to look for his pal, Boyd saw some big bruiser with a chair in his hands just ready to take a swing at Albert. Boyd was close enough to reach out and grab the man by the necktie and pull him off balance. With the tie pulled tight around his neck, the man quit worrying about swinging the chair and started trying to get the necktie loose. Boyd gleefully kept tugging him around, keeping him off balance. "Hell, I'm breaking him to lead," he crowed, and with the man struggling and gagging he went out the door and down the street.

Albert got himself disentangled and hurried after Boyd. "Wait, you damn fool, where you think you're going?"

"I got him broke to lead. I'm going to take him down to the corral with the other jackasses."

The man was choking and wheezing and trying to loosen the tie. Albert dug out his pocketknife as he went along and reached up and cut the necktie above Boyd's grasp, then cut it at the knot.

"Now what did you want to go and turn him loose for? I just got him broke to lead." Boyd complained. The man sat on the ground still gagging and wheezing.

"He's not going to want any more fight for a while, let's go back and get the bird that started this."

But then the law arrived. The sheriff and a deputy closed in on the pair and started asking questions. They weren't exactly arrested but they were eased off to their room and made to promise to stay there until morning. "Oh well," they reasoned, "Maybe we missed all the fun, but we didn't have to find ourselves in the jug."

Along in the fall when the stretch of fence was done and before hunting season and roundup work had made Bill need his horse, the two horse thieves came riding down the river and stopped at the Redrock ranch.

"Bill, your horse came into camp with ours. We figured he belonged to you so we kept him there to bring him back to you." they said with the greatest truthfulness.

"I can't tell you boys how much I appreciate that," Mr. Redmond told them. "If you hadn't caught him I'd have had to go clear over to Crowheart fir him. I got him from Nippers over there, and you know how those reservation horses are determined to get loose and go back."

Yep, the boys knew all right. He sure had been determined to get out.

Another Charter-Nelson prank was carried out when two female schoolteachers arrived in town and spent their first night in the local hotel. Boyd and his co-conspirator had found out which room they would be in. It was still the day of the chamber pot into which they dropped a package of Alka Seltzer tablets, guaranteed to fizz in liquid. The results fully met their expectations as the girls' screams were heard by many.

The year after the "Necktie Party," when Boyd was eighteen, he was trailing some horses on the road high above the Gros Ventre when he heard what he thought was a wagon coming up behind him at top speed. His horses spooked and left the country and what he saw instead of a wagon was a whole mountain sliding into the river. He had noticed that Guil Huff had been riding just about parallel to him in the valley on the other side of the river. He saw him now riding at breakneck speed trying to outrun the slide. He saw him pull up at a fence as the slide passed him not thirty feet away, opening the gate for him! Its estimated speed was 50 miles-per-hour. Boyd watched the slide split, part going up a side canyon and the main part pushing a column of water 30 feet high. It formed a dam which caused a flood and formed a lake. Seeing that the Huff ranch was mostly under water, he rode at top speed the two and a half miles up Horsetail Creek to the ranger station. Dibble the Forest Ranger was able to rescue Mrs. Huff and her small daughter and take them to the ranger station in his Model T. The news spread rapidly and those in the vicinity worked through the night to save the Huff's worldly belongings and those of a neighbor whose house was also filling with water. Everything was taken to the ranger station and then moved into Jackson by pack horses. A week later the rising waters reached the ranger station which ended up floating on the lake. The river bed was dry at first and it was thought that it wouldn't flow again for weeks, but it resumed normal flow in two weeks. Because of the seepage the dam burst two years later, in 1927, flooding the town of Kelly, literally sweeping it away. Six people died, 30 to 40 families were homeless and hundreds of cattle were lost.

It was also about this time that Boyd's friend Albert Nelson, who in addition to cowboy leanings had aspirations of becoming an artist, decided to spend a few winter months in Denver studying art. Boyd decided to go with him to study the models. In addition to ranching Albert did become a very credible artist, painting mainly the wildlife and breathtaking scenery he grew up with. My favorite picture of his is of an Indian on horseback in a dust storm.

Working for the game department was year 'round and in winter the mode of travel was by snowshoe. Boyd said it took a while every winter to get one's muscles adjusted and hardened, but once in shape he could really cover the territory. There was great rivalry between those who insisted skiing was the best way to cover mountain terrain in a hurry, and those who claimed the same for snowshoes. This rivalry resulted in numerous races and a lot of betting.

Boyd told of one winter when one of the oldtime trappers had not shown up for too long a time. He and Fred Deyo volunteered to snowshoe to his cabin. Fred Deyo was the veteran game warden who taught Boyd all he knew. They were formidable partners in "crime" when it came to practical jokes but they were tops at their job and this time their job was to find the old trapper. They made the challenging trek into the mountains only to find the cabin was empty and signs showed the trapper had not been there for a long time. There were also no tracks outside to indicate what direction he might have taken, so there was nothing to do but turn around and head home. About half way there, they sat down to rest on a mound of snow under a trail sign. The next spring they discovered they had been sitting over the frozen body of the trapper.

Boyd was working for the Game and Fish Department when the first elk feeding ground on the outskirts of Jackson was established. He spent numerous winters feeding the elk. Boyd was good friends with Bob and Heather Domingas who had two little boys about three and four at the time. They lived on the feeding ground and when he and Bob Domingas were working together, he was a frequent visitor to their home. One evening as they were approaching the house, the two little boys came running through the snow to greet them—stark naked.

Boyd's most gruesome job for the Game and Fish Department was to shoot elk on the feed ground and butcher them out. The elk had fared so well on the winter feeding programs that they had overpopulated their range and it was necessary to drastically cut down the herd. The meat and hides were to be auctioned off and anything left given to the needy. The impact of killing and butchering so many however brought about a violent reaction among those who had to do the slaughtering. The elk livers were stacked up in a great pile and the butchers started throwing them at each other, ending up in a vicious liver fight during which Boyd vowed they almost killed and certainly bloodied each other.

A practical joke that the townspeople of Jackson never forgot happened one winter about the time that the winter doldrums commonly known as cabin fever set in. Boyd and head game warden Fred Deyo had caught a poacher and were bringing him in to the jail as he had nowhere else to stay. The undersheriff Dewey Van Winkle lived in the back of the jail. Figuring it would be a quiet night, he had a lady friend in with him. Boyd and Fred walked in on him, demanding to know whose feet those were sticking out from the blankets. They declared it a crime, and having nothing better to do they locked him and his lady friend in the jail with their poacher. Then they decided that things had been pretty dull around town and needed livening up. So they proceeded to call in turn Justice of the Peace Lee Johnson;

The Charter family coat of arms (BELOW); the Jackson school "bus" (MIDDLE, RIGHT); Bert Charter's freight wagon in Pinedale, Wyoming, circa 1905, courtesy of Virginia Cooper (BOTTOM, RIGHT); the Charter family home in Baggs, Wyoming; Berniece and Boyd Charter (TOP, LEFT)

Dr. Huff the coroner; and County Attorney Wilford Neilson, giving each an urgent reason they should come to the jail immediately. As they arrived they were ushered into the jail and locked in. Then Fred and Boyd dropped the key on the outside and left town. They didn't dare return for at least two weeks. When they did return, the heat had cooled a bit and they managed to survive. But the doctor said, "If I ever get those two on the operating table, I'm going to castrate 'em."

Practical jokes entered every phase of their lives and were self-perpetuating, as the victims always had the incentive to get even.

Ned George had a "get even with Fred" story to tell. Ned was an old-time friend from Wyoming days, now ranching near Winston, Montana. He stopped by the day Mike Wardell was taping an interview with Boyd. As Ned was deaf and his hearing aid not working, the ensuing conversation was often hilarious. A thought would come to Ned or he'd catch a word that would set him off on some tale that was completely foreign to the ongoing conversation. He did come up with some good stories though, including this one in the practical jokes department:

> This Fred Deyo was quite a hand at joshin' people. He was a game warden, but he was always playing pranks on people. I forget what he did to this old Jack Ellis, but he played some kind of prank on him. So Jack went into town one day and said 'Deyo, there's an old bird fishin' up there on Spread Creek at a beaver dam without any license.' He said it in such a way that Deyo believed him. So, Deyo went up and got in his car and drove all the way up there. I think it was 42 miles. The old bird fishing without a license was a pelican.

Boyd followed Ned's tale with this story of a night in line camp:

> There was this old homestead cabin, this guy took up a homestead there, oh, years ago, an old log and dirt roof outfit. It was built just like this. See, this was one room and there was another room just off there. All it was, was just inch boards, the partition was just inch boards. This woman had papered with newspaper, papered these boards, but that other room out there, wasn't kept up at all, holes going out there, the roof was bad too. So that night we all made out beds down in one room. Well, this Deyo went out and got everyone's chaps and coats and everything, and hung them all on the wall on the outside there, on the other side of the partition there.
>
> So, every time we'd come into camp, we'd shoot. We had pistols and we'd shoot at targets to see who cooked the meal. You'd see a target and you'd say—'I'll shoot ya' to see who cooks dinner.' Then we'd get through eatin', then we'd say—'I'll shoot you to see who washes dishes,' and all that kind of stuff. And I don't know why we did, but everybody carried a pistol. Everybody that was ridin' had this god damn pistol. Then when you'd go to bed at night, you'd take it out and put it under your pillow.

So next morning, Fred Deyo wakes up and said, 'I'll shoot you guys to see who's cooking breakfast!' So everybody was kinda sittin' up in bed, ya' know and had their pistols out. 'Let's shoot at that spot right over there.' So we all wailed away at this damn spot then got in a big argument over whose bullet hole had won. 'Oh, well, let's shoot at that other one, that big one over there.' And god, we must have shot forty-five, fifty shots at that one spot. And so finally we got breakfast and we were leaving, by god, here was our coats and chaps and everything we owned hanging on the wall out there, and we had shot the whole god-damn outfit full of holes.

There were often old men who were still good cowboys but suffered some of the ailments of aging. As everyone slept in bed rolls on the floor, it was not easy to wend one's way through the bodies if one had to get up at night, so one afflicted with this necessity often had a coffee can by his side. It caused a con- siderable disturbance the night someone punched holes in the bottom of the can.

So much for the humor of the West. After all they didn't have TV! They had to provide their own entertainment.

It would be hard to differentiate hobbies from work, but if Boyd had a hobby it was running wild horses. His son Tom along with his good friend and partner Tom Hope, followed in his father's footsteps when it came to running the wild ones into areas where they could be corralled. Boyd ran his in the Wind River County of Wyoming, Tom in Eastern Montana. I'll let Boyd describe his part:

There were thousands of them. Thousands of wild horses in there where Crow Heart Butte is. You know, where that Butte draw, Sand draw, and all them draws is? We used to have big wild horse corrals there. I could name you 25 guys from around there—Buddie Stall, Frankie May, and, oh Christ, Billie and Jimmie O'Neil, and oh, god, let's see, Matly and Richard Green, George Gross, Nobe Harris, and Abe Harris. I could name them for hours. Most of them half-breed Indians. We used to run them goddamn horses out there, and you can believe it or not, but we corralled high as 500 head on one job.

We'd take out the young studs, make geldings of them, and any other that would make saddle horses. Then we'd run elk down them draws onto the feed grounds on them, or at least I did on mine. When I got them horses broke, I'd sell them to some cow outfit or I'd maybe trade one good young horse for two old ones. Then I'd take the old ones and sell them to the dude outfits.

After his father died, Boyd had to settle down to running a ranch full-time. In the spring was calving and branding and trailing up to their mountain range. In the summer it was putting out salt licks and keeping track of cows. Fall meant the gather and the trail home and selling off the calves which were usually trailed over the pass to Victor, Idaho. During the summer, brother-in-law Olin was in charge of putting up hay as well as his normal sheriff duties. Winters consisted of feeding in the snow with a team pulling the wagons.

The first time I saw the ranch, we stopped at the big corral where they broke their horses. Boyd told me this story about his father.

He bought one of the first Model Ts in the Valley and it was delivered to their ranch. "Put it in that there round corral," his father said. "Reckon the Missus and I will have to break it in." For a while they drove it together round and round, he steering and working the pedals, she on the throttle. Finally, he yelled, "Open the gate!" and out they went lickety-split through the gate and out onto the road. It took them awhile to get it stopped.

After telling me this story Boyd took me into the house and showed me his old bedroom where he had heard the Cassidy stories. This was the last time we saw the ranch while they owned it as it was sold before we returned to Jackson.

This was the summer of 1942 and Boyd had agreed to sign up for the Navy as soon as the cattle were down from summer range. He knew there was a possibility of the ranch being sold, but thought it might be better that way. He didn't relish the idea of spending his life running a ranch with a brother-in-law he didn't get along with.

The summer had a surprise ending for him. He got married!

PART III: INTRODUCTION TO MARRIED LIFE

THE WAR YEARS

Our time together as newlyweds was shortlived as Boyd was off to join the Navy. I traveled home to St. Louis, living with my family by Christmas. The honeymoon ended on that cold, miserable, windy day when I stood on the corner of the bus stop in Laramie, Wyoming, waving good-bye. Boyd was off to boot camp.

On being inducted, Boyd fell in line with some recruits from Chicago. They were all young and city-bred; he was 35 and Western. But among them he found Tom McCarthy who had been a mounted policeman, and somehow the two of them smelled horse in each other. They became lifelong friends. Tommy, also an artist, made his post-war living designing and painting signs. Each year he sends a Christmas card with his "signature" rendition of a bucking horse or Western scene. We have them all on the walls of the cabin.

From boot camp Boyd was sent to Coeur d'Alene, Idaho for basic training. He found himself in the fire department, at first riding the trucks then as dispatcher. The driver on his first truck was a character named Bella. Boyd told of one hair-raising ride when Bella was going too fast and came to an unexpected turn. Bella let out a bellow to himself, "Toin, Bella, toin." And Bella "toined" just in time. He and Boyd became friends and we often did things together when they both had leave. Bella was impressed with the diamond ring my folks had given me for a graduation present. His comment was, "Geeze, dem rocks!"

I headed for Coeur d'Alene as soon as I learned Boyd would be there for three months. On arrival I got the last available hotel room. The first day Boyd could get away from camp was the same day his mother arrived for a visit. Having no place to stay, Nanny as she was called, moved in with us. In spite of this I was nice to her and she in turn, decided I might not be *too* bad for Boyd. She had taken a wartime job in Spokane, Washington, and feeling useful, was the happiest she'd been since her husband's death.

When Nanny went back to her job, I found a barely livable room with kitchen facilities and a shared bathroom. Fortunately the renter on the other side of the wall wasn't there very much. The camp was not far from Coeur d'Alene and Boyd joined me whenever he could get leave. Coeur d'Alene was not the glamorous resort city it is today and its attractions were few. The landlocked sailors only saw the lake when on leave and were subjected to "cat fever," a bug which they thought had something to do with the location of the camp: just down the road from the mining camp of Wallace, Idaho. Boyd and I rented a rowboat once, but we didn't feel very nautical. Boyd didn't like being in water, but he did like being at sea.

As there was nothing to do in the town and nowhere to go or at least no way to get anywhere, I took the nurse's aide training course and worked in the hospital as a full-time volunteer.

On completing his training Boyd was assigned to munitions ships in the Pacific. His first ship was the *Cape Igvack*. As these ships endangered the convoys, they had to travel alone. Boyd was on numerous ships all during the war. Of his sea adventures, Boyd talked of only one time when a Japanese plane flew low over their ship, firing on them. He was the first to reach the gun, but the sailor who had secured it had tied it down wrong and the cord wouldn't release. So Boyd missed his only chance to shoot down a plane. One time their ship arrived at Saipan just after the invasion and they went ashore after it was secured. He told of how it was going onto those islands strewn with the dead and of how dehumanized one became. They thought nothing of collecting Japanese teeth as souvenirs. Boyd brought some back in his "medicine bag," along with shells he had made into necklaces and some photos taken by his mates.

There was little Boyd could say in his letters which arrived months apart, but he did telephone me whenever his ship came into port in California. Twice I joined him when he had a two-week leave — the first time in San Francisco, the second in Ventura. His main gripe about the Navy was the "90-day-wonder" officers they put over him. Of all the officers there was only one he respected, and he of all things had been a jeweler in California. Boyd said not only was he a great guy, but he was the kind of man you could trust with your life.

While Boyd was at sea, I was living comfortably at home in St. Louis experiencing pregnancy for the first time and then motherhood. It felt strange being married and yet living in the surroundings of my childhood, and still living up to the expected customs of society. Two weeks in the hospital was not enough. I had to have a baby nurse for another two weeks. My daughter Katherine (Kit) was brought in to me at nursing time and I was carefully rehearsed in bathing techniques and how to shield her from germs: always keep a clean blanket between the baby and your shoulders or lap, everything must be sterilized and re-sterilized. After Miss Sibly left (the same nurse who took care of me as a baby), there was a routine established for naps, feeding, bathings and airings, and how to keep the baby from crying when grandma's bridge ladies came over. Kit was a cute baby, and once past the colicky stage was a delight to all. She enjoyed having grandma make a fuss over her and teach her the usual baby tricks, peek-a-boo and patty-cake, etc..

Then came the great day when Boyd came home from the war to a wife he had hardly seen and an 18-month-old baby. He was among the last to be discharged and the waiting seemed as long as the war.

My darling mother, oblivious to the situation she was creating, planned a dinner party to welcome him home, and invited shirt-tail relatives Bob and Nancy Smith. Bob, too, was just back from the war. He had traveled with sister Louise and me on our trip to Austria and we were all good friends. Louise and her husband were also invited. What my mother hadn't taken into consideration was that Bob had been a high ranking officer and Boyd a seaman and that not enough time had elapsed for them to feel comfortable in their civilian roles. It was a difficult evening, but we somehow survived it without another war being declared.

Anne Charter holds daughter Katherine "Kit" Charter in July 1944, in St. Louis, Missouri.

The Navy sent Boyd Charter, age 35, to Coeur d'Alene, Idaho, for basic training in 1943.

The mid-winter morning we left to drive to Jackson in his pickup was as bleak and dreary as the one when he left for the Navy. The weather turned from bad to worse with icy roads and snow squalls for most of the journey. Between being a mite spoiled and in an alien environment, baby Kit was a real mess. If she wasn't trying to pull off her daddy's hat she was on the floor of the pickup throwing a tantrum. In the midst of this tense situation, we passed a sailor hitchhiking. Boyd slowed down. I let out a scream—"You aren't going to pick him up! There's hardly room for us."

"He's a sailor," Boyd said. We stopped and picked him up. Our hitchhiker actually cleared the atmosphere: he played with the baby, talked Boyd talk and diverted our attention from the unpleasant aspects of our trip. We were sorry when we reached his destination.

We finally reached ours: Boyd's sister's house in Jackson. As we got out of that cramped pickup, the first thing Kit did was stick her tongue out touching the side of the pickup. Her yowls announced our arrival in Wyoming.

THE POST-WAR YEARS

Boyd's first thought on arriving home was to get a job. I'll let him tell about it:

I was in the Navy for four years and when I got back to Jackson our ranch had been sold and all my damned horse gear, pack saddles, hell everything had been sold or thrown away. By god, even our picture albums. I didn't have a darned thing left. I needed a job. It was no time to be ranching. After World War One there was quite a panic, everything just went to hell. I remember that panic that my dad went through trying to keep his head above water there with the ranch. So when I came back I told Anne, goddamn it, before we go into any kind of ranching venture, I said we'll wait a few years and see what the hell happens. So as soon as I got back the Game and Fish Commission wanted me to go back to work for them. They had hauled several hundred elk out of Jackson's Hole and planted them at Big Piney, Wyoming. What they was trying to get them to do was migrate from the mountains to the desert like they had a long time ago. But the damn elk went to the mountains in the summer and when they come back that fall, they stopped at the first haystack.

So Boyd took the job. But knowing there had been no game warden in Big Piney for a long time, he sent down word in advance that he would arrest his own grandmother if she violated the game laws. Then Boyd went ahead of us to find a house, and put together a string of horses. He bought a house on the edge of town [population about 100] for three thousand dollars. It must have been furnished, as we had no possessions at the time. Then Boyd returned to Jackson to get us and what meager chattel we could gather together.

On our way to Big Piney we couldn't get through the Hoback Canyon because of a snow slide so we stopped with the Albert Feuz's overnight. Albert Feuz had bought the Frank VanVleck ranch after Frank's death. Roy and Frank VanVleck were among the earliest settlers in Jackson Hole. Roy started VanVleck's Hardware and Frank the V-V Dude Ranch even before Charters had settled in Jackson.

When the Feuzes heard we were about to set up housekeeping they asked us if we needed some china. They had just bought new china for the ranch, so we were delighted to get what remained of their heavy white mugs and dishes. We still have some of those mugs, still unbroken after almost 100 years of use.

Up early our first Sunday in Big Piney, Boyd looked out the window and said "Hum, I think there's work to be done." Francis Tanner, mayor and hardware store owner, lived right across the road from us. Boyd watched him take off with two cronies heading up country for what looked like a bit of forbidden winter fishing. After waiting a short time, Boyd left and followed their tracks to where they were fishing through the ice and making a great haul. He arrested and fined them even though Tanner wasn't his grandmother. Of course it became the town joke and everyone entered into the fun. A few days later when Francis Tanner opened a refrigerator for a customer, he found it filled with slightly putrid fish. There also was much discussion about a justice of the peace who had to appear before himself. Boyd had made his point. No hard feelings. Friends were friends.

Another story about his tracking ability had a different ending. Boyd was on his usual weekend tour of the mountain streams looking for poachers or fishermen with over-catch. He saw tracks leading into a remote area and followed them until he heard voices coming up from behind a low ridge. Parking his pickup behind some trees, he inched his way up the ridge on his belly. Peeking cautiously over the top he sighted a group of women skinny-dipping in a mountain pool. If anything could have been stealthier than his approach, it was his retreat.

In spite of his tough stance, Boyd could make exceptions in enforcing the letter of the law. He found it hard to arrest a man who lived off the land, so to speak, especially when he was enjoying his hospitality. This was the case with one of the Hanson brothers who inhabited the mountain regions above Big Piney.

Returning home on horseback one evening after hazing elk out of haystacks, he came upon one of the brothers about to partake of his evening meal. He invited Boyd to set and have something to eat. The smell of sizzling elk steak and steaming coffee was irresistible. He had just one plate which he gave to Boyd. Then he looked around until he found a large, flat well dried cow pie which served as his plate. Boyd said "We ate our fill and talked until the fire turned to embers."

Boyd's favorite story about the Hanson brothers was of the night they came into the Big Piney Hotel. Like all small town hotels of the day it was uninsulated and heated only by a huge pot bellied stove in the lobby. On this particular night it was 40-below-zero and blizzarding. As usual, most of the transients and salesmen had been frozen out of their rooms and were gathered around the stove. The Hansons walked into town from their camp, and when they entered the hotel they had icicles hanging from their beards. They immediately joined the men around the stove causing one to ask which room had they come from?

The Big Piney jail consisted of an iron cage, all that remained after a fire had destroyed the jailhouse. I never heard of its having been used. The sign on it saying Big Piney Jail was perhaps enough to deter crime, especially in winter.

I felt safe that first winter, even when Boyd had to be away overnight. He had picked up a frozen coyote which he positioned by our gate. It stood watch with one paw raised and a terrible snarl on its face. Even our friends would side-step as they came through the gate. Boyd also used the coyote to protest the use of the predator poison 1080 which had surfaced during World War Two.

My role as wife of the game warden was mainly confined to home and children. The first winter we lived in the house, anything freezable left on the floor did freeze. We had wood stoves, but it was hard to keep them going all night and still get a good night's sleep. When my family got word that I was pregnant, they made us a present of the latest contraption in the heating industry; a propane-gas floor furnace. To install it, Boyd had to tunnel under the house and dig a pit big enough for the furnace to fit in. This was not an easy task. When Joe was born, we put his crib next to the furnace at night. I later learned that he could have been affected by toxic fumes, but he came through unharmed. He had numerous close calls however. He learned to crawl and climb simultaneously. One day I found him reeking of cleaning fluid which he had dragged off of the top pantry shelf. In a state of shock I called the town doctor who said, "Well if he's still alive he didn't swallow any, so wash him off good and he'll be All right." Our doctor was a genial man, but he was past retirement age and fond of his liquor.

Residents of Pinedale and of Big Piney decided to build a small medical clinic in each town, so they could together hire a medically trained missionary Episcopal priest who was available. He would alternate weeks between the towns, serving both the clinics and the established Episcopal churches.

Ours was a nice little church but unfortunately there were scarcely a dozen attending members including children. I took mine to help fill the empty spaces. Kit at age four wanted to learn the Lord's Prayer so she could talk in church.

Our poor doctor/priest didn't have much to keep him busy. Most people went to Jackson for any serious illness. The only place he could go for companionship was the bars and he, too, soon succumbed to alcohol. At this point, we moved to Jackson so I never learned the outcome of his story.

Big Piney social events were rare, but the various clubs put on an occasional dance or costume party. The biggest event was when the women decided to put on Shakespeare's "Taming of the Shrew." As all available women had been recruited, our only audience would be the men. Our director, promoter, organizer and constant source of enthusiasm was a young woman who had come to Big Piney with a troupe of traveling actors. She fell in love with a local rancher and remained behind to pursue her romance. She had a good sense of humor, was a fun director and, of course, our production was a howling success.

I was kept close to home, but Boyd was expected to be everywhere at once. One of Boyd's jobs as game warden was to see that wild animals made into pets were not abandoned. It is well known that wild animals that become tame usually come to a bad end. A rancher in Boyd's district had a deer that fancied itself a sheep. He found it as a fawn. Its mother had been shot, so he took it home and fed it in the barn with the bum lambs. It never seemed to realize that it wasn't a pet sheep until the rancher sold out and moved away. Boyd's job was to take it to the wildlife park. As I said, it had been a family pet all its life and was as docile as a lamb. Boyd went up to it, petted it and put a rope around its neck. He led it up a ramp into the back of his pickup and all went well until he had to tie its legs so that it couldn't jump out. At that instant, all its natural instincts for self-preservation came to the fore and it gave one mighty kick with its razor-sharp hoofs, neatly ripping the seat out of Boyd's pants. The deer spent that night in our garage with plenty of feed and water and by morning was calmed down enough to continue its journey to the wildlife park.

Not long after the deer episode, Boyd arrived home with a baby badger. "I know this is not a good idea," he said, "but I just couldn't leave this little fellow to die." The animal had been hit by a car and one leg was injured.

He recovered with only a slight limp and became a household pet. He could flatten himself and get under the lowest piece of furniture, so that often we couldn't find him, but he'd come out when he got hungry. He was good with all the family, children included. But if a stranger came to the door, his hackles would go up and he'd be on the fight. In fact, he got so aggressive we felt we'd better keep him outside. Boyd made a harness for him so we could chain him to the clothes line. He could run from one end to the other and seemed quite content. We called him our garbage disposal for he would eat anything, and if there was too much for one meal, he'd bury it for future use.

One day, around noon, a stranger knocked on my door and asked me if I had a .22. When I asked, "Why?" He said he was delivering something to the Budds, our next door neighbors, when he noticed a badger was digging into their chicken house. There was no one home he said, so he thought he ought to shoot it for them. "No need to," I said, "You go inside and bang on the wall." While he banged on the chicken house, I pulled Badge out by the tail, picked him up and went back to the house.

Quite a tale was being spread at the bar that afternoon about the game warden's wife, when in strolled Boyd with a female beaver draped over his shoulder. It was one he had trapped to relocate, but she was so tame that he let her ride in the pickup with him all day instead of caging her. She spent the night with us and was taken to her new home in the morning. It suited her fine and she immediately began to gnaw down willow trees for a dam.

Not so, poor Badge. Boyd decided that we couldn't keep him now that, like Houdini, he could slip out of his harness or anything else confining. He took him and a large cache of food on a long trip back into the mountains and turned him loose. Some months later a rancher told Boyd that a badger with a lame leg had come right into his yard and made himself at home. He said he had to shoot him because of his chickens. Another sad ending.

Boyd spent much of his time herding elk out of haystacks. He'd drive 'em off, and the ranchers would call us again, "The elk are back." Off he'd go again. He had to show ranchers how to put up panels to elk-proof their stacks, and was responsible for assessing any damage. One time he told a rancher that he would have liked to see all those elk down on their knees eating from the bottom of the stack like that. The damage had been done by rabbits.

Boyd realized he was not going to make much progress just running the elk around horseback. The problem was discussed in the bar where he met Miley, a recently returned World War Two pilot. They discussed the possibility of running the elk by plane. Miley had a single-engine Cessna and offered to teach Boyd to fly. I'll turn the story over to Boyd:

> Well, the first winter I was down there, Jesus, the area I had must have been 100 miles long and 100 miles wide. Christ, I just couldn't move them goddamn horses fast enough. Some guy down here would raise hell with the elk eating up all his hay, and then 75 miles over here, one would start yelling about elk in his stacks. Them horses couldn't get from one ranch to the next fast enough. So the next year I went and

bought me an airplane. It was a 90-horsepower Piper Cub. It was a light plane, but it had a lot of zip to it. God, it would just fly up over them hills and in that backwoods country. Later, I got a Cessna. I run them elk all over with that goddamn plane for three years, and I had it out over the desert, too.

To move them, I'd dive down over them to get them a goin'. I'd have as many as three bunches of elk goin' at the same time. There'd be snow in there, and I'd get them started, see, and get them out of the foothills, and out of the deep snow. You could keep them a goin', maybe five, six miles until they started to play out — they'd tire and start laying down on you. Then I'd quit that outfit, and go over 50 miles and get another bunch started, take them 'til they tired. Then I'd quit that bunch, go over another 50 miles and get another bunch started. When they got tired, I'd go back to the first bunch. I moved some elk 50 miles or more.

The worst part was getting them across the goddamn highway with all the cars and trucks. They'd see the elk, they liked to see the elk anyway, then they'd see this plane di-doing around up there, then they'd all stop right in the middle of the road. I'd take the goddamn elk up the highway or down the highway, but Christ, they couldn't cross with all them cars, then they'd either run down the edge or back where they come from. I'd go down and run the wheels practically over the top of them goddamn cars, but they'd just look up and away.

The worst day was when I had another guy with me, (Miley). He was a World War Two fighter pilot. He was the best pilot I ever saw in my life. Anyway, he and I were out one day in this goddamn Piper Cub, and we had the skis on so we could land in the snow. The skis just fastened onto the wheels. So we was runnin' this bunch of elk out across this big basin and they started getting played out. So we decided we'd land in this hay meadow and drink some coffee while they rested up a bit. And so we came down to land and one of the skis hit a hidden rock and broke. Miley was flying the plane and when the tip of the ski struck he gunned the goddamn plane back into the air. What was left of the ski was twirling round and round taking the plane a little sideways. I reached back in that tool box for a Crescent wrench and a piece of fishin' line and tied that wrench on that line. There were some jagged cracks in that broken ski and I kept fishin' down there 'til I got the line through one of the cracks. So I held this goddamn ski up and got it stopped from whirlin'. So, we went over the town there at Big Piney, 'cause we knew we was going to have a hell of a time landing. The airport was two miles past there.

I said, 'Lets go down there and buzz the house.' Just about the time we'd hit the house, we'd gun it, beroom! and we'd miss the chimney about that far, then we'd look back to see if she's coming out. We knew damn well she (Anne) was in there cause the car was settin' there, so we'd buzz her again. But no one showed up. So then we buzzed the town, and I guess a dozen people or so picked up that something was wrong, and they all came up there at that airport to look at how we landed that plane. Nothing happened. We landed her coming down on the inside, scooted along and turned about halfway around. Everything was allright. When I got home I was madder than hell. I said, 'Jesus Christ, it looked like you'd come out of that goddamn house at least!'

My version: I had conditioned myself not to think about it when Boyd was up in his plane herding elk, for if I did I would be a nervous wreck. People had called me up to say they thought his plane had gone down in the desert because they'd see it disappear over a rise and then wouldn't see it again. He was probably flying low and he always came back. The day they buzzed the house, I knew he was with Miley and I had complete trust in him as a pilot, but I also knew the two of them could be up to high-jinx. My reaction was, those smart alecks, won't they ever grow up? I'll be darned if I'll go out and wave to them. When Boyd came home all hot under the collar and told me what had happened, I told him he'd better be grateful that I didn't come out of the house, for if I had known the situation I would have probably had a heart attack.

After three years the elk were pretty well conditioned to their migration, and Boyd was transferred to Jackson. Another warden was sent down to carry on. But after a few years, he opened a firing line for hunters near the highway and that ended the migration to the desert. We never had the heart to go back to find out the details.

When Boyd was transferred to Jackson, we were able to sell our house in Big Piney and buy one in Jackson almost at the base of Snow King Hill.

Having a baby and two preschoolers didn't give me much chance for a social life. In fact, it was not much different from living in Big Piney, except that I could watch the skiers from my yard. In 1947, after living in Jackson for about a year, I wrote the following tribute to its four seasons.

Winter
King Winter once in robe of white
Stalked Snow King Hill both day and night
But now in daytime it appears
He decorates his robe with skiers.
Spring
Spring brings its crop of calves and grass
For cattlemen still tarry
Suppressing longings for the past
As old and new now marry.
Summer
Summer comes in all its grandeur
Dudes dress western to philander
A summer's romance with the West
Jackson offers as its best.

Autumn

In autumn comes that time when
Jack Frost throws the switch again
aspen gleam among the pines,
Nature-rivaling the neon signs.

We spent what turned out to be our last summer in Jackson Hole in the Moran Ranger station. It was just far enough off the highway to give the feeling of being in the wilderness. We got our water out of a spring, and one morning as I went down with my bucket, I found a moose had gotten there ahead of me and was taking his morning drink. It was a magnificent sight and I just stood there for a moment and stared. Then I turned around very quietly, and returned to the cabin to await my turn. After all, he'd gotten there first.

I loved that cabin. It was just one big long room. We slept at one end, cooked at the other and lived and played in the middle. But the thing I will never forget were the walls. The cabin was made of hand-hewn logs and the inside walls were as straight and smooth as if made of milled boards. They glowed in the sunlight and lantern light and felt as smooth as silk when rubbed.

The land surrounding us was untamed wilderness and Tommy, just over a year old, had a bent for taking off for parts unknown. Boyd fenced in a yard for us which allowed me some peace of mind. For something to do we often went on excursions. The next inhabited place was a wildlife park a few miles up the highway, and further on was a ranch we called the Kitty ranch. On one of our visits it happened they had some kittens just the right age to give away. That's how the ranch got its name, and we got a couple of little fur balls. One day, I decided we should pick sarvis berries on the mountainside. Everyone picked faithfully except Tommy who kept rolling down hill. It became a dance retrieving Tommy without spilling any berries. On the way home to declare his independence once again, Tommy threw his bottle out of the car window. "O.K. Tommy," I said, "that's it — No more bottles."

Sometime in the middle of the summer, Boyd was sent a "helper." A greenhorn from the east who wanted to become a game warden. Boyd's job was to train him! Boyd had been in charge of CCC recruits when working for the forest service, but he said this greenhorn had no equal even to his raw CCC gangs. The first thing this kid did was carry a pistol, which was not exactly part of the uniform. About the second day out on horseback, he shot himself through the foot. That ended his "help" on horseback, so he was relegated to the pickup. Boyd suspected that poachers were working between our cabin and the wildlife park and figured they were working at night, so he was trying to do a little night duty. One day he told his "helper" that he had to be away overnight, showed him where to park the pickup, and where he might expect the poachers to appear. The next day his helper said he had heard the poachers coming in, but when he switched his headlights on, they had turned around and gotten away. That was the last straw. Boyd sent him back to headquarters assuring them he could perform his duties best without any "help."

I never felt nervous being alone, even when Boyd had to be away overnight, until one night which seemed different from the others. It was a pitch dark night, and our dog Iggy kept going to the windows staring out into the darkness. It was downright spooky and I told Boyd about it when he got home. He said that he had stopped at the Wildlife Park on his way home and they told him a rough looking character had stopped by their house the night before looking for a handout. They gave him something to eat and sent him on his way. But they knew I was alone that night, and so followed him down the road and sure enough he had turned down our road. He was stopped in time and followed on down the highway to a point of no return. Did Iggy sense this danger or was there an animal prowling around? I've often wondered. After that, Boyd made me sleep with his pistol under my pillow when he was away. I had never shot a pistol, but he must have figured a gun in the hands of a nervous woman would put fear into the heart of the most hardened criminal.

Then came the night that changed the direction of our lives. It needs a bit of background. Two things had plagued Boyd ever since he began working for the Game and Fish Department: the sale of beaver hides — when some of the revenue found its way into employee's pockets, and the discrepancy between actual hay inventories and the amount supposedly bought for the winter feeding programs. Part of his job included supervising the sale of hides and the purchasing of hay, and many times he came home saying that something was rotten in Denmark. He reported it to his superior with no results. The only one who seemed at all concerned was a Board Member from Rock Springs who was a friend of his, but even he did not seem to be able to get to the bottom of it.

On this particular day there had been a big Game and Fish Department meeting in Jackson, and once again Boyd expressed his concern, but he got no response or any indication that something would be done about it. They told him, "We'll just transfer you somewhere else, if you don't like it here." That really made him mad. So Boyd told them, "Like hell you'll transfer me. I don't want to have anything more to do with any of you bastards." He threw down his badge and walked out. Later, his friend who had been on the Board found out that the corruption went all the way to the head man in Salt Lake City. Boyd arrived home in the middle of the night and said, "Anne, guess we'll be packing up and moving out tomorrow, I just resigned my job." I was glad he did, after the first shock wore off, but now what?

We had always dreamed of getting back into ranching, but the possibilities seemed remote. Game Department wages were not very impressive, but when we had a spare nickel we salted it away. I had a few stocks and we put what small interest they paid into savings. Boyd said that after WW I, the price of land had gone down and maybe it would now, but instead, it kept going up.

And now here we were with no job, no future--perhaps it was time to think ranch. Boyd had heard the only land that might still be worth its price was in Montana. But where did one start looking?

I wrote my family about what happened and that we were thinking Montana. Always supportive, they sent us names of two families we could contact. One, the Al Henry's, had a ranch near Absarokee and were friends of my sister Louise. The other family, the Newt Pierson's, my mother knew of through a college friend of hers who knew Newt's mother. They ranched near Shepherd, just out of Billings.

Armed with contacts we set off in our new little Buick which my family had given us. It was the only new car we ever owned. We didn't get far that first day, as we found we had to make numerous stops to pacify three restless kids. We stopped at a motel and as I tried to get Tommy to go to sleep, I turned Joe and Kit out to get some fresh air. When I looked out the window, I saw Joe picking up gravel and pelting the motel with it. After a restless night, we turned around to drive back home.

I managed to find a woman who would stay with the kids and Boyd's sister and his niece, Ollie, who had kids the same age as ours agreed to keep an eye on them and to help. So off we went again.

Our first destination was the Henry's. Louise had written them about us and they gave us a warm welcome and insisted we stay the night. They had three great kids, school-age and ranch-minded. Jean told me she didn't care how dirty her kids got, but as they went barefooted so much, she had one rule; that they had to wash their feet before they got into bed! For some reason, that made quite an impression on me.

They owned a beautiful ranch on the Stillwater River with prime fishing at the edge of their hay meadows. The next morning they took us to Absarokee and introduced us to Kratz, the most energetic ranch Realtor in the state. He took us in hand and drove us all through that country which was very beautiful, but as Boyd said too rich for his blood. Boyd also spotted a lot of larkspur which is poisonous to cattle. He had seen too much of it in the Gros Ventre Mountains. Kratz was a great talker and sensing Boyd's desire for a more down-to-earth working ranch, told him about a ranch he had listed north of Billings. He'd had his eye on it for a long time, thinking it the best buy in Montana. Unfortunately, no one with a family would want it, as it was too isolated and primitive. But what a buy: $150,000. Of that, $10,000 was to be paid as earnest money, with $40,000 to be paid on date of purchase, and the rest on a 20-year contract at four-percent interest. Three hundred head of cattle were included. How could anyone go wrong?

Finding nothing to suit us, we thanked Kratz and bid him good-bye. "Let's head for Billings," Boyd said, and off we went, staying in a motel, studying the map to see how to get to Piersons's place. Again, we were given a warm welcome and introduced to a man who had just stopped by and had a ranch he wanted to sell. It was Lon Marsh, owner of the ranch Kratz had told us about. He asked Boyd if he'd like to see it. Boyd said he would, so off they went while I stayed and visited with Ruth and Newt. When they came back Boyd said, "That's our ranch. Tomorrow we'll get a lawyer and pay the earnest money."

The earnest money was what we had in our savings account, and we'd have three months to come up with the balance of $40,000. Tom Burke was the lawyer recommended, and he turned out to be the best thing that ever happened to us.

Back in Jackson before a week was up, we were faced with the reality of having to raise $40,000. I asked my father to sell my stocks and we put our Jackson house on the market. Boyd traded his Cessna for a stock truck, once more sold his horses, and we waited to see how much money we could realize. It was the only time I lost weight worrying. I'm not much of a worrier, but I lost ten pounds during that wait. I worried in vain as is usually the case for my stocks brought in $30,000 and our house was $10,000 cash. So the day before the deadline, Boyd drove to Billings and with Tom Burke at his side, paid the rest of the down payment, signed contracts and the ranch became ours. Lon Marsh was livid. He had us marked as two more suckers who wouldn't be able to come up with the down payment, and he thought he'd be another $10,000 richer for it. He never forgave us for "stealing" his ranch. We had just bought the last ranch in Montana worth the money. When this realization hit us both, we stared at each other in disbelief. We each felt that there was a power guiding us and influencing us, much greater than chance or coincidence.

RANCH LIFE IN MONTANA

After the war, larger atomic bombs were tested in the Nevada deserts. One night we experienced what turned out to be a weird electrical storm. We thought it was the world coming to an end.

Boyd had stepped outside and called me to come quick and asked me what I felt. My hair seemed to be standing on end—he had the same sensation. The night was absolute, oppressive darkness, broken by flashing lightning coming as regular as clockwork and illuminating the full circle of the horizon. Our sense of fear that this was caused by the atomic blast turned into an argument. I insisted that it would be better to be asleep if the world came to an end. Boyd retorted that we should stay awake in case there was something we could do to save the children. It all ended when the complete low-lying cloud cover collapsed into a torrential rain.

The world was not only changing around us, but it would change our lives and the ranch too. Realizing our dream of buying a ranch was not the end of the rainbow; there was much to be done. To begin with, we had used up all our resources and had no money to live on, or to run the ranch until we could sell our yearlings the following fall. Again, I turned to my father and he agreed to loan us $10,000, a debt never paid but instead deducted from my inheritance. He did the same for my brother when he wanted to buy a house. We paid some nominal interest to keep it a legal loan.

Then came the move. We piled all our belongings into the stock truck, including a beautiful antique chest that had been brought to St. Louis from New Orleans by river boat when my great-grandparent Brushes moved there. Our car too was crammed to the roof. Quite a few treasures had to be left behind, but we had the essentials.

The first night we stayed in a rather crummy motel just outside of Billings, but were glad to drop exhausted into bed. Early the next morning, we set out for the ranch. It was only 40 miles from Billings, but from Shepherd the road had never been graded. The overloaded stock truck could only creep along and the low-slung Buick barely straddled the ruts. It took us some two hours to drive that road. We eventually had a steel plate welded to the bottom of the Buick to protect the gas tank which we had replaced numerous times. One time when headed for town we suddenly realized we were out of gas. Boyd got out to check the gas tank. No tank. We found it on the road about a quarter of a mile behind us; we had coasted that far without it. We learned later from the Marshes that although the ranchers in that area paid the same taxes as everyone else, the county had never seen fit to do anything about maintaining the road that led to their ranches and on through to Musselshell. Some years later, complaining to some of his Wyoming friends, Boyd was told of a similar situation in Wyoming where the ranchers had paid their taxes in escrow until the county agreed to maintain the road, and that it had worked. He proposed to our neighbors that we do the same, but oh no, that was too risky. We did it without them anyway, and from then on the county did grade and maintain our road.

When I viewed my new home for the first time it looked very small and drab. It had that brown-brick patterned asphalt siding that some enterprising salesman must have sold to every rancher in eastern Montana. Across the road was a large wooden tank that had once served the railroad. I learned that it held our water supply. The windmill next to it pumped water into it. The water flowed into the house, courtesy of gravity. Behind the house was a tall, three sided tower that once supported the wind charger that supplied the house with DC (direct current) electricity. Now there was just the tower and one lone wire on the top. One day I came out in the yard to find Joe almost at the top. I said "Joe, you'd better not go any higher, there's an electric wire at the top. You might as well come down now." With that I went inside. He got down safely without a nervous mother watching him. This antic did not surprise me. While still in Big Piney when Joe was about two, I found him sitting on the ridge pole of our roof. A ladder had been left leaning against the house. It was lucky his Daddy came home for lunch that day and could rescue him, as I was very pregnant at the time,

Four-year-old Joe was the one most relieved when we arrived at the ranch. He had worried at every stop we made that our dog Iggy would get lost or perhaps that little Joe would get lost. I realized how upset he was by the move when he started wetting his bed. It didn't last long, however, as all the children seemed to enjoy and fit into their new surroundings.

We entered the house through the back door, going up a few steps into an enclosed porch where a gasoline-run washing machine with a hand wringer stood. On into the kitchen which included a sink with running water and a stove and refrigerator both run by propane gas. The usual cupboards stood against the walls. One door opened to the basement stairs, an open doorway led to the dining and living area. Two small bedrooms opened off the living room. The boys were in one, Boyd and I in the other and the end of the back porch was curtained off for a bedroom for Kit. In the middle of the living room was a floor propane furnace just like the one we had in Big Piney. We had a big tub we'd fill with water and put over the furnace. When the water got hot, it became a bath tub.

On the walls for lighting were propane gas jets that had to be lit. Why the kids didn't turn them on I'll never know, but I don't remember even thinking of the possibility.

To unload, Boyd found he could back up to the front end of the house which had an open porch. So as fast as we could, we moved in our furniture and I made beds and stored away the food we had brought with us and the fresh things bought in Billings. Everything was in except the handsome old couch I had inherited from 21 Brentmoor, St. Louis, Missouri. We had twisted and turned it to no avail. Then all of a sudden visitors began to arrive, all of the Marsh families who were our neighbors, and the front door was blocked by the couch. Never mind, said Mildred, all you have to do is push. Push she did, and the couch went through the door with a big tear on one arm.

Everything was moved in but hardly in place, so everyone draped themselves around as best they could. I made coffee and found some store-bought cookies. Tommy and Marilyn Marsh were the same age, eighteen months, so Marilyn with her golden curls and Tommy with his Indian black hair were put in the middle of the arena so that everyone could ooh and aah over how cute they were. They were just standing there looking at each other when Tommy walked boldly over to Marilyn and knocked her down.

After that crisis the conversation turned to horse racing and we soon learned racing was the Marsh's main interest in life, especially Lon's. We agreed to let Lon pasture his horses on the ranch until the racing season began. He would in turn leave Shorty, his hired man, to take care of them and help with chores.

As we bid them all good-bye, we heard a crunch. One couple had come in a stock truck and accidentally hit our new Buick on the way out, so it too was initiated that night.

Boyd's most immediate concern were the windmills. We had hundreds of them (well, at least twenty) and Boyd knew nothing about them. Some just depended on the wind, but some had gasoline engines to do the pumping. I bemoaned the fact we were living in a country where I had to wish the wind would blow. I hate wind!

The Marshes had told us that our only non-Marsh neighbor, Bill Weggner, was a good windmill man, so Boyd went to call. He found that Bill had a small ranch which he could run easily by himself and have time to spare. He agreed to work for us by the day when needed, and would initiate Boyd into the maintenance of windmills. Having an open winter that year so cows could graze without being fed hay made for a successful ranch beginning. However, there were other factors we had to deal with. Lon was bound and determined to get his ranch back. He would come by to visit when Boyd was away, telling me that Boyd didn't know what he was doing and if we kept on this way we'd go broke. He said that he'd be glad to help us out though, and he'd buy the ranch back for the best winter wages we'd ever made. This made Boyd just a trifle angry, and he told Lon he was never to come on the ranch again when he was not there. He said, "If you have any business, you have it with me, and you'd better leave my wife out of it." But Lon did not heed the warning. He drove up one day in his pickup, Shorty by his side. I saw him coming and met him half way. Now I don't get mad very often, but when I do I guess I can put on a pretty good show, for Shorty's description of Boyd's wife telling Lon off must have been pretty graphic.

We figured this would be a poor way to have to live for the next twenty years until the mortgage would be paid off. So our attorney Tom Burke advised us to refinance with a bank as the debt could be paid off without penalty. Lon Marsh would be glad to get his money, since he couldn't get his ranch back. We originally opened an account with Lon's bank, but decided to refinance with Security Bank after Tom Burke introduced us to the president and to the head of the agricultural section. Negotiations would entail numerous trips to town by both of us, so I took the kids back to St. Louis for Christmas with the understanding they could stay an extra week while I went back to tend to the business at hand. Sister Louise would bring them back and see our ranch for herself.

I returned on schedule and we transacted our business with just one more day to finalize everything. That was the day we met Louise and the kids at the train station and informed her we had a hotel room where she and the kids could wait,

Family visited the ranch in the summer of 1953. Left to right (FRONT ROW) Joe, Kit, and Tommy. (TOP ROW) Grandpa holds Steve, and Aunt Irene.

Joe attempts pole vaulting at the track meet at Marsh School in May 1958.

Ranch life provided the children with many playful distractions.

A painted photograph of Tommy by Susan Wadington.

while we finished up. She just gave me a look. She had been on the train with them for over 24 hours and Joe had gotten sick in the dining car, sitting next to a strange man.

We rescued her shortly after lunch and to make up for all her trials, we decided to stop at Piersons so she could meet them. We were given the usual warm welcome, had a good visit, and on leaving were presented with a dozen fresh ranch eggs. Not knowing where else to put them, she put them on the shelf above the back seat. Bump, lurch, bump, we were on the road for home. All of a sudden a shriek came from my sister sitting in the back. A nice fresh brown ranch egg had just fallen into the collar of her fur coat. And yes, it broke.

The next morning we awoke to our first light snow fall. At barely the break of day, Louise was the first to venture out to the outhouse (wrapped in her fur coat). Again came the now familiar shriek. Louise had found the outhouse door open, and entering in the dark had sat down in two inches of fresh snow.

All this time Boyd was having to adjust from being a carefree, range-riding Wyoming cowboy to a ranch owner with a family. The next biggest adjustment was the terrain: from mountain ranges to dryland prairie; from the live water of rivers and creeks to windmills. He didn't mention the windmills to any of his friends back home for a long time. A Wyoming friend did stop by the ranch that first year, however, and asked Boyd what he'd been up to. "Oh, nothing much," he said, "Just breaking stick horses for the kids."

I had a few adjustments of my own to make and many things to learn about living on a ranch. Boyd was quite helpful: always have several weeks of groceries on hand in addition to the home canned variety and staples; always be polite and hospitable to anyone who stopped in and if at meal time, feed them; any other time a cup of coffee will suffice.

There was a time when a salesman came to the door looking a little wild-eyed. He had been driving for hours over country roads or tracks as you might call them and had surfaced here. But where in the world was here, miles from anywhere? I asked him in, produced freshly made doughnuts and coffee, and reassured him that he was only about 40 miles from civilization on our mildly rutted road. He was so grateful he left without trying to sell me anything.

But the real test of hospitality was the day Paul James arrived horseback about noon. Paul was an old bachelor who was the only surviving homesteader that we had heard about. Of course he was a "character," usually went barefoot, had horses in their late teens which he called his colts, and was as much a part of the land as the grass that grew on it.

He told me who he was and I invited him in. Of course Boyd was off fixing windmills or fences and wouldn't be back before dark. Paul turned his horse into the corral, apologized for arriving late—it was just after noon—but said it had been many years since he had ridden this country and there were fences he hadn't known about. His cabin was about 10 miles as the crow flies and his pastures bordered ours. He was on a visit to new neighbors.

As luck had it, this must have been just after Easter and I had a propane refrigerator full of delicious leftovers and could produce quite a meal. When Boyd returned that evening I couldn't wait to tell him all about it and the wonderful meal I had produced. His response, "Did you feed his horse?" "Well, no. Was I meant to?" "Of course, a man always wants his horse taken care of first." So much for my day of triumph. But I learned what Boyd meant when I discovered this obituary in the Jackson Courier, 1950 for Harry Scott:

"Harry Scott hauled freight and mail over Teton Pass from Victor Idaho into Jackson 1919 through the 1920s. No matter what happened Harry always took care of his stock. His horses were properly fed and watered or Harry didn't eat himself. It is as fine a compliment as one could pay in the last of the old West."

The next year the identical thing happened. Paul came riding up around noon. Boyd was off for the day fixing windmills and fencing. I greeted Paul and said, "I'll go to the barn with you, there are oats and hay for your horse." Paul looks at his watch, "Not time for him to eat yet, I'll just turn him into the corral where there is water." Imagine my triumphal account of this Paul James encounter. I felt completely vindicated from any wrongdoing the previous year.

Eventually, our city friends were our banker, our lawyer and our doctor, and later some of the cattle buyers. But those first few years Boyd found just one friend he could really relate to, Ressa Clute, a one-time rodeo bronc rider and cowboy from Wyoming. He was running the Grass Haven Ranch for two partners. It adjoined us, but our houses were about 10 miles apart. I'm not sure what Boyd would have done if Ress had not been in the country.

Ress was the only one who spoke Boyd's language. They didn't see each other very often but when they did, could they ever talk. Sometimes I think they stayed up all night.

One afternoon Boyd announced that his Jeep engine wasn't firing just right and that he'd better take it to the Shepherd garage to have the spark plugs checked. He'd be back in time for supper. Supper time came, it got dark—no Boyd. I told Kit, "You'll have to look after the boys for me while I go and look for your Dad. He might have broken down." I drove all the way to Shepherd—no Boyd. I went to the mechanic's house. Yes, Boyd had been there and the Jeep was now in good running condition. I stopped by the bar. No, Boyd had not been there. I drove home looking to the right and left for the non-existent tree he might have hit or the non-existent ravine that had swallowed him up. My imagination was running wild. Suddenly I realized he might have stopped at Ress' for a visit. I drove into Ress' road, but the cabin was pitch black, so I figured Ress was asleep and maybe Boyd had gone home. But when I got home, no Boyd. What was I to do? Go wake up Ress and ask him to join the search? But just then headlights appeared, and in drove Boyd. He and Ress had seen my headlights come and go and figured I might be looking for a lost husband. Boyd had stopped in for a visit on the way home. They put on a pot of coffee and began to talk, not even noticing when it got dark. Guess they could spin yarns as well in the dark; it didn't seem to make a difference.

Ress didn't talk much about his past, but when he and Boyd started swapping tales, one got glimpses of this man born in Indiana of Scottish ancestry. Ress was a "hot" basketball player in high school, and he never lost his love of the game. With his schooling behind him, Ress headed for the wide open plains of Oklahoma and

Texas, as cowboying was the only thing he wanted to do. When visiting a sister in Colorado he met some folks with a dude ranch near Medicine Wheel, Wyoming, where he worked for four years. After that, Ress worked on the Two Dot Ranch for Lloyd Taggart near Cody, Wyoming, and spent other good years on some of the big ranches on the Crow Reservation.

RANGE COWBOY TALES

Ress shared many of his stories from these cowboying days with us. One of his favorites was when Sarpy Sam was wagon boss for the Frank Heinrich's Antler outfit. This is how he told the story.

The Antler wagon had been shipping beef, a trainload of four-year-old steers at a trip to the stock yards. So they pulled in this evening to the pasture where they were going to gather more beef the next day. So with no cattle to watch over that night, the cowboys all turned their horses loose for the night for the night hawk to watch over with the rest of the cavvy (horse herd). Sam, the wagon boss always kept up a horse on a stake rope in case something went wrong.

About twelve thirty or one o'clock at night, after filling up on grass the horses would go to sleep, some standing and others laying down. There were two or more bells on the horses in the cavvy. Since these were all ranch horses they would be bunched pretty good. With rep horses (reps are cowboys from neighboring ranches) these would have to be watched closer as some would want to go home. But with these horses the night hawk didn't have to worry, so when all the horses were sleeping, if everything was quiet with no storm or big wind to worry the horses, he would ride in to the wagon to get some coffee to help keep him awake.

On this particular night, he done just that. He then went out to where he had left the horses, but there wasn't a horse there, and he couldn't hear a bell. Of course he couldn't even see a track, especially in the dark. So he commenced riding the area but he couldn't find a trace of them.

So, of course, the cowboys had breakfast at 4 o'clock as usual and were all waiting for the horses to come in. Soon the night hawk came in and said he had lost all the horses. So after his breakfast Sam saddled up and went with him to look for the cavvy. They rode all morning without a clue to where the horses might be, so they come in about 10 o'clock for the noon meal. They were sitting around talking about the situation when an old Indian came riding up, and seemed to look the situation over. He questioned, 'Heck, cowboys not working today?' So of course, Sam told him the situation, so he looked far and wide and pretty soon said, 'Me know the country good,' (which he did) 'maybe me find them. How much?' With a hundred head or so in the cavvy, Sam had to pay one dollar a head. So the Indian rode off in one direction. In an hour here come the cavvy, all from another direction, with three Indians driving them. The cowboys got their horses back, but they had lost a whole day of gathering beef. The conditions had been perfect for the Indians to hide the horses from the night hawk."

Another story Ress tells was about a cowboy's cat.

After Frank Heinrich's death, E. L. Dana & Co. acquired most of his holdings. He didn't get the Antler brand, but with the extra lands it was a large operation. He would have five or six camps scattered around and a couple of cowboys would stay at a camp during the winter and break ice and check on the cows. Maybe a hay crew had come through and put up some hay for their horses during the summer. So the cowboys would pick up any cows that weren't doing good and bring them in and then take them to the hay ranch where they were feeding. In most of the camps there would be an old tomcat. They'd come in during the winter, but the cats would make it on their own during the summer when the cowboys would be gone, branding and later shipping cattle. But this one cowboy didn't want to turn his cat loose, so he decided he would take his tomcat with him on the roundup wagon. He carried his cat over to where they were camped, and while moving cattle he put the cat on the bed wagon to ride to where the next camp would be. So after a few times, Tom would jump on the bed wagon by himself every morning. He got to be a friend of all the cowboys. So this particular time they moved as usual, and just supposed that Tom had jumped on the bed wagon as usual. But when they got to the new camp, no Tom. They thought he had jumped off a mile or so back when he'd seen a mouse or something, and they thought he would show up later. Still no Tom at bed time.

Cowboys were funny. They would stand guard for hours some night watching the cattle. Of course, they would maybe be cold and wet and cuss the whole world but that was their job. But with no Tom, that was a different story. Some cowboys would quit over something less than that. They woke up and had breakfast at 4 o'clock as usual, but some of the cowboys still grumbling about not having Tom back. They saddled up as usual, and the wagon boss knowing the situation said, 'Boys, we'll scatter out and ride back to our last camp and see if we can find Tom.' So they did. And they found Tom at their other camp. They rode back to the wagon with Tom and all the boys were happy. But by then it was so hot, they couldn't do any work with cattle that day. But it was worth that wasted day to make the boys happy. Even when the big boss Dana heard about it a week or so later, all he said was, 'I'm sure glad they found old Tom,' as he knew some cowboys might have quit, and that would have left them short-handed.

Cowboying in Wyoming included rodeoing, and Ress was no exception. He became a saddle bronc rider of no small repute, following the rodeos around the country. This good life came to a sudden end in Tucson, Arizona, when a spectacular ride ended in disaster. His leg was badly smashed and Ress was hospitalized until it could mend. Like everything else in his life, Ress made the most of his stay in the hospital, making himself a welcome patient.

Boyd's good friend in Jackson, Eddie Hodgson, had an outdoor chuck wagon restaurant where people were treated to an authentic cowboy feed of stew, beans and sourdough biscuits. He had a small building for preparation and cleanup work, and inside were a few tables set for bad weather. There was a large teepee-tent where you could get out of the weather or just sit around by the fire.

The main cooking was done outside in Dutch ovens and the customers would go along the lined-up pots, filling their plates as often as they wished. During the 1960s, it proved a little much, because often the hippies hadn't eaten in days!

On one of our visits to Jackson, our family was almost as unwelcome as the hippies. Our whole family was lined up with people ahead of us and behind us, when Boyd suddenly calls out at the top of his lungs, "Hey, Eddie! What's this piece of leather halter doing in my stew?" Implying, of course, he was eating horse meat. The dudes didn't know what to think.

Eddie visited our ranch in Montana and became friends with Ress Clute. When Grass Haven in Montana was sold, Ress Clute went into semi-retirement. But retirement didn't fit him well, and he let Eddie Hodgson lure him down to Jackson Hole where he worked as a Dutch-oven cook for awhile.

Ress remembered Boyd's tales of trailing cattle up the Gros Ventre. So when he was offered the job of riding with an outfit as they trailed to their mountain range up the Gros Ventre, Ress was quick to take up their offer. He wanted to see the place for himself and spent the next several summers on the cattle drives to and from the mountains.

Ressa Clute was a role model for our kids. Each of them wrote about him when the time came for the school essay, "the person in my life I most admire outside the family." He was a true gentleman which made him seem quite old-fashioned. He respected women as the gentle sex, enjoyed children of all ages and was genuinely interested in them. His strongest invective (in the presence of women and children, at least) was "gracious." He made a lasting impression on our kids one time when we were trailing cattle parallel to a highway. A funeral procession passed us, and as it passed, Ress stopped his horse and took off his hat.

Our youngest grandson is named after him: Ressa Clute Charter.

When fall came around that first year, we had some prime yearlings to sell. One carload of black white faces went by train to the Hershey Farms in Pennsylvania, which paid us a premium price. Lon was one of the first to buy black Angus bulls to breed to his first-calf Hereford heifers. This had two bonuses: the calves were smaller which made calving easier, and this first cross proved to be terrific. We were told that when they arrived they had gained back the weight lost due to trucking and shipping. This was a happy ending for an interesting if challenging first year.

THE HOMESTEADER LEGACY

The first question people usually ask is how many acres in your ranch, or how many cattle do you own. The latter is like asking how much money you have in the bank, the first answered by; we think in sections, not acres. After all, it's a semi-arid country which takes 20 to 40 acres to maintain one cow. It's country where it's possible for cattle to graze out year round, if you're lucky. We were lucky those first few years when we had no hay or supplementary feed to fall back on. A bad winter could have wiped us out as it did the Texas trail herds that got caught in Montana's fateful winter of 1886-87.

Adding to our luck, the ranch had not been over-grazed and there was grass a-plenty. The winter pasture consisted of three south-facing ridges, so it was the first place to thaw off after a snow storm. Neighbors were often feeding hay while our cattle were grazing on the hard winter grass. "Gotta be the best ranch in South Central Montana," Boyd would say.

In the early part of the century, it had been covered by homesteaders who were lured there by the railroad and government to help settle the West. They could claim 320 acres and if they lived on it for three years, it was theirs. They were mostly farmers who came with their families, their pigs and their chickens, planning to make a living raising wheat or corn. The wheat depleted the soil and the corn grew according to the rainfall. The (manipulated?) rise and fall of grain prices together with the growing conditions made farming a poor gamble at best. Trying to beat the odds, as in other parts of the country, these small farmers often turned to making bootleg whiskey, as "grain" in a liquid form was quite profitable during Prohibition. One could usually tell who was bootlegging by their hogs. The left over mash was fed to the pigs who would then get tipsy and ill-tempered. Chewed ears and tails were the telltale signs that there had been a pigs' version of a drunken brawl.

We found many signs of these homestead days as we became familiar with the terrain of our ranch. There were coils of copper tubing in secluded areas; rank patches of coarse crested wheat grass planted by the government where failed wheat crops had left the soil barren; the remains of a rock foundation or root cellar; a lone chimney where a house had burned down; a cemetery nearby for the children who had been left in the house.

There was a story of a homesteader who was an enthusiastic piano player without a piano. Finding that he could buy a grand piano in Billings he planned his house around it. He laid the foundation, framed it up, and then bought the piano on installments. He positioned it in the room where he wanted it and then enclosed the room and the house around it. When the merchant came to repossess his piano, there was no way to get it out of the house.

Not many of these homesteaders survived, but a farming community did grow up around the town of Shepherd which could boast of a school, a post office, general store, garage and possibly for a short time, a bank. The area farmers produced enough hay and grain to winter their cattle but there was no longer open range for summer grazing. To remedy this the Bureau of Land Management (BLM) turned the government land that had not been homesteaded into grazing districts. Each farmer was allotted a certain number of cattle which he could turn out in the grazing district for a designated period of time.

In the meantime, the homesteaded land was going back to the county for taxes and was bought up for fifty cents-an-acre by ranchers who put together rather sizable spreads. Soon these grazing district sections were surrounded by private land and were inside the borders of a ranch. The rancher had no choice but to turn his cattle in with the cattle from the valley. Bulls became a very touchy subject between rancher and farmer: the ranchers wanted the best, while the cheaper ones suited the farmers fine. The farmers also knew that ranchers would look after their cattle, and in so doing would keep an eye on the farmers' cattle as well, so they figured all they had to do was turn out in the spring and help gather in the fall.

This is what we were faced with when we bought our ranch, for it contained three government sections. The full shock came in the first few years when we realized that more than the allotted numbers had been turned out and that these pastures were consistently overgrazed. Each grazing district member had a tendency to sneak in a few extra head over his allotment just in case his neighbor did the same. It had a snowballing effect, and the only thing that kept it under control at all was lack of grass.

We had to persistently bring this to the attention of the local BLM, which finally agreed to have a delegation from Washington, D.C., come and look into grazing districts in general and our complaint of overgrazing in particular. No solutions for "cooperative" grazing were forthcoming at the time, but we were eventually able to trade section for section — our private land that could be fenced off separately outside the ranch — for government sections lying within it.

Within our original 40 sections was an area we called "40 Mile Flat." No matter when we trailed cattle across this area, it always seemed to be hot, dry and endless. When the children would complain that they were thirsty, Boyd would say, "Cowboys don't complain, they suck a pebble." In our family the answer to almost any complaint became "Oh, go suck a pebble."

Below the ridges in the winter pasture was another endless flat with a reservoir in the middle of it. One dry spring the water got so low that the cattle had to wade knee deep in the mud to get to where they could drink, and we had to check it regularly for cows that would get stuck in the mud. One exceptionally hot day we did find a cow bogged down, and as it was a million miles from anywhere, we stripped down to wade out in the mud, threw a loop over her head and dragged her to shore. Right in the middle of the operation we heard a Jeep approaching. I hightailed it to our Jeep, got on the leeward side, and, still covered with mud, pulled on jeans and shirt as best I could. I threw my underwear in the Jeep and emerged looking as innocent as possible as some Soil Conservation men came driving over the trackless grasslands, assessing range conditions. We had a long talk about the drought, mud holes becoming traps and so on, and they eventually left none the wiser, I hoped. Boyd managed to pull on his jeans and was real busy with the cow.

Tom Burke, our lawyer who became a trusted friend, saw us through many a land deal. He once turned to me and said, "You know, Boyd's only interested in acquiring the land that joins him!" Boyd's answer was, "I don't care about making all that money, I just like putting a good ranch together."

First it was half a section here, half a section there that we could trade with the grazing district. Then the Fisher Ranch, joining us to the North, came up for sale. It was a gem of a little ranch, and when we drilled a well to add to our watering holes, we found it had a river running under it, providing an endless source of water in this land of low rainfall. An added bonus for me was the round oak table with extra leaves, and the old fashioned wood stove that were left in the homestead cabin. The table we took possession of immediately, the stove we left for a time we might have use for it. It would have been perfect for our cabin on our Bull Mountain ranch, but by the time we acquired the ranch, the stove had been stolen. The thinking seemed to be, if it isn't lived in, come in and help yourself, and it could be anybody from antique hunters to those who made their money from stolen goods. In fact, the country had its share of shady characters and cattle rustling was not unusual. Cows with unbranded calves were often in neighboring pastures. If discovered, the excuse was that they had just gone through a couple of fences; if not discovered the calves were branded at weaning time and the cows turned out to find their way back home. One time Boyd helped a neighbor brand who had all Hereford cattle. After branding all the little red-white faces, he brought out some black-white faces, a Hereford-Angus cross. When he got home that night Boyd said, "Damn it, you know what I had to do, put so and so's brand on those black-white face calves and I know damn well they were mine." We were running Angus bulls with our first calf heifers. We had found the answer to the question of why so many cows turned up dry, or why our tally at roundup time was always short, but we were the strangers in a strange land and there was not much we could do about it. This was peanuts, however, to what almost happened on the Fisher Ranch.

We were staying in the Bulls where our cows and calves summered, and had a hired couple at the home ranch. There was no communication between the ranches except by Jeep or horseback. So when we arrived horseback in full force early one morning to work through the yearlings on the Fisher Ranch, we took our help by surprise. They seemed a bit flabbergasted when Boyd told them his plan, and begged off having to go with us, as they had arranged to take the ewe they had raised to the sheep sale. It all sounded a bit phony, so we were not too surprised to find all the yearlings gathered for us in one corner of the ranch. They apparently were all ready to be loaded onto stock trucks and spirited across a state line.

After we had bought the Fisher Ranch and the Gentry Ranch in the Bull Mountains, Frank Mackey put his ranch on the east side of Highway 87N up for sale. He had been a big sheep man and had put together a big spread on both sides of the highway by buying up land from the county at 50 cents an acre. He later switched from sheep to cows, but was now ready to retire. Although land prices had naturally been going up through the years, Boyd would average the cost out with the $5 an acre we paid for the home ranch and figure we could still make the mortgage payments with the increased cattle we could run.

A RANCH TOO BIG

Then the day arrived when Boyd suddenly realized he had blocked in a ranch of almost 90 sections (57,000 acres). We had to have two hired couples in addition to our six-member family unit to run it. It became nothing but a headache. So we put everything up for sale except the Bull Mountain Ranch which was where our hearts were. After making the sale he decided the only safe place to invest money was in land, so he bought the smaller Mackey Ranch on the west side of the highway. We could own it outright, no more mortgage payments. He had sold his breeding herd as well, so Boyd decided to run yearlings, and those he would buy himself. Thus, we began to spend a good deal of time at cattle sales at the Billings Live Stock Commission Company (known as Billings Live). Later, when his health failed, we took in cattle to pasture or leased the land out.

With the idea of keeping the land intact as a ranch, and being able to pass it on to our children instead of to the government, we went through a lawyer's dream of incorporation and shares, thinking we could give the ranch away through giving shares to the children until they owned it, as permitted by the IRS. Boyd and I would keep a debenture that would give us enough income for our modest living needs. Unfortunately, Boyd did not live long enough to give all his shares away, so we were burdened with a sizable tax. But that was spread over enough years that we were able to hold onto the ranch.

I was able to give all my shares away, so three children, all with very different personalities and interests, found themselves owning a ranch together. They decided to go into a cow-calf business again. But as happens on many family ranches when those who inherit it try to run it together; it simply doesn't work. So, the children have divided the ranch among themselves and are running it separately, even though no solution has been found as to how to get out of the corporation. It turns out the government changed the laws about the kind of corporation we are. We didn't have sense enough to know it, and our attorney and accountants neglected to inform us, assuming I guess, we'd never want to change the status quo. But, who knows, if we stall long enough, the government might change its policy again. It's happened before.

Anne Goddard Charter

FROM DUDE TO RANCH WIFE

One thinks of horses when one thinks ranch, especially when working or trailing cattle. My first experience as a ranch hand, however, was on foot.

We arrived on our ranch mid-winter and there was work to be done, so ignorant but blissful, I was ready to help work cattle. After all this was the life I'd been dreaming about. Now working or trailing cattle take up much of a rancher's time, except of course, when he is digging post holes (preliminary to fencing); oiling windmills; pulling up well pipe (pipe dropped down the well means additional hours trying to fish it out); feeding hay; and under certain circumstances, digging cows out of snow drifts.

Cutting cattle can mean you are working out the drys, the early calvers, the pregnant two-year-old heifers, the heifer calves from the steer calves, or cattle to go to market. One could mention a few more, like treating for foot rot or pink eye, and, of course, the big social event of the year, branding.

I'm not sure what the reason was on this bleak day in January, but some were to go out into the pasture, and some were to stay in. I was positioned on foot as guardian of the gate. "Anne, how in hell do you think you can watch the gate with your hands in your pockets." I took them out and waved my arms as the milling herd came towards me. "Anne, stop waving your arms, you're spooking the cattle," and so it went, as I tried to stop an exiting cow at the right moment or let one through the next.

When the job was done Naomi Marsh, Lon's wife, and I and the kids went inside to warm up over a hot beverage, while the men rode off to trail the cattle to some distant pasture. Naomi's first remark was, "Anne, how do you do it? When I try to help, and Lon yells at me, I can't help crying." I said, "Oh, men! You know how they are. I don't pay any attention to their carryings on."

On the trail drives from Texas, they say the cowboys would sing as they rode around the herd at night to keep the cattle from spooking. But yelling seems to be an intricate part of "cutting cattle," if you have family as help. Daughter Kit, being the oldest, was her father's top hand well before she was 10 years old. One day he took her with him to help the neighbors, a rather elderly couple. Boyd was doing his usual yelling at Kit, who was urging her pony to the left and right, holding the herd, and only occasionally letting one get by her. When it was all over, Gladys Carpenter laid into Boyd, telling him it was disgraceful for a grown man to talk that way to a little girl. Talk? Who was talking?

Some years later, Boyd heard of a rancher who was selling the kind of bulls he'd been looking for. He decided to drive out to look the bulls over. As it was an interesting drive to the ranch and a beautiful day, we decided to make a family outing of it. When we arrived, their whole family was out in the corral, and we could hear papa yelling even before we got out of the car. One of our kids turned to the others and said, "I'll bet they are nice, they sound just like us!" We had a good visit, made new friends and bought some bulls.

Of course, cutting cows from the herd is done by the rancher on his top cutting horse. When we bought our ranch, included in the deal were five head of horses; no top cutting horse, but four usable cow horses and the fifth one, I could ride. Paint had a broad back, but he had reasonably smooth gaits and tolerated dudes. The day came when Paint and I were stationed at the gate. Boyd yelled, "Out!" I dug my heels into his ribs and reined him to the side. Instead of moving quickly out of the gate, Paint rose majestically up on his hind legs. Would I had taken my hat off and bowed to the cow herd. We found later he'd been trained to do circus tricks, but we never knew the signals or when to use them.

Boyd seldom missed a horse sale and was constantly buying and selling horses trying to improve his string. One time he came home with a matched pair of buckskins that had been square dance horses. We kept Buck, who turned out to be a good cow horse; but the other was prone to crow-hop and had no cow sense, so was sold. Boyd decided to try Buck as a cutting horse the next time we worked cattle in the corral. Things were going smoothly until Buck broke into a square dance; he wouldn't stop until he had gone through his whole routine. So much for a cutting horse. Even the cattle looked on in astonishment.

It was while talking to the horse trainer connected with the Dustin Hoffman movie, "Little Big Man," part of which was filmed on our ranch, that we learned about training trick horses. Although they are slow to learn, once horses do learn a routine, they never forget it and will see it through to the finish. That was Buck all right; now if we could only find some one to explain the signals.

He was a good all-around horse, one that anyone could ride. But not knowing what the starting signal was, we had to trust to luck that he wouldn't start dancing. There were no further incidents until the day our cowboy friend Ress Clute was helping us trail cattle to the mountain pastures riding Buck. Nobody had thought to mention Buck's square dancing talents. Ress was pleased with his mount and all went well until we decided to quicken our pace on the homeward journey. All broke into a lope, except Ress. His horse began to dance instead.

"Gracious," Ress remarked. We all reined around and watched the performance with straight faces. We let the horse complete his performance, before filling Ress in on Buck's secret life.

On one of my first rides trailing cattle, I asked Boyd how one rode Western, as all my riding had been done with an English saddle; clamp your knees, heels down, toes in. Boyd's instructions were, ride anyway that comes natural to you. Well, I did learn and became quite fearless when trailing or working with cattle, but to the end, I hated those return trips when kids and horses began racing each other for home.

In the early years, I was not always the greatest help.

"Anne, why didn't you stop that cow from breaking out before she got going." How did I know she was going to break out? says I a bit resentful. "All you have to do is watch her ears." I guess I was a slow learner. But Boyd didn't give up on me, I was the only help he had. He decided a better horse would make me better help.

So, he bought Comet, a top cow horse, half quarter horse, half Arabian. The Arabian breeding gave Comet a wonderful disposition and comfortable gaits, but that was just the half of it. Comet revolutionized my ability to help. From the beginning, I learned that if I could stay on top of him, Comet would do the rest. We might be gathering cattle, when suddenly he'd take off for a clump of trees where a foxy cow thought she was hiding. I hadn't seen her, but we brought her in. He knew just how to circle a grazing bunch of cows and get them headed in the right direction. And he was usually in a calf's way before it had time to break back. He must have watched the cows ears, too, for one seldom broke out on us. Comet was the love of my life and riding him was just pure pleasure. I had other good horses. Copper was a close second, but no horse could quite take Comet's place.

Our best horse story is about Croppy. One day Boyd came back from a horse sale and told me to come out and see his new horse. Well, was he ever homely — crop eared, short legged, no redeeming features whatsoever. Boyd said nobody wanted him, he was going for canner prices. But, the little horse reminded him of a crop-eared horse he'd had once, and he looked like a right tough little cow pony. He thought he'd give him a try.

Well, Croppy was an uncomplaining, going machine. He was not the smoothest thing to ride and when bored was inclined to stumble, but he'd go-go-go. This is the story of Croppy, as Boyd told it to a reporter for the Jackson Hole News:

> In the big spring blizzard of '56, after three days of not even being able to get to the barn, Boyd set out to see if he had any cattle left alive. He played out two horses he had in on feed, and hadn't found any of his yearlings. The next day he caught Croppy, who had been 'wintering' out in an adjoining field—all the coulees had drifted full and most fences were drifted over. He made a complete circle of the ranch on Croppy, some 35 miles, found the yearlings huddled against the farthest fence, dug out cows and calves that had been drifted in, and returned to the home base on Croppy, who was ready to go again the next day. At that point Boyd made his horse a promise — he would always have a home and the best the ranch had to offer.
>
> Tough horse, tough man with a soft heart.

Kit, being her Dad's top hand those first years, had a special pony called Blackie. In the spring, we would gather cows and calves out of the winter pasture, and brand the calves in a corral which also served as the gate between the pastures. Boyd and Kit would set out in the morning and gather as many pairs as we could handle in one day. I would arrive about noon, with a picnic lunch and three small boys. Boyd fixed a small pen in the corner for the boys until they were old enough to help.

Boyd would pound a stake into the ground, wrestle down a calf, tie one hind foot to the stake, stretch the calf out, and sit on its head. From this position he could dehorn, ear mark, and castrate. In the meantime, I'd brand and inoculate. Kit got so she could bring me the branding irons, a lazy C hanging J. We had two sets, so that one could be in the fire while the other set was being used.

The first spring when Kit was just seven, Kit was doing so well that Boyd let her out of his sight to bring in some cows. Kit added, "And I'm doing so good I don't think I'll get bucked off anymore," a term kids use when they get unsaddled. The next day, when rounding the last bend coming home, a jack rabbit jumped out in front of Kit's horse. Blackie leaped to the side, leaving Kit in mid-air.

Kit was also the first one to break a colt. All the kids had been fooling with it in the corral, leading it around, slapping it with the saddle blanket until it learned not to spook. One day they all came in very excited, crying, "Skeeter doesn't buck! We put Steve (about age 3) on his back and held him on and led Skeeter around. He didn't even try to buck!"

Joe turned out to be a natural with horses. At an early age he could ride most any horse. One day Boyd returned from a horse sale with a retired race horse. Joe, not yet in his teens, named him Fox, and elected to ride him. All went well until we began an easy loop on the way home. Fox thought it was the start of a race. He took off at full speed determined to be in the lead when he reached the finish line, home. Joe, tugging with all his might couldn't stop him, until he steered him into a tree. We decided Fox should have been named Sea Biscuit. Tom, too, had his colts to break as he grew up to the job.

Our neighbor, Mae Segar, had the esteemed reputation of being meanest woman in the Bull Mountains. Boyd read her crudely lettered sign on the side of her barn "BEWARE OF MEAN DOG" as "BEWARE OF ME AND DOG"

She was a good friend and liked to help the children with the colts they were breaking. She often rode with them and was full of good advice. One day, however, she rode over leading a colt. As she dismounted the colt pulled back — Mae jerked on the lead rope to get control, but the colt lurched up, then over backwards and broke its neck. Mae looked disgusted, took off the halter and left us to deal with the corpse.

Art Segar liked working with the kids too. He was Mae's opposite; easy-going, good natured. He wasn't overly ambitious at home, but he sure liked to work with the neighbors, especially when we were trailing cattle.

Tommy, two-and-a-half years younger than Joe, and five years younger than Kit, always wanted to do everything they did. So, at an early age, he got a colt, Biggy. He begged to ride him one day while we were moving cattle. Art volunteered to lead Tommy on his colt, and what a sight that was. Biggy chose to crowhop most of the way, but Tommy stuck it out to the end. Tommy turned out to be a top hand, as well as a rodeo cowboy. He idolized Frank Stevens, who trucked our cattle to market. Tommy often rode with him to the livestock market and it was from Frank that he learned to drive a semi-truck. He drove the ranch truck as soon as his legs were long enough, and when Boyd began to collect bucking horses, he started helping Dale Small around his rodeos and soon began driving the rodeo stock truck. Both Joe and Tom got the rodeo bug, Joe riding saddle bronc and Tom bareback. Tom also went in for steer wrestling. Boyd and I of course went to all of Dale Small's rodeos to see both our horses and our sons perform. I could watch our horses, in fact cheer for them, but I could never look when our boys rode.

Of course, we tried to get Steve on horseback as soon as possible, so I too could go along on the rides. Boyd bought him a good sized Shetland pony. He had no trouble staying aboard, but to get that pony to move was something else. Kit would jump on Jolly, and between kicks in the side and a stout switch, could get him to go quite well. But Steve just didn't have the strength.

Jolly did follow along after the other horses, however. So, one day when we were to trail cattle from the lower ranch to the mountain, we decided Steve could come along. Everything went smoothly, until it got hot. Jolly found a nice pine tree and proceeded to lie down under it. Nothing would budge him. Finally, I had to turn my horse around and lead him back towards home. No more Shetlands after that. Steve graduated to the two tallest horses on the ranch, Coyote and Pirate. For some reason the tallest horses make the best little kid's horses.

Coyote loved children, the smaller the better, and he would let them do anything, including shinny up his front leg. But if a real cowboy tried to ride him, Coyote would do his best to buck him off. Coyote and Steve got along fine. No more lying down under trees. One day Steve's saddle wasn't cinched tightly enough, and while we were trotting along, it slipped under Coyote's belly. Steve fell on the ground directly underneath him. Coyote stopped immediately, and didn't move a muscle until someone came to the rescue.

Steve gave his version of those early days in his sixth grade autobiography. He included a picture of himself on Coyote, one small figure behind a string of cattle that stretched to the horizon. His title: "My father owes his success as a rancher to child labor."

The summer before Steve left for boarding school in the ninth grade, he broke a brown and white pinto named Frosty. He came along fine, and Steve was riding him on all occasions before he left. When he returned from Shattuck for summer vacation, Steve got on Frosty and took off for a test ride. All went well until he came to a gate. Steve got off to open the gate and remounted. But on impact, Frosty blew up and bucked an unsuspecting Steve off.

Frosty enjoyed the experience so much that, from then on, he would buck on all occasions that suited him. If his rider stayed on too long, he would start snorting. He was not a wicked bucker, but a showy one. In fact, he put on such a good performance and seemed to enjoy bucking so much that Boyd decided to add him to his bucking string. Frosty was a great success. The crowd loved him, and he loved the crowds.

BUCKING HORSE VENTURES

We never missed the Miles City Bucking Horse Sale. I enjoyed the camaraderie, dancing in the streets, the good fare and eating with the local rodeo celebrities. It was the weekend of the year for Miles City with motels filled, and restaurants serving round the clock. Of course, they had to hire a lot of temporary help. One morning about eight of us were gathered around a table waiting for breakfast. A young girl waited on us, and one could see she was a bit nervous and new to the job. One of the bronc riders had a brand new Stetson, which he politely took off at the table and set carefully on its crown by his chair. (One reason that cowboys wear their hats at the table is so they won't get stolen.) Our waitress, while putting his ham and sunny side up eggs in front of him, saw them slide off the plate into his hat. She let out a scream, fled to the kitchen and was never seen again.

At that sale, Boyd bought a bucking horse that had made a name for himself but had stopped bucking. His name was Top Cat and he bucked well for us for quite a few years. Eventually, Boyd got out of the bucking horse business and sold his entire string to one owner. Top Cat wasn't bucking well then, so he was turned out to pasture for a year and his name changed to Rip Cord. A few years later, Rip Cord won the title of top bucking horse of the year on the rodeo circuit. Boyd felt like a proud papa.

Eddie Hodgson, a friend from Jackson, had a cherished quarter horse stud named Stormy. When he could no longer pasture and care for him, Eddie asked Boyd to give him a home. Until then there had just been geldings on the ranch. Stormy was a magnificent animal but a bit of a nuisance. After a few years, Boyd decided to buy him some mares to breed. This turned out to be more of a scenic attraction than anything else. They became the wild bunch. Stormy herded his mares and colts just like the wild-horse herds on the open range. This added a wilderness touch to the Bull Mountain ranch and everyone got a kick out of seeing Stormy herding his mares. Everything was fine until the third set of colts arrived and suddenly there were too many horses for a small ranch. The wild herd had to be rounded up and sold. It was no easy job and a sad ending to a noble experiment. Stormy died of old age on the ranch and thus added to its productivity in another way.

COUNTRY SCHOOL COMMUTING

The Marsh School was located halfway between two Marsh ranch houses. Our children were the first non-Marshes to attend. The Lynn Marshes lived south of us and brought Marilyn, who was Tommy's age, as far as our house. We provided transportation to the Fred Marsh house, and then their oldest drove the whole lot up the draw to the school. The teacher lived at the school in rather questionable quarters. We had a variety of teachers, most of whom were supporting husbands. The husband of the year would bring his wife to our house on Monday morning and then come get her on Saturday morning.

One early-spring Saturday morning, it rained and snowed so much that Fred Marsh couldn't get the current teacher to our house in his pickup. Fred said she could make it out if she was willing to ride horseback. He volunteered to accompany her and she agreed. They got safely to the gate between the two ranches when Fred noticed he had a heifer calving and she needed help. He opened the gate for the teacher and told her, "I can't go any further, but you'll be fine, its only about a mile down the road."

Fred put the teacher on a gentle mare, not taking into consideration that she was riding into Stormy's pasture. Stormy spotted her in no time and took off in pursuit. The mare took off at full gallop running away from him and soon we heard shrieks coming from down the road. Everyone ran outside to see our teacher arrive with skirts billowing, hanging on to the saddle horn for dear life. Luckily we turned the mare into our gate and closed it before Stormy caught up.

Kit was in the second grade at the Marsh School the year Steve was born. The Christmas program was scheduled for his two-week birthday. Of course, we couldn't miss Kit's first performance, so we bundled everyone up and put Steve in the time-proven safe carrier. But unlike the basket Moses was in, Steve's was equipped with the customary hot water bottles and newspapers for insulation. Then we all loaded into our canvas-topped Jeep that could get us through the deep snow. There were no casualties, either during the performance or the journey. It was a good start for the Christmas season. That year Boyd cut down our tree on Christmas Eve and dragged it into the yard roped to his saddle horn.

One year when the children were in the Marsh School, it was decided that the Moore School and our Marsh school should have a joint picnic and track meet in the spring. We drove for what seemed like hours on the county road toward Musselshell, and then more miles up a ranch road to get to the school. I got out looked around and said, "Who in the world could ever live in this godforsaken place?" Hum. I lived in a "godforsaken place" too. But it was my "godforsaken place," my home, the center of my universe.

A red-letter year for the Marsh School was when the Tempero children joined the student body, bringing attendance to twelve. George Tempero was a "flying farmer" with a small ranch in our school district. He flew his children to and from school each day.

Altogether, my family added four pupils to the Marsh School, though we arrived at the ranch with only three. Then came those "famous last words." While Boyd and I were discussing the pros and cons of the ranch we had just bought in Montana, I happened to say, "Well, at least we won't have any small babies to worry about." It was just a year later that Steve arrived.

Now, the two things I hated most about being pregnant was that big bulge and people asking "When is that baby going to arrive?" I would not only have those two things to plague me, but the baby was due in early December and I knew that my family in St. Louis and everyone I knew would be worrying about whether I'd be able to get to the hospital. So instead of setting the due date as the first week in December I said somewhere around Christmas. In fact, I said it so often I came to believe it myself, but I did pack an overnight bag ahead of time, just in case.

On December 4th I asked Georgia Marsh to come stay with the kids, while I went to Billings for a doctor's appointment and Christmas shopping. The doctor said to come back in two weeks. I managed to complete my shopping in spite of the fact that the store aisles had become narrower. On getting into my car to return home, I suddenly cried, "Oh, no." I was having real, honest-to-goodness labor pains. I drove myself to the hospital, wondering how I was going to let Boyd in on the news. We had no telephone.

As I staggered into the hospital, I remembered that our neighbor and windmill man, Bill Weggner, was at the cattle sale. At the desk, I said, "I'm in labor, but I have to make a quick phone call." They thrust a phone at me, and I had the Billings Live Stock Commission page Bill. I gave him the message, and told him to tell Boyd to bring me my suitcase.

The baby arrived before the doctor did and a few hours later, Boyd showed up with a suitcase the size of a trunk. It was the one from under the bed — with all our summer clothes.

THOSE RANCH DOGS

It is hard to imagine a ranch without kids and dogs. Like the kids, the dogs worked side by side with us on all the different ranches. It would be impossible to think about the dogs in our lives without starting in Jackson with Poochie, Boyd's constant companion at the same time he had his horse Spider. When we got married and Boyd was faced with the date he would be joining the Navy, he had to part with both his horses and his dog. This parting marked the change in his life from free-wheeling cowboy to family-oriented rancher.

In 1942, Boyd sold his string of horses to a friend, and gave Poochie to close friends up the Gros Ventre River so that he would be in the country he knew.

You can tell that dogs, like horses, were very much a part of our life by the unusual number of rocks in a sheltered spot under the pines not far from our cabin in the Bull Mountains. It's the dog cemetery where the pines stood watch over many a solemn funeral service.

Our first dog Iggy was named after the *Cape Igvack*, the first ship Boyd served on in the Pacific. When he was assigned to the job of game warden in Big Piney, Wyoming after the war, the first thing Boyd did after finding us a house to live in was put together a string of horses and find a good cow dog. Iggy proved to be a good family dog as well, subjecting himself gracefully to the affectionate maulings of the very young. He was Boyd's faithful companion accompanying him on his long, solitary rides both in his pickup and on horseback.

After the war, the poison 1080 appeared on the market, put out for coyote bait or for anything deemed undesirable. The only trouble was that it had a domino effect; it spread to non-target species as one predator ate from the carcass of another. Boyd fought as hard as he could to prevent its use, but it was widely available and there was no law against it. There was not much he could do.

Boyd did raise holy hell when he found someone had put some in a haystack not far from our house and the school yard. Iggy must have gotten a small amount of 1080 by chewing on some dead critter, as he began having fits and almost died. For the rest of his life, Iggy was subject to seizures, and he failed to live to a ripe old age, dying soon after we began ranching.

Our next dog was Scotty, a ranch puppy of mixed breeding, but mostly border collie. He ate eggs out of the nest and killed chickens, so he was given to us as we didn't have any chickens at that time. When Scotty was about a year old Boyd decided to test him out as a cow dog. He wanted to gather his horses out of a small horse pasture and corral them. They were pretty well scattered out. Scotty had followed Boyd when he gathered the horses on horseback, so he pretty well knew the routine. Boyd said, "Scotty, go gettum," pointing to the far corner of the pasture. Scotty took off at a run, gathered the entire pasture and brought in every horse. Of course, the horses knew the routine too, but we knew Scotty had the makings of one good cow dog.

Boyd had Scotty well trained, and he obeyed orders, but we learned he also had ideas of his own. One day we were cutting out some cattle from the herd. We were gathering them in a fence corner and didn't need Scotty's help, as all six family members were on horseback, so Boyd told him to go lie down. He went over and laid down by the edge of the creek bank, close to where we were putting the cattle we wanted cut out of the herd. They went over the bank, down into the dry creek bed and were content to stay there. We were so occupied cutting out the right cows and holding the others, that no one noticed Scotty inching his way on his stomach over the bank, and we were slightly startled when Scotty proudly brought all the "cuts" back into the herd.

A rancher in Ryegate raised blue heelers, their original pair coming from Australia. The first blue heeler we bought from them, "Pup-pup," raised many pup-pups with the assistance of Scotty. All of our near and far neighbors soon became the proud owners of this most-successful blue heeler-Scotty cross. We gave them away like kittens.

HOME RANCH

Bringing up children on a ranch had many advantages, although as they became high school age, the children felt it had some disadvantages. We drove out to the ranch every weekend to help, making it virtually impossible for them to participate in sports or other school activities.

At first, the ranch was their whole life. We were a ranching family and they were part of the operation. If asked when they learned to ride, they'd probably say that they always knew how. It was different with becoming cowboys. One day when we paused for lunch on a trail drive, Tommy said he wanted coffee to drink, and his Dad said, "Okay. Coffee it is, to go with the beans." So I fixed their cups with plenty of milk and sugar. Tommy was very proud. With a bit of a swagger, he said, "Now we're real cowboys." Tommy's favorite book was "The Little Cowboy," with a picture showing the little cowboy sitting at the campfire, drinking coffee and eating beans with the rest of the cowhands.

It wasn't all riding and working with cattle. When not in school, it was a small house full of four kids. I used to wonder how people raised children in town. When they got too noisy or drove me crazy with their bickering and fooling around, I would turn them outside. Of course, for a time in the winter that meant putting on and taking off snow pants, coats, boots and mittens about a dozen times a day. This I could have done without. I performed all household chores, but with little gratification. I looked on Boyd's niece, Ollie, with awe the time I watched her gain satisfaction and pleasure out of hanging her baby's "cute little things" in artistic array on the clothesline. Oh, to be able to enjoy such simple pleasures! I did rather enjoy cooking, though, and canning the vegetables I had raised. I guess my kids ate them, for they didn't have much other choice in those days. Fast foods had not been invented.

The second or third summer on the ranch, the St. Louis grandparents came to visit, and stayed in Billings at the Northern Hotel which had original C.M. Russell paintings hanging in the lobby. My dad entered into ranch life with enthusiasm, bouncing all over the range in the Jeep with Boyd. He even talked of investing in cows.

My mother put up with us because of her grandchildren, but I can't say she actually approved. I was still a daughter who had to be occasionally set straight. One morning coming in about ten she found us drinking coffee at a table full of breakfast dishes. She couldn't help saying, "Anne, this is not the way you were brought up."

"We had important things to talk over and decisions to make," I replied. "Dishes can wait."

Boyd, however, didn't take things as lightly as I did, so there was constant friction between him and my mother with her domineering tendencies. No one, especially my mother, was going to tell him what to do and certainly not in his own house. The fact that their priorities differed didn't help matters. She thought he should provide his family with a better house to live in, while he thought it more important to keep his ranch afloat as it was our only source of income. We had a roof over our heads didn't we? My father being a business man understood. He was supportive rather than critical.

It didn't help my mother's state of mind when "Dusty Roads" followed her up the back steps and right into the kitchen! Dusty was our first "bum" (orphaned) calf. He became the children's pet. They'd learned to bottle feed him, and give him rides in their little red wagon. And as he got bigger, he learned to follow them around.

We kept him for about five years, an impressive looking steer, and it was fun to have him in the herd, that is, until he began getting down on his front knees to suck a milk cow! After he learned this trick there was a necessary but tearful parting.

On a subsequent visit, Mother became even more horrified over a bum lamb that had been given to us. He too liked to come in the house. The first thing he always did was jump up on the couch and deposit a few little round calling cards. It was not only my mother who didn't like this, you could hear me yelling a mile away, "Get him out of here."

The lamb took up with the dogs, and if a car should happen by, he'd chase it along with his pals. When we had to move into town to send the kids to school, Maa-Maa, by then a full-grown sheep, had to go to market. But no one would take him in. Guess who ended up with the job? Hard-hearted Annie! The kids wouldn't eat lamb for years, afraid they might be eating Maa-Maa. There was another episode when "hard-hearted" Annie was needed. I call it, "To Market to Market to Buy a Fat Pig."

In one of his weak moments, Boyd bought a bred sow thinking it would be fun to raise some pigs, and a good way to use up some grain we had on hand. The old sow soon produced numerous piglets, including the usual runt which was nudged away from the tits by its more energetic siblings. The children adopted it immediately and it fit in just fine, playing with the kittens when the children tired of treating him like a doll; dress up, baby carriage and all. Of course, piglets grew into pigs, using up all the grain, and school time was approaching. It was time to take the pigs to market. For some reason Boyd was loathe to part with that old sow. "She's not only mean tempered," I argued, "but we have nothing to feed her."

"Well if you're so all-fired anxious to get rid of her, you load her up."

"I'll just do that," I said, and got Tommy and Joe to help me. It wasn't an easy job, and we ran her around and around and around, but not up the ramp into the pickup. Finally, we backed the pickup into the gate of a small corral where we were letting her rest. The bed of the truck didn't quite fill the gap, so I was to hold the end-gate across the hole. Tommy got into the corral, then jumped to safety on the fence, then down again, got her facing toward the pickup, and finally got her running in the right direction. To my horror, instead of escaping into the pickup, she'd spotted light under the end-gate and headed for that. I was squashed flat on my back as she ran over me and the end-gate, heading toward her relative freedom. When I bared my bruises and injured pride to Boyd, he laughed at my misadventures. I wanted to murder him on the spot. He escaped just in time, leaving me to lick my wounds while he loaded up the old sow and took her to town.

Before my children grew big enough to herd pigs though, my father died. I went back to St. Louis for the funeral. I felt I should hurry home as I had left Boyd with four children to take care of. When I got home I was greeted with, "Why did you come home so soon? Dad fixes us wonderful meals. We've just had rice with bear sign," which translated into rice and raisins.

Boyd recited just two major incidents while I was gone: the first, when the kids were walking down the road with Steve on Kit's shoulders. They came upon a huge rattlesnake coiled and ready to strike. The second was when Boyd couldn't find Joe and Tommy one day. He found their clothes beside the overflow pond by the windmill. Fortunately, they were not in it. He was frantic, about to climb into the Jeep and start searching, when he glanced up the road and saw the boys sauntering home, stark-naked.

Shortly after my father died, my mother came out to visit us hoping a change of scene would help her get over those difficult days. It was a spur-of-the-moment decision, so I did not have much time to get things shaped up. One thing I felt I had to do was paper the boy's room where she would be sleeping. I got the paper the day before her arrival and stayed up most the night putting it on the painted walls. The room looked very nice and fresh and clean.

I left early that morning to meet her at the airport. On arriving home, I ushered her into her room. Every bit of the paper had curled off the walls and lay on the floor. I later learned the walls had been calcimined and wallpaper won't adhere to it. Luckily, my mother had a sense of humor and we laughed and cried together over it. One of her favorite bits of advice to us as we were growing up was not to lose our sense of humor. She did have one complaint during her visit. The windmill squeaked and it kept her awake. She was used to sirens and revving motors, but not country noises.

One evening, mother took the whole family to dinner at the airport restaurant, which has subsequently burned down. Its view of Billings and the distant mountains from atop the rims was spectacular. My mother felt the children should learn how to act in public. They actually behaved very well. She let them choose from the menu. Joe chose the frog legs and ate them with gusto. Pretty sophisticated, I thought.

The time came when she felt she must go home but she dreaded going back to an empty house. She decided to take Joe with her and send him to Community School for one term. Her brother, my Uncle Floyd, brought him back and then stayed for a visit.

About this time I wrote in a letter to my Aunt Anne that on her visit, my mother "threw herself with energy into her visit with us this spring, but unfortunately, it was a time when the house was constantly invaded by our working crews and ranch activities."

My letter continued:

> All seemed to be going at a hectic pace. It has been a taxing year for us, for although our lot has been improving, it does not come without exacting its toll. The decisions involved in buying our two new ranches were not easy ones. Although as financially sound as anything can be

this day and age, they greatly add to our responsibilities and involve hired help which we were long overdue in getting. Hired help has its problems, too. Our two major blows of the year were the spring blizzard and a short calf crop. The blizzard, the worst ever known in this country, made us wonder for several days whether we would have any cattle alive when it was over. As it turned out the death loss was negligible, but it set the cattle back. A summer hail storm in the Billings area missed us, but caused over four million dollars worth of damage in Billings alone, and wiped out many a farmer's entire crop. These two freaks of nature cannot help but impress upon one how fragile a footing agriculture rests on. The short calf crop was due to an abnormally hot, dry summer.

The good side of the ledger is, that due to an abnormally cool and wet spring and summer, we have never had such a sea of grass as this year. The cows and calves are thriving on the new mountain ranch. They are up to their knees in lush grass and amply provided with water by springs. Although it looked like an impossible job, we were able to put up two hundred tons of alfalfa hay on the mountain ranch and a sizable amount of crested wheat grass on the Fisher ranch.

Out of a clear blue sky while Mother was here we got an oil lease which compensated for our short calf crop and makes it possible for us to hold over our yearling steers and make use of the abundant grass.

But Boyd, having shouldered all the responsibility, labor and un-certainty of the last four years, is now experiencing the letdown — first cousin to a nervous breakdown. Nature's warning to take it easy. That is our present hurdle, but one I trust we'll be able to take as we have the others. So that is the picture of ranch life. A bit windy, I fear, but leads me in to attempt to explain why I have not written before.

Your generous Christmas check did come and it has been put to good use in a much needed second youth saddle as Joe too has started riding with the cattle. Boyd now has two homemade cowboys to help him. Even I had a chance to ride over the mountain while mother was here, a rewarding experience for me. All four children are thriving, brown as berries and as healthy as they come. At the moment they are cooling off in the stock tank and from the noise it would seem as satisfactory as a fancy swimming pool.

The blizzard referred to in the letter was the spring blizzard of 1956 that made Croppy the horse famous. It snowed and drifted for three days before anyone could get out to do anything. Heifers kept in the barns couldn't be reached as the doors were snowed under. You had to tunnel in to find the doors. Cows and calves huddled together and were surrounded by deep snow, and the ranchers had to dig it out to get to their animals. When Boyd couldn't find the yearlings he was afraid they were snowed under in some coulee. But our cattle didn't suffer this fate, though many animals were lost that spring.

It was the first and only time I experienced what it meant to be snowbound. Boyd warned me when we first moved on the ranch to always have a month's groceries on hand, and luck was with me! I had just been to town and had stocked up. I could even loan a neighbor coffee when on the fifth or sixth day he rode over horseback to see how we were faring and exchange horror stories. We had no telephones and were lucky we had no electricity, as the powerlines were down. Our power supply was propane gas. The county never did plow our road. After Easter, when Boyd did finally make it into town, he had to dig out the drifts as he came to them. There were six-foot drifts against our yard fence. When the storm was over the children made the most of them, making forts and slides. Snowball fights took on many forms.

In spite of the state of our road, with weather permitting, I began taking the children into Sunday school and church. Shepherd had a Lutheran mission church and a wonderful young minister just out of seminary, Reverend Carlson. He had been brought up in Madagascar where his parents were missionaries. He had a wife and a couple of little ones about the ages of ours, so we hit it off from the start. He was interested in us as isolated ranchers and wanted to meet Boyd. He said that if we could gather a few neighbors together he would come out Sunday evenings for a Bible study. Boyd was agreeable as were the neighbors. All went well until the day of the downpour. The creeks were running and crossed the road in numerous places. His first remark when he finally arrived that Sunday evening was "And I thought Madagascar was primitive!"

I told him when I encountered these creek crossings, I'd close my eyes and gun the engine, pleading to the Lord for a safe landing. I called it "Coming in on a Wing and a Prayer," borrowed from a WWII song.

Boyd and pastor Carlson got along fine and although Boyd didn't become a churchgoer, the sermon following one meeting, inspired by Boyd, was on stewardship and conservation.

In early March, Boyd left me in charge to go to Jackson for his mother's funeral. It was bitter cold and I had the "flu" and would have liked to have taken to my bed. Instead I had to go out and do the chores including milking the cow. I not only managed to survive but recovered more quickly than usual.

The oil lease that we got that year followed a couple of years of fighting with freelance seismographers. They would come unbidden on our land and drill holes to blast and see if there were indications of oil. Such blasting could affect the water wells as well as our springs. At one point, Boyd went after them on horseback. Once the ranch was leased to a company, however, this trespassing stopped. We hit pay dirt with the lease money, but they didn't hit oil.

BOYD'S BLUE PERIOD

Boyd was a worrier. I tended to focus more on each day as it came. Boyd didn't have anyone to talk things over with, except me, and everything I knew about ranching I had learned from him. One day in exasperation he said, "Anne why can't you help me worry?"

I said, I would, if it would help. And if I say so myself, I did a good job of it. After about two weeks, Boyd got down on his knees (first and last time) and begged me to stop. I did stop worrying about how things would turn out for the ranch, but I was becoming more and more concerned about Boyd's state of mind.

It was becoming harder for him to make decisions and to get things done. I tried to understand what the undercurrents were that led up to this state of depression. His mother had always dinged into him that he should stick with a regular job, because he would never make it on his own. On the other hand, my father had loaned him the money to operate that first year. Boyd found my father's confidence in him overwhelming. He was pulled between proving his mother wrong and my father right.

But the stress of knowing he could have lost his herd in the blizzard and the constant demand for water in our semi-arid country made him aware of how unsure our future was. He'd never know, one year to the next, how it would turn out. But one thing Boyd didn't credit was the confidence his bankers had in him. They trusted his hard work, experience and judgment.

The summer of '55, Rives Holcomb, a friend from Jackson, came to work for us on our new Bull Mountain ranch. That helped. Rives had been a cook in the Navy and the children were fascinated watching him wipe down the table and counter tops as he talked. He sure kept a trim ship, and made a mouth-watering stew that became known as Rives' stew. He had a special skill and a lot of patience braiding rawhide ropes, whips, bridles and halters. Rives was a good cowhand too, of course, and we would have liked to keep him forever, but he had a home to go to. Though he lived on the Fear ranch in Big Piney country, he was his own man.

That fall Boyd became more and more depressed, but refused to seek help or go to a doctor. I also had no one to go to for advice. Our minister friend had gone off on a foreign mission. I read all the helpful books I could find and ran across a line from a poem that made an impression. It ended, "God is my tranquilizer." I prayed a lot but didn't know what to expect from my prayers. Several times Boyd's talk was suicidal and one night, in desperation, I threw his gun in the stock tank.

We both were chain smokers. It seemed Boyd always had a cigarette in his mouth. I had given it up several times to show how much will power I had. But every time something went wrong or I got mad at the kids or myself or Boyd, I'd light up a cigarette. I needed something to turn to besides cigarettes.

It had come to the point where I had to go everywhere with Boyd to monitor his moods. As we were crossing the ranch in the Jeep one day, I started to light one cigarette from the butt of the one I had been smoking. I couldn't bring it to my mouth. I put it back in the pack, never smoked another cigarette, never needed one, never wanted to. My dependence on cigarettes was gone: my dependence on God began. From that moment came the realization that God was real, that He cared for me, and that I could turn to Him in my need. This didn't solve our problems, but it enabled me to cope with them.

Finally, I had to have Boyd committed to a clinic in Denver, the same one he had taken his mother to when she had a nervous breakdown after her husband's death. It was the worst nightmare I ever went through. This must have been in March, for he was in the clinic for three months and during that time we had to move the cows from the winter to the summer pasture and brand the calves.

I hired our neighbor Fred Marsh and his son Gordon to help. Our kids weren't very big, but they knew the routine, and the Marshes had a hard time keeping up with their pace. Working in the corrals that spring, I was so acutely aware of Boyd's absence that everything around me felt alien. It was the lonesomest feeling I've ever had.

All I was getting from the clinic were bills, and I began to wonder if they were just keeping him there indefinitely. So once again I called on Georgia, the oldest of the Marsh children. She stayed with the children while I drove to Denver.

When I arrived, I learned that they had been giving Boyd shock treatments and keeping him sedated. Then they said, "Mrs. Charter, we hate to tell you this, but he almost hit a doctor this morning."

I said, "He did! That's wonderful. He hasn't shown that much spunk in over a year. I'm going to take him out of here. He's going home."

They said it would take several days to free him from the sedation, but that I could stay in the room with him and take him out on short drives. So we drove around in the mountains and finally headed for home. But I wasn't prepared for the outbursts of hostility directed towards me and my mother. At first he insisted it was all my mother's doing, for that was the St. Louis way, and she had led me into it. It took a while to convince him that she had nothing to do with it, for I hadn't told anyone what I was going to do. Then his rage was directed at me.

He was very embittered and enraged at what he was put through. He was sure his chances to run a successful ranching operation were over. No one would have any confidence in him again. Fortunately, one of the officers of our bank had gone through a similar experience and was back on the job with no stigma attached. Once Boyd was back on his feet, neither his credit nor credibility were questioned.

However, it was not easy resuming his normal life. He felt embarrassed and dreaded meeting people. To add to his misery he was often disoriented on the ranch as a result of the shock treatments. This gradually wore off, but the resentment lasted. Life would seem to be going along smoothly until something would trigger a memory or he would have too much to drink. Then off he'd go into a rampage of accusations which went far into the night.

I don't know how we were finally reconciled, but Boyd eventually conceded that I had acted out of love, and that even if I did the wrong thing, which I well might have, I did it out of desperation, not knowing what else to do.While our relationship was mending, life on the ranch went on smoothly. Our operation was now an ideal situation, with wintering on the home ranch and summering on the mountain.

Anne Goddard Charter

THE MOUNTAIN RANCH

The mountain ranch became the focal point of our operation, the place we spent our summers, and because it had been bought with Boyd's inheritance, it became a continuation of the Jackson Hole Charter ranch, a heritage to be kept and passed on.

We went back each summer to Jackson to steep the children in the atmosphere that Boyd had grown up in. We took two vehicles, so we could divide up the children, mixing and matching to avoid bickering. There was something about the movement of wheels that encouraged this animosity, or maybe the close quarters. To offset this on the way to Sunday school, we sang Negro spirituals and other lively songs.

It usually took us two days for the one-day trip to Jackson, as we stopped a lot. When we went through Ryegate, we'd stop to inspect the hotel with the two-story outhouse built onto an outside wall. We would spend the night in Gardiner, if we went that way, or in Cody if we took the other route. The Cody Museum was a must and the old hotel a museum in itself. We always counted bears going through Yellowstone Park and stopped for all the views and oddities of nature.

On arriving in Jackson, the first place we went was the cemetery located at the base of Snow King Hill. While we visited graves, we listened to Boyd reminisce about the history of Jackson and the oldtimers he knew. He had a story about everyone he had known or heard of. Once when we came to Fred Deyo's grave there was elk manure on it. Boyd's observed that they had come to visit Fred and decorate his grave. "He'd sure like that," he said, "It sure beats flowers for old Fred."

From the cemetery we'd go to the elk feeding ground which flanks the town to the northeast. The kids wanted to know if it had always been there.

"Hell no," Boyd said, "Years and years ago the elk used to migrate clear out of Jackson Hole and all that country, those mountains in there. They migrated to the desert and wintered on the hard winter forage. Then when civilization came in, all these ranches and towns, then the elk quit migratin' and that's when they holed up there in Jackson Hole country."

I asked him if the elk were there when they moved to Jackson.

"Now you can believe this or not, but when we first came to Jackson Hole, right around our house and right around the town of Jackson, in the spring of the year when the elk would start calving, they would start dying and it would stink so bad you couldn't hardly stand it. There were hundreds of elk lying there dead every winter. Christ, they got hemmed in there and that snow was nine feet deep, and hell, they would just starve to death. That's when they started feeding them. I worked many a winter feeding elk."

We'd visit relatives and friends, make the rounds of the town, visit the museum where Boyd's father's silver-mounted saddle and bridle were displayed and then return home by the route we hadn't come.

By this time, Kit had outgrown the Marsh School and had to go to Billings for junior high. Delia and Celia Ryan were twins a few years older who lived on a ranch in the Bulls. They were attending school in Billings, staying with relatives who agreed to take Kit in too, for room and board.

It was a tough time for poor Kit having to adjust to a large public school while living with strangers under less-than-ideal conditions. There were tears when I drove her to school early Monday mornings and then tears of relief when I picked her up on Friday for the homeward journey. The plus for these weekly trips during the short days of winter was when our drive coincided with those magical times around sunrise and sunset, when the sun turned artist and transformed the bleak expanse of land into glowing contrasts of light and shadow and colors known only to this prairie country.

"Just like a C.M. Russell," we would say. The tall grasses on curing can shine bright yellow in the sun. As winter wears on, the gold becomes tarnished and drab, but a light snowfall can transform it to white gold.

One junior high problem that Kit brought home was what to do for a science project. Boyd had just shot a badger that had invaded the chicken house. He speculated that if it could be reduced to bones, Kit could wire together a badger skeleton.

He skinned it. I cooked it. The odor was potent. I hastily threw in all the pickling spices and other aromatic herbs I could find. After that, every time I cook a ham, I think, badger! Well, with lots of fine wire and a bit of help, a fairly respectable badger skeleton was produced and taken to school. A unique contribution to say the least.

It was the same year that five-year-old Stevie dove into a corner of the kitchen after a rolling apple, hit the cord to the deep fat fryer and the fryer fell to the ground spilling hot grease down his back and one arm. I yelled for Kit to get her Dad, tore off all his clothes, put him on his stomach on a sheet in the car and took off for town. He must have been in shock as he didn't even let out a whimper on the way in.

The doctor who examined him said he would be all right, and as he would be sedated I might as well go home. The next day, he was swathed in bandages and released. Our instructions were not to remove the bandages and return in a week. By the end of that week, I was thinking spices again. He smelled almost as bad as that badger.

When the bandages were removed, he was cleaned up. The healing had begun but he still has the scars. Some lessons we surely learn the hard way.

Our friends the Temperos underwent a much greater tragedy. Their little girl had also graduated from the Marsh School, and her father flew her to Worden to continue her schooling. While returning one Friday evening with his little girl and a visiting friend, the plane crashed and all were killed instantly. The shadow of this tragedy spread over the whole ranching community.

Not long after this happened, we had to trail our cows from the home ranch over the mountain. Our planned early start had been delayed, so when we began the ascent from Railroad Creek to the top of Dunn Mountain it was growing dark and the cows figured they had gone far enough. It was almost impossible to keep them climbing, and as a last resort we'd get off our horses and push or bat them with sticks.

By the time we reached the top, a full moon had risen. This was also after the disastrous fire which had turned the slope down Black Canyon into a landscape of stark, black, skeletal trees. With the memory of tragedy so fresh, we felt the eerie presence from ghostly apparitions which cast long shadows in the moonlight. Only the herding of the cattle kept us linked to reality.

This much-used trail from Black Canyon to the top of Dunn has changed its appearance as the land has responded to the ravages of nature and the imprints of man. Left standing through flood and fire is the toilet tree so named because of its great girth. It provided privacy for those responding to the call of nature. Wish we could comprehend the stories that tree could tell us.

For the children, working or trailing cattle was serious business, but riding was also just for fun: playing cowboy and Indian, breaking colts, racing and whatever else young minds could think of doing on a horse.

Riding did not take up all their time. There were always plenty of outdoor activities. They built hideouts, tree houses, "lived" in caves and climbed rocks. They liked to collect the clay from nearby clay banks and become potters.

The kids "help" in the garden was usually at watering time so they could squirt the hose. The rest of the time they ran their trucks in their construction site, a corner of the plowed earth where they could dig, tunnel, build or just make tracks. Of course when they got big enough to really help, they preferred being Indians and took off to the hills.

My children learned to swim in the stock tanks or shallow end of the reservoirs while on the home ranch. But the mountain ranch had more inviting swimming holes.

Before becoming a rancher, I had been warned never to learn to milk a cow or stack hay bales. I milked in emergencies, but stacking, no thanks. But then Art Seger came along and offered to teach me how to build a perfect stack and I soon became engrossed in working out the patterns that would hold a stack together, keep it from leaning and form a top that would shed water. It wasn't long until I was the official stacker. Boyd would bring in the bales and heave them onto the stack or put them on the little bale conveyor that would hoist them to the top. One of the kids would be with me to pull the bales with a hayhook to where I wanted it positioned.

My cousin from St. Louis, Mary Augustine, came to visit us several summers. On the first occasion we left her in charge of the children while we went on a short vacation. Mary reported that the children thought they had been left in charge of Mary, as they instructed her just what to do or not do.

A subsequent visit coincided with haying. Mary and I were positioned in the stock truck to pile the bales in an orderly fashion as they came over the edge propelled upward by the bale conveyor. Art was in charge of loading the bales onto the hoist. He took great delight in loading them on so fast we couldn't possibly keep up, and Mary became so buried in bales she couldn't move.

Art also liked to take in the sights. One of our meadows lay over the hill from their house. When raking hay there, I would often wear my bathing suit, hoping to get a tan, and so attired, I could break the monotony by pretending I was sailing. On such occasions Art would inevitably find an excuse to come riding over the hill to enjoy the unusual "harbor view."

The ultimate in haying years was when the grass grew so tall and abundantly that we could cut it for hay in the pastures that had not been grazed. Our stack grew so long we called it the steamboat. There was more hay than we needed, steer prices were on the up, so Boyd decided to buy enough steers to winter on the hay. This meant staying at the cabin all winter to feed the hay to them.

They did well until it came time to sell. The price of steers plummeted. Our summer's work was for naught. The hay had not made us one single cent. Boyd took a solemn oath never to hay again, and he never did.

In 1958, when Joe reached junior-high age, we moved to town. We also bought another ranch, the Mackey ranch on the east side of the Roundup highway. With it came a valuable asset, Joe Miller who had been ranch manager. The Miller family became our good friends. Boyd bought some 400 head of cows to stock the new ranch. As Joe Miller ran the operation pretty much on his own, we only helped on special occasions, such as the time we tried to trail calves across the ranch to the home place. It was like trying to control autumn leaves in the wind. The feeling was of holding one's breath and riding on tip toe. The slightest sudden movement would set them off. As we neared the end of the trail we were doing well until suddenly, directly in front of our tentative herd, a man appeared as if from outer space: an invader, a hunter, a trespasser!

Our calves exploded, scattering in all directions. It took so much time and effort to gather them back into a manageable herd that we never did know who the catalyst was.

WILDFIRES AND TEAMWORK

We started ranching during a drought period. Being new to the country, we thought it normal weather but Boyd worried about the grass. He took out his frustration by digging holes to see how far down it was to moisture. He figured if he could only line up all the holes he had dug, he could put in a division fence. My frustration came out thus:

Thunder Storms
High, dry, sailing by,
Thunderheads in the sky.
Bolts of lightning coming fast
Thunder rumbling, rain at last?
Not a drop, clouds retain
Every bit of precious rain.
Lightning ugly, thunder snarling
Could it be they're giving warning?
Heat so scorching, air so dry
Electric bolts rend the sky
And there it is
Fire on the ridge!

Legend has it that the Indians periodically burned off the country to keep the ponderosa pine from growing so thick they would become fuel for an uncontrollable fire. They also noticed the grasses came back more abundantly for their horses, the buffalo and other game after a fire. But fire is a scary thing.

We raced to a tree that has been hit by lightning to put out the fire before it can spread. One time, from a high spot on Brunner Mountain, we spotted over a dozen fires started by lightning in a matter of a few minutes. Luckily, like us, every rancher in the area was out spotting fires. Most of these spot fires could be put out easily, but sometimes they would smolder and burn underground. Undetected, fed by tinder dry pine needles, then caught by the wind, the fire would rise up and sweep through the country, destroying grass and trees in its path.

When this happened, all the ranchers and many town people would turn out, doing what they could; dig fire guards, saw down burning trees, start back fires or just beat the burning grass with wet gunny sacks.

Our two big fires were in 1959 and 1984. The fire of '59 started west of us. George and Paul Meged and Art Seger had been putting up hay, and saw smoke coming from the direction of Fred Johnson's ranch. They spread the word and every rancher in the area turned out with shovels, chainsaws and water tanks in their pickups.

Often, the whole family would turn out, and those too young to work stayed in the pickup. The women's main job was to provide food and beverages at the fire line. Hams and roasts were cooked and made into sandwiches. Hasty trips to Roundup were made for more supplies; bread, mayonnaise, sandwich fillings that would stick to the ribs, but no peanut butter, thank you. The heat and sweating from the fire made one thirsty enough! Watermelons and beer were a must. The long nights spent guarding the fire line was a good time for camaraderie and swapping tales. Boyd had lots of experience fighting fires as he had been in charge of the Civilian Conservation Corps fire-fighting crews near Jackson Hole and Yellowstone Park during Roosevelt's New Deal.

Fires were the community social gatherings of the 'Fifties and 'Sixties. Ranchers and their families tended to do their own work. There were few free days for visiting. One summer when son Tom was about twelve, he commented, "Sure wish we would have a good fire."

"Tommy, how in the world could you say such a thing?" I responded.

"Well," he said, "It's the only time we get to see our neighbors."

Tom was a gregarious kid, and life on the ranch during the 'Fifties and 'Sixties was pretty isolated. It wasn't like the homesteading days, when people lived close enough to go to the local school house for regular dances and social events. We went to only one dance like that, in Musselshell. We loaded the kids in our car, instead of on a wagon. But, as in the old days, they slept on the benches along the wall while we danced.

RANCH KIDS GO TO TOWN

When Kit reached high school age, the children and I moved into a rented house in Billings. It was in a new residential area and there were a lot of pre-school kids on our block. When Boyd came in from the ranch, he would sit on the porch steps, and kid with the children as they played in the street. When supper time approached, the mothers would start calling their children in. Boyd said it was like the cows mooing for their calves. They were "mothering up."

The next year we bought a house that was ideally located, within walking distance of both the primary school and the junior high. It was after acquiring this "town" house, that I was able, for the first time, to unpack my wedding presents! And I was finally able to join a church.

My father's family were Unitarians, and my mother's were Presbyterians. The children joined the Episcopal church, where they went to Sunday school and were baptized. I was married by a Baptist minister. I was instructed by a Lutheran missionary. So, in all this, I chose Grace Methodist Church, perhaps the only denomination that could assimilate the mix in my background.

It was a new, fairly small and very friendly church which had a succession of fine ministers. Here, for the first time, I was in the midst of women friends. Until this point, I had lived mostly in a man's world. I soon became integrated into the Women's Society and eventually became its president. I became aware of the role a small town plays in lives of so many women during these years of traveling to church conferences. Small towns, with their rich variety of names and histories, introduced me to many interesting women.

Ranch friend LaVisa Golder and I attended a seminar in Wyoming where Evangelist Reg Goff opened his session saying "Ladies, don't come here to pray for your husbands, because they aren't here. And don't come here to pray that they might change. Pray for yourselves for your own attitudes, while you are here, and find what a world of difference this will make when you go back home."

I dropped out of all extra activities for almost a year after it reached a point that Boyd felt neglected and became resentful.

Our possession of the Mackey Ranch was short-lived. Boyd had created an impressive ranch, but he discovered he wasn't happy with one he couldn't run by himself. In 1961, we sold our cow herd and all of the ranch except the Mountain Ranch. Feeling that the only sensible place to invest money was in land, Boyd bought the part of the West Mackey ranch that runs along Highway 87N. We now had a winter range that balanced the summer range on the mountain, and a ranch we could run ourselves.

Boyd started buying calves to stock the new ranch. In the fall, we'd spend all sale days at the Billings Live. We sat above the sale ring and he did the bidding. It was up to me to keep track of how much money we spent. These days, plus evenings spent at the Spur Bar, kept Boyd in touch with a number of Montana cattlemen.

My church-going activities and bar attendance with Boyd started at about the same time. This made me question the appropriateness of my drinking. The Methodist stand on alcohol had softened; it didn't prohibit drinking, but cautioned about doing anything that might be a harmful example to another person. For a time, I just drank Cokes, which by two a.m. had a harmful effect on me. I soon decided there wasn't anyone present whom my drinking would harm, and that I could drink in moderation.

This was easier said than done, for the custom of the day was for each in the drinking circle to set up drinks in turn for everyone. There would often be multiple drinks set up in front of me. I learned to push them to my right or left or just to ignore them. No one was the wiser except the bartender, who might have been serving me mostly water anyway. This did make the time go slowly, and I wasn't always interested in or included in the conversations swirling around me. There was a Hamm's Beer sign over the bar. It showed a canoe going down some rapids and on down the river until it disappeared from view, and then it reappeared at the top to head down the rapids again. I watched this by the hour, becoming mesmerized and numb. But I resisted complaining or even appearing disagreeable.

My reward came with one of the best compliments I've ever had. My "admirer" was a rough character from the rugged and wild Missouri River Breaks country. Boyd always greeted him by saying, "Well if it isn't the biggest horse thief in Montana," and he'd grin and seem flattered. Once after a long evening, he turned to me and said, "Anne, I'd sure go down the river with you anytime."

Our gift to Kit when she graduated from high school in 1964 was a summer in Europe. On returning, she married Henry Nilson, just a year out of school himself. Boyd liked Hank, but considered them too young and couldn't bear the thought of losing his little daughter. He couldn't bring himself to go to the wedding, and got drunk instead.

Once they were married, however, Boyd accepted Hank into the family. They agreed to live in the cabin on the mountain ranch and take care of the cattle. This was about the time nearsighted Kit rode up on a mountain lion feeding on a dead carcass. Needless to say, neither of them held their ground.

They moved into town where Hank was always able to get a job and for the arrival of their baby girl. By the time Kasey Anne was about four, however, they decided Hank would go to college so he could get a white-collar job.

In 1968 they moved into our town house, where Kit ran a nursery school to help finance Hank through college. While Kit was running her nursery school, Steve was in Shattuck, an Episcopal military prep school in Minnesota. He became a rebel of the 60's. Joe was in the Navy in Vietnam, and Tom, with a deferment, was working on the ranch. I began to feel the empty nest syndrome.

Anne Goddard Charter

OUR BULL MOUNTAIN SANCTUARY

Boyd and I spent most of our time in the cabin after the kids left the roost. Accompanied by our two dogs, Fred and Ted, I walked the many ridges which stretched out in every direction from our cabin. One high rock above the dog cemetery made a good starting or ending point for a walk. One could stand on it and look across the valley to the rock that towered over the coal vein in the "40." It's easy to imagine Indians sending smoke signals from those rocks.

The "40" is forty fenced-in acres, where a coal vein surfaces along the face of a cliff. The footing beneath the vein is crumbly, but this does not discourage the young from hunting for leaf fossils along its surface. Boyd discovered part of a dinosaur bone in the creek bed a little further down, after a flash flood washed away some of the bank. Coal lines the bottom of the "dry" creek bed, but water runs below the vein and springs trickle out here and there along its banks. A "test" hole dug by the Consolidated Coal Company, planning to strip-mine in the area, filled with water to a certain level and couldn't be pumped dry. The coal is the aquifer for most of the country. We asked them how they would strip-mine the vein in the cliff. They said it would be easy; they'd just blast the rocks down.

Dams were put in twice at the end of the ridge, making a wonderful clear water swimming hole, but in time flash floods took them out. These floods seem to come in mid-summer, often breaking a drought or following a fire. It was very exciting when the floods came. We would race out into the torrents of rain to hear what sounded like a train coming down the canyon, and watch the wall of water which filled the creek and flooded the land. This inspired me to write:

Cloud Burst 1968
Black clouds - blue sky
Dirty clouds scudding by
Dust swirls - awfully dry
Scorched grass about to die.
Then
Rain pelts - like hail
Big drops that flail
Comes hard, takes your breath
Dark and noise scare you to death.
But
We're so glad must run in it
Drenched clear through in a minute
Splash to creeks to see them run
Oh lordy - this is fun
Oh well
Tomorrow fence will need repairing
Cattle out - but who's caring?
Oh Lord who could complain?
You gave us rain - you gave us rain!

My walks with Fred and Ted took me far beyond the "40," to destinations which have acquired names of their own. If we followed the road which climbed up the mountain and down into Railroad Creek, we came to the wooden windmill, a relic of the past with the well no longer usable. If we started the ascent, we'd come to Buffalo Skull Spring.

Our alternative, if walking beyond the "40," would be to turn right on the tracks just beyond the towering dead pine tree. This "road" led to Black Canyon, a small reservoir. The dam of the original reservoir had washed out, but the ranch needed the water hole, so we had one dug and a new dam with a good overflow was built further down the creek. It was fed by underground springs and by a small surface spring at its upper end. It made for a wonderful swimming hole, and we kept it stocked with trout for the kids. This water hole lasted until the flash flood which followed the fire of 1984. The erosion caused by the flood after the fire filled it with muck and debris. It was a bubbling cauldron of composting material for several years, but finally cleared up enough for swimming — if one did not stir up the bottom. The creek bed above the reservoir is a gorgeous tangle of wild roses in the spring.

We made many trips by horseback from Black Canyon to the top of Dunn Mountain. The mountain was named after the family who lived there during the homesteading days. From letters we found in a sealed jar, we deduced from his elegant script and his grammar and spelling that Mr. Dunn had been an educated man. The letters were written from the penitentiary. He had killed his son-in-law with a ballpeen hammer.

Dunn built his cabin on top of this high plateau and raised wheat. Our neighbors, the Segars, would tell of his trips to town in his wagon. If he was not hauling grain, he would take his girls with him, locked in a cage in the back of the wagon where they would be safe while he went about his business.

We found the remains of the cage near the homestead site. Enough of the cabin was still standing to make it an interesting place to rummage. We found some of the shoes Dunn had made for his family out of old tires; miscellaneous bits of tools, furniture and farming equipment he left behind. Outsized fence posts were presumably set by the girls, and he had a lookout tower from which he could scan the country in case of invaders. His main fear was probably young men, as he considered his daughters his property. Which explained his ill-will toward his unfortunate son-in-law. There was a spot near the cabin where some thought there were graves, but no one wanted to look further.

The "40" was a focal point, and if we were working cows horseback, and not headed for the mountain, we would turn right and follow the fence line passing by the "Fat Woman" place. She must have been quite a character to have her homestead remembered by name. There was part of a root cellar and a few foundation rocks to identify the spot. The only other homesteader to have his place identified by name was Sam, of the "Sam Place." It was actually a mini-ranch — a beautiful mingling of flat rocks along a stream bed good for picnics and playing, a small pond for swimming, pine woods for shelter, open meadows for grazing and a boggy, brambled creek running at the bottom of the hills. It was a favorite place for chokecherry picking and mosquito bites. In reading the abstracts for our Bull Mountain ranch, we were fascinated by the entries that Sam had refinanced his place with a different person every year that he owned it.

After passing the Fat Woman and ascending the trail to the Three Tanks Windmill, one could go through a gate into the Sam Place or proceed straight ahead to Elk Pass, going past the Two Reservoirs. If one followed the trail to the right it took you into Number 9, the only place on the ranch identified by its section number. Many ranchers knew their ranches and identified locations by section numbers. Boyd refused to use these numbers in daily conversation, making use of them only when poring over maps. Number 9 was a railroad section, and its identification as 9 passed on to us.

"Lake Louise" was a good place to go mushrooming after a summer rain. It derived its name from Art Segar, who had accompanied us the first time we trailed cattle from the home ranch to the mountain. It was also the first time our children got a chance to see what the new mountain ranch was like. It was quite a contrast from the flat plains country they were used to. Going up the first steep ascent, some yearlings took off over a steep bank into a heavily wooded ravine. Kit being the good cowhand she was, took after them and brought them back up to the trail. But she was in tears, she had lost her hat and her glasses, and received numerous scratches. It took her a long time to get over "hating the mountain." Art tried to recapture the peace by telling the kids all sorts of stories about our new ranch and what it was like. They wanted to know, is there any place they could swim? "Well, there might be a place not far from the house."

"What's it called?" they wanted to know.

"Well, we might call it Lake Louise," he said. It turned out to be a live spring which made a sizable water hole for the cattle, but was not deep enough for a swimming hole.

One other favorite walk for my faithful dogs and me was to climb the ridges southeast of the cabin, and follow along the top of them to "the hole." Its name describes it well; it could only be entered by descending steep banks, and cattle did not find this little paradise easily. If they did find it, we often missed them during the fall roundup. The grass was lush, it was a beautiful, protected spot with live springs which we developed into watering holes. The banks one slithered down or scrambled up were a great source of prehistoric leaf prints in rocks. One had to pause and contemplate the formative years of this country.

I'm telling only of the changes I've seen in my lifetime. If only the rocks could tell about the changes they have seen, like how this country was once sea, for we've found fish and shell fossils; and how it became tropical and inhabited by dinosaurs, for we've found their bones on our ranch. This land is testimony of being spared by the glaciers and so became a mountainous area in the midst of plains country. It holds many secrets of the past.

THE BATTLE OF THE BULLS

The Bull Mountains rise out of the prairie to around 4,000 feet, forming the divide between the Yellowstone and Musselshell river valleys. These hills are mostly timbered with ponderosa pine and cedar, intermixed with grassy meadows in valleys between sandstone outcroppings.

The Bulls are dryland mountains: the few streams are usually intermittent. Ranchers who live in the sparsely settled area depend on springs and ground water as their primary water sources. There is abundant wildlife in the higher pastures, including deer, elk, and wild turkey.

The ecology of the area is fragile. Rainfall is limited and water is always scarce. During long, dry summer periods ground water is the only supply available to ranchers. The Bulls are underlain with sub-bituminous coal, some of which was mined by underground methods. Past mining had an adverse effect on water tables and springs; only after the end of intensive mining in the Bulls did the water tables rise and the springs begin to flow again.

One has to understand the division of the land here, also. At the height of the Civil War, when President Abraham Lincoln signed the 1864 Northern Pacific Railroad Land Grants, Congress conditionally granted the company 40 square miles of public land for each mile of track laid. The land was laid out on either side of the railroad's mainline right-of-way, in alternating sections (640 acres each). In Montana alone, the NP was granted 20 million acres.

Contrary to the conditions of the 1864 and 1870 land-grant acts, the Northern Pacific did not live up to its obligations. In 1924, Congress launched a five-year investigation of the NP land grants. It found that the NP had spent $70 million in building the railroad, but had made $100 million in net land-grant receipts by 1927. It also concluded that the NP had violated the Congressionally mandated terms of the original land grants by not selling stock to the public; not building the railroad on schedule; not opening its lands to settlement; wrongfully receiving 13.3 million acres within Indian reservations; had fraudulently classified more than a million acres as mineral lands in order to claim prime agricultural or timber lands in lieu of those holdings; had illegally diverted funds to the building of branch lines; had claimed 1.4 million acres too many in Washington state; and had delayed surveying vast portions of the land grant to avoid paying taxes. But Congress did nothing to remedy the fraud and the railroad's land empire remained secure. When the railroad sold its surplus land to settlers or ranchers, it usually retained the subsurface mineral rights.

Because of the checkerboard division of land ownership, the situation we faced when the coal companies invaded the West was that we owned the surface land without any mineral rights on every other section. The alternate, adjoining sections we leased for grazing from Burlington Northern, successor corporation to Northern Pacific after the 1970 merger of three railroads.

133

Anne Goddard Charter

The lease we had with the railroad, once considered the best private lease one could have, turned into a nightmare when Consolidation Coal Company tried to get control of the Bull Mountain coal field for strip-mining.

Had coal even crossed our mind when we bought our mountain ranch? Yes. We knew that the railroad controlled alternate sections in the Bull Mountain coal field. We knew there once had been a coal mine and small settlement on what we call Railroad Creek. We'd seen the grave markers, collected oxen shoes from the site, and a rattlesnake from the cellar hole of an old saloon. At that time, locals were contracted to cut railroad ties for a proposed railroad to be built toward Huntley. However, the mine was abandoned when more accessible coal was found near Red Lodge, and the tie cutters were left with their wooden ties. One can still find a few barns built from them.

What we didn't know or hadn't bothered to find out was that the Bull Mountain coal field was part of the Fort Union Coal Formation which contains some of the richest known coal deposits in the world. What we didn't even dream was that we, like the other folks living in this coal rich area of eastern Montana, would become the targets of the strip-miners.

LEASE HOUNDS AND SMOOTH TALK

When the coal company land men descended on us, they came in the guise of oil men, much as the wolf in the fairy tale comes in sheep's clothing. "It will be free money up front, and you'll never see us again," they said. We had already received an oil lease on our home ranch that had enabled us to keep yearlings to two-year-olds and had put us ahead in paying off the bank.

Fortunately, no oil was found on our ranch. The town of Melstone was not so lucky. There is a grim story of two brothers who had been ranchers all their lives, that is until oil was struck on their ranch and they became rich. Having no work they had to do to survive, they ended up drinking themselves to death.

The landmen told us that all they wanted was to core-drill on our land. They tried to make it sound like an oil lease: they would give us a dollar an acre for our land, and two cents-a-ton royalty if coal was mined. (Later, we learned the landmen were promised ten cents-a-ton royalty for their efforts.) The coal was worth about $15 a ton then. We sent them away, contracts unsigned.

Soon, they were back. They informed us that all of our neighbors had signed up and that if we didn't follow suit, we'd be in the unenviable position of being an island of nothing in a sea of plenty.

Boyd reminded them that fifty years ago the mountain folk of Appalachia, in response to a little sweet talk and some up-front money, signed away the rights to their land with an "X." He allowed that although he had just gone through the fourth grade of school, he'd be god-damned if he'd put his X on any of their papers. "Oh yes, they'll go over here and tell my neighbor that, oh, I'm going to sell to them and that I've done this with them," Boyd explained. "That first guy that came here with the card, he told me that they wanted permission to come in here and core-drill for coal, and he had this contract all made out. And that contract gave them the right to core drill anywhere they wanted to on this land. And if need be they could build roads. Like if they wanted to get a core drill up there on top one of them mountains, they could go and bulldoze a road up there. And they would have the right to go through a fence anywhere they come through it, in other words they wouldn't have to go a mile or two down the fence to come through a gate. And they would compensate me one dollar-an-acre for the right to do that. Now this is the first guy that came here. So, when I get mad I don't use very good language. I said, Why you son-of-a-bitch, why, if you think I'm going to do anything like that, give you the right to come in here and tear this god-damn place up, go through anywhere you want to, in the winter or anything else, and I give him a right damn good cussin' and he left. And he went right straight over the mountain there to Mrs. Pfister, a widow woman, and he told Mrs. Pfister. She read the contract, and of course, she didn't cuss him, she said, No I won't sign that. He said why not, all your neighbors have signed it. And she said which one of my neighbors has signed that? And so he had a list of the people who signed this contract, and my name was the second one on there. And she said, Charter over there signed that?

And he said yes. So she come over here and asked me about it. So that's one way the sons-of-bitches do it. We don't go to town very often, but I happened to be there in town and the phone rang. I was there alone so I answered it. Here was this woman that I know, she's a friend of my wife through the church, and she comes out here every once in a while to spend the day. She said, oh my goodness, I heard something the other day that sure made me feel bad. And I said what's that? She said, I just heard that you'd sold your ranch. I said, we ain't sold nothing, who-ever told you that is full of beans. Well, she said, the story is going around that you sold out to the coal company for an enormous amount of money. They get that thing that I've sold out, see, and I'm one of the last hangers on, so it's a hell of a lot of good propaganda. Huh?"

Not knowing quite what to make of this ornery man, the front-men left, only to reappear once again. This time it was three of them with brief cases arriving over our rut-filled road in a fancy car. This was enough to set Boyd's teeth on edge, but he went to the door and said, "Come in gentlemen, won't you join us around the kitchen table. Anne, you have some coffee, haven't you?" I poured the coffee as they introduced themselves. One was Del Adams, vice-president. He allows that its a mighty good cup of coffee. Boyd says "Hell, my wife never made a decent cup of coffee in her life."

They try again for a little small talk. Looking out the window seeing a pasture full of horses, "Are those horses you raised?" one asks. "Oh yes," says Boyd.

"They are certainly fine horses."

Boyd says, "I've read that you coal men told the Appalachian hillbillies what fine pigs their razorback hogs were. Those horses that you see are jug-headed, raw-boned, mean-tempered bucking horses and most of them came down from Canada."

They left without opening their briefcases.

Boyd could look the part of a hillbilly, and he played the part too. Our mountain house was a two-room log cabin, kitchen and bedroom, with a lean-to added on for another small bedroom, bath and front room.

In the meantime, having been told we had no recourse, as there was an eminent-domain law for mining in Montana, the telephone lines were hot between the Bull Mountain ranchers. We all agreed they were bastards and not to be trusted and we'd better find out what our rights were. Bob Tully said a Musselshell County Cattlemen's meeting was coming up and he'd see if he could get the county attorney to come and answer questions.

We all went to the meeting only to be told by our county attorney that we indeed had no rights, and we'd do well to accept their offer, for it was the best we could expect to get. We learned later that the county attorney had already been hired as one of Consol's lawyers. We also found out that this was normal practice for coal companies in mining areas throughout the United States.

THE BULL RANCHERS BUNCH-UP

The next day, Boyd and Bob Tully decided we'd better all get together to see how we could fight this thing. A meeting of ranchers was called at the Tully ranch. We decided we all had best work together and stick together and the best way to start was to become an organization. So we called ourselves the Bull Mountain Landowners Association, elected officers and agreed to present a united front to the coal company.

Bob Tully was elected chairman, and as I was the one living in Billings with the kids during the winter, I was elected vice-chairman. My job was publicity. The only thing I could think of doing was to call the *Billings Gazette* and give them the news that we had formed an organization, what our purpose was, and the names of our officers. I was referred to reporter Dave Earley who listened to my spiel, asked a few questions and then, silence.

Being a woman, I had to fill in that silence, so I blurted out that Lou Menk, chairman of the board of Burlington Northern had just bought a Bull Mountain ranch and we were considering (tongue-in-cheek) asking him to become a member. His ranch was actually outside the coal field but he was still a neighbor. Dave seemed to appreciate a good joke, and he asked me to bring him some maps the next day. When I presented him with the maps he informed me that Mr. Menk would have to decline our offer to make him a member of the BMLA.

"What offer?" I cried, we haven't even talked to him. "Oh but I did," says Dave, "I telephoned him to see what his reaction would be. He told me that he was a true conservationist at heart, but that his first duty was to his stockholders."

That incident provided us with about a year's-worth of publicity. Dave Earley followed up every aspect of our publicity and every story with a reference to "Menk in the middle!" This gave us confidence in our ability to be noticed and make a difference, and it kept up the momentum.

Another incident that brought Mr. Menk into the picture was when he was asked if he would use the leases to put pressure on the Charters to sell out. His reply was that such was not their policy, but of course, there could be mitigating circumstances.

More of the company attitude was revealed in the early 1970's when a reporter asked one of Consol's men if they would reclaim the land if there was no law requiring it. The answer was, "no, it would not be economically feasible." The law did make it economically feasible by requiring the same from all the coal companies. But through the intervening years the industry has tried to undermine federal and state environmental laws.

We continued to hold meetings, usually at the Tully ranch, discussing and cussing and planning strategy. We invited the Pfisters over for our second meeting, and also Consol's representatives. Boyd took it upon himself to make the introductions.

"This is Mrs. Pfister, who has a daughter, Ellen, but if you think you're dealing with widows and orphans, you'd better change your mind. Mrs. Pfister here is as tough as old shoe leather and her daughter just happens to be a lawyer."

Mrs. Pfister was a proper old lady, intelligent, educated, and with old fashioned manners. Out of the corner of my eye, I saw her struggling to keep a straight face. Her reaction surprised me, as I had expected her to be horrified. Instead, from then on she accepted Boyd wholeheartedly as co-conspirator and battle companion.

Consolidation Coal Company invited Mrs. Pfister to come to their office for a consultation. They were trying to find a "weak link" and they thought they might find one in her. They offered to send a car out to her ranch. She declined. She could drive herself, she said, but she didn't mention that she would bring the Charters along, too.

Boyd recalled that meeting:

> I said, you people think this old lady is an old lady that you can put one over on, and I want you to understand that we don't figure you're anything but a bunch of dirty, lying sons-of-bitches. Well, they didn't know what to do. These men kept looking at each other and then pretty quick, they went back and opened up a clothes closet and out walked this man. One of them said, I want you to meet Mr. Del Adams, the vice-president for the western district of Consolidation Coal Company. And I said, well you son-of-a-bitch, you've been hiding in that closet. He had a tape recorder. He was going to record all this stuff, so that if they caught the old woman in a weak moment, they'd say, yes, you said you'd do it. Here is your tape.

Our strategy wasn't limited to confrontations with Consol. We made our plight known whenever and wherever possible. One evening in town, I stepped over to the neighbors to tell them what was in the air, as their sixth grade daughter, Jannie Burchell, was a visitor to our summer cabin in the Bulls who loved horses and riding with our kids.

As I unfolded my story to her parents, I was not aware that Jannie was sitting at the top of the stairs listening. The next day at school during their creative hour, she told the story to her class, suggesting that everyone write a letter protesting strip-mining in the beautiful Bull Mountains.

The following day, Jannie presented us with some thirty-plus priceless letters that made their impact not only locally, but as far away as D.C. and New York. Jannie also enlisted the help of classmates to get people attending the first Earth Day celebration to sign a petition against "stripping in the Bulls." I believe we ended up with 4,000 signatures.

Earth Day couldn't have been better timed as far as we were concerned for it carried our momentum to a new high. We had a booth, circulated petitions, and managed to get on the same TV coverage as the Chamber of Commerce. We even had the incredible luck of introducing the program.

Our Earth Day presentation consisted of a slide show of the Bull Mountains narrated vivaciously by neighbor Vera Beth Johnson. The Chamber had the immediate disadvantage of not being able to repudiate what we had said or defend their position. All they could do was to present their wonderful plan to make grass seeds available to anyone willing to participate in their environmental effort which was for everyone to scatter seeds along the highway right-of-ways. This of course was something we could willingly agree with and participate in.

We managed to give the impression that the Chamber was in perfect accord with us on preserving the beauty and productiveness of our land, when of course they had the completely opposite view. They were for mining and jobs, regardless of the cost. The sad part, we learned much later, was that Consol never really intended to mine and they could care less about jobs or the impact on the community. Their only intent was to put a negotiable value on their coal reserves in order to sell them for a profit.

We lucked out with many of our strategies, but the most lethal ploy that we had to combat was that of divide-and-conquer. Mining companies throughout Montana and the nation use this relentlessly. The bait they dangle sets neighbor against neighbor, family members against each other, and in our case, the town of Roundup against area ranchers.

Consol promised to revive the once flourishing coal-mining town through the creation of jobs and the spinoff of mining activities. Roundup was proud of its coal-mining history, and rightfully so, as Tony Boyle, national head of the United Mine Workers Union, was a native son. The prospect of growth and prosperity returning to the area and regaining some of its traditions looked good to the town.

Unfortunately, we were aware of the history of boom towns and the usual disastrous results, so we regarded Consol's promises as just pie-in-the-sky. After all, their offices were in Billings and most of their employees lived there. Maybe they'd share the spinoffs, but the people who got the well-paying jobs would be brought in from outside with the huge machinery.

There was also the problem of getting the coal to market. Either a railroad would have to be built into the heart of the Bulls, involving all the right-of-way disputes and the destruction of scarce bottom land, or the coal would have to be trucked to a railroad, providing jobs of course, but raising the problems of the use and maintenance of rural, county, state, and federal roads. The mining area is a long distance from any existing railroad and the continuous flow of trucks would not only disrupt normal traffic flow but be an additional concern where school bus and truck routes intersect. These concerns were seldom addressed in public meetings, and often buried in the seldom-read back of environmental impact statements listed under "public comment."

The idea of building a railroad to take the coal out of the Bulls made us paranoid at times. One morning in the early 70's, Boyd and I were jolted awake by the sound of a train whistle. A train? It can't be a train. They couldn't have laid tracks overnight. Could they? Of course not! But we had to find out where a train whistle had come from. We hastily dressed, jumped in the pickup and headed toward the eerie sound. We found a monstrous machine equipped with this whistle.

Why? To scare us? Weird. And they were about to do some core-drilling on our private land. Boyd won the heated argument and they left. We returned to our cabin for some strong coffee.

As with all bad situations there are moments of humor to lighten things up. A public meeting organized by bureaucrats was held in Roundup on some aspect of the mining situation. There was the usual danger of the government men monopolizing all the time, leaving no chance for public input. This did not please my husband, so he did what he did best, which was to interrupt with questions and comments.

At one point I felt he was being a bit too obnoxious so I nudged him with my elbow and whispered, "Give the poor man a chance to get at least one word in edge-wise." Boyd turned around and said, "Anne, stop beating up on me," and continued his tirade.

That week, the *Roundup Record Tribune's* front page headline read, "Wife Beats Up On Husband at Public Meeting." I learned to let Boyd be Boyd!

We enjoyed another good laugh when Consol offered to sponsor the girls high school basketball team. They provided the girls with jerseys carrying the logo, "The Roundup Strippers."

Then there was the time Ted Hanks, representing Consol, was to come to the ranch and have Boyd take him to some of the proposed mining sites. He brought his wife with him, and not anxious to bump around in the pickup, she stayed with me. We went on a walk during which she commented that the country was much too beautiful to be strip-mined. Later, I had an opportunity to quote her at still another public meeting in Roundup.

To counter the corporate technique of divide-and-conquer, we kept refining our "hang-together" policy. Ultimately, we informed Consol that to have any further communication with any of us they would have to go through our lawyer first, and then come to a regular Bull Mountain Landowners Association meeting. That about ended Consol's attempt to invade the Bull Mountains, with one notable exception. They came once more to our door in Billings, walked in with their briefcases, and without much fanfare pulled out a signed check. They asked Boyd what was his price. Boyd recalled: "They came to buy my ranch. But I told them, you'll always be four dollars and sixty cents short of being able to buy me out. This Del Adams walked out that door, he got ahold of the doorknob and he said, 'You get as hard-boiled as you want to, but in the long run we're going to get you. We are bigger than you are and we can last longer.' Those were his very words: 'We're going to get you.'"

Granted, they outlived Boyd, and other companies came in and tried to succeed where they failed, but none of them ever came up with the necessary four dollars and sixty cents.

COWGIRLS IN THE CAPITOL

Perhaps our most significant undertaking as the Bull Mountain Landowners Association was the Washington, D.C. adventure. As none of us had any previous experience in politicking, organizing or public relations, we were prone to do just about anything anyone suggested. We were told that hearings on strip-mine reclamation were being held by a House of Representative's committee and that we should try to get in on it. We wrote, received the reply that they were filled, but there would be another hearing later on. We were turned down for that, too. That made Boyd mad and he said, "Call Senator Mansfield and I'll talk to him." These were House hearings and he was in the Senate, but Boyd said that didn't make any difference. And it didn't.

Senator Mansfield got us in on the hearings. Our men suddenly had a lot of pressing ranch work, so three women were delegated to go. It was decided that Vera Beth Johnson, young striking looking rancher's wife, would explain the situation in the Bulls. Ellen Pfister, with a law degree, would tackle the actual reclamation problems. I, the grandmotherly type, would come up with a speech made up of "it doesn't make sense" most of which could still be applied today.

Ellen did her homework, part of which consisted of ferreting out information from the Agriculture Department at Montana State University, which was reluctant to come up with information, as much of their financing for the research had come from mining companies. There was no "right to public information law" then.

In D.C., our initiation to the hearing was to sit through several hours of listening to Representative Steiger of Arizona harass those representing the Navajo Tribe in their protest against the infamous Black Mesa strip-mine. They were accused of agitating on the reservation, and being backed by communists. You could feel the hostility in the air of the hearing room.

When our turn came, it was getting close to the noon recess. All three of us wanted to get our two-cents-worth in, for by then we were fighting mad. Vera Beth was first up with a map, and all her best school teacher skills ready to present our situation. She noticed that Steiger was talking over his shoulder to an aide and was paying no attention, so she called out "Representative Steiger, do you know where the Bull Mountains are?"

At first, there was dead silence, then the whole room dissolved in laughter and the press corps practically rolled under the table. The chairman rapped his gavel saying, "Mrs. Johnson, it is not customary for the witnesses to ask the questions. Please proceed."

Completely undaunted, Vera Beth proceeded and from then on we had everyone's undivided attention. No one seemed to mind that we ran over into the noon hour. Afterwards, the coal lobbyist came up and said, "You ladies should come more often, you do liven things up." The Chairman told Vera Beth she reminded him of his daughter, and Steiger said he guessed that if it was his land, he'd meet them with a shotgun. We began to feel good, and when our fellow believers

From left to right, Anne, Vera Beth Johnson, and Ellen Pfister talk with U.S. Senator Cliff Hansen, Wyoming. The trio from the Bull Mountain Landowners Association travelled to Washington to testify before a committee of the U.S. House of Representatives on strip-mine reclamation. Senator Hansen was a friend of Boyd's.

began to gather around us, we felt better and better. We gathered for lunch to become better acquainted and became friends and helped each other through the years.

We staged a money-raising reception that was a success both in raising money and spreading the word. We met more people from states being strip-mined. Those from Appalachia were especially vocal. Members of our organization made numerous trips to this shameful example of coal-mining exploitation.

The most memorable gathering was the National Conference on Strip Mining organized by Louise Dunlap of the Washington D.C.-based Environmental Policy Center and sponsored by Representative Fred Harris, Democrat from West Virginia. It was held in Middleboro, Kentucky, a typical Appalachian strip-mining area. Representatives from all the strip-mining states attended as well as the local miners who had been given the day off for the occasion. Fred Harris acknowledged the presence of the miners when he opened the meeting, and said they would have equal time to express their views. They had intended to break up the meeting, not participate in it. But there were no disturbances, and few views expressed by the miners, but it did give them a forum.

During an intermission, I talked with some of the young men standing around. Their response, rather than issues, was about our sex. They said they would never send their wives out anywhere, especially across the country, to represent them.

The only response that I could think of was that our men had work that had to be done on the ranches back home, and besides, I was too old for my husband to have to worry about me. I added that their wives were probably young and beautiful. Fortunately, we were saved by the bell.

Many of those present believed strip-mining should be banned completely, and they stuck to their guns, as the conditions in Appalachia haven't improved. We felt that banning was an unattainable goal, so were concentrating on getting the best federal and state reclamation laws possible.

We soon realized we had upset apple carts all through the mining community. No more secrecy, no more getting a foot in the door before they could either be held responsible or stopped. On the strength of this impact, we were urged to try to get in on the Senate hearings to be held the next day back in Washington.

Senator Clifford Hansen of Wyoming was in charge, and because of his friendship with Boyd, would probably feel obligated to get us in. It turned out that I was the only one able to stay over. Cliff said that although the hearing was filled, he would fit me in at the end.

Dumb me; I hadn't done my homework. Before strip-mining, we hadn't concerned ourselves with politics and how politicians stay in office. I just assumed that Cliff, having been brought up on a ranch in Jackson Hole, naturally shared Boyd's feeling for the land.

On that assumption, I rewrote my introduction, saying that Cliff and Boyd had grown up on neighboring ranches in Jackson Hole, and that whereas Boyd had stayed on the land to protect it, Cliff had opted to protect it in Washington.

Cliff gave us the red carpet treatment throughout our stay, taking us to lunch in the Senate dining room, introducing us to all who passed his table, including

143

Senator Hubert Humphrey. He gave me a proper introduction at the hearing, heard me through, and thanked me with no indication that anything was amiss.

Imagine my chagrin when I stopped by his office to leave a message of thanks for his kindness and saw the walls lined with posters of support for the oil and coal industries. I quickly learned that Cliff was pro-development and didn't look favorably on environmental laws that might hinder the progress of the energy companies. But that was not the only time I found myself in this kind of situation.

On returning to Billings, filled with excitement and enthusiasm about the success of our trip, I couldn't wait to broadcast the good news. The opportunity came through my church.

Hearing of my Washington adventure I was asked to tell about it at the next general meeting of the Women's Society. I gave the full report, which seemed to be well-received. But later, someone told me that I had really offended Audrey Rice. She did not think it was seemly for a church to sponsor such controversial issues which could threaten the very jobs of members. I was dumbfounded. I found out that she and her husband, Roger Rice, a senior geologist for Western Energy Company, had joined our church while I was in Washington. The last thing I wanted to do was to cause dissension in my church, so I decided that would be the end of airing my views.

But I still felt uneasy about my relationship with Audrey. We were on polite if adversarial terms with Roger whom I saw in church each Sunday, but Audrey headed the children's church service and I seldom saw her. A lay witness weekend solved the dilemma. It ended with us being divided into groups of four. Audrey and I were in the same group. Our task was to explore our spiritual journeys and their effect on our lives. A common bond brought us together so that we parted with hugs and tears. I thanked the lord for his guidance.

Roger's vindication came after his retirement. A Coal Board hearing was held to determine whether or not to terminate Carol Ferguson's job by merging the Hard Rock Impact Board and the Coal Board. She was doing her job too well in seeing that environmental laws were enforced. Roger Rice, as President of the Montana Mining Association, chaired the board of five members. Two voted pro, two con. His was the deciding vote. He voted against the merger and resigned from the Mining Association, saying he'd spent his life trying to reconcile mining and the environment and wasn't about to undo everything he'd worked for.

For the sake of immediate action, our membership organization, the Bull Mountain Landowners Association, was at first limited to the involved landowners. However, we had lots of support from other ranchers and many people in the Billings community, and we were becoming aware that similar situations existed in other parts of eastern Montana. Only the names of the coal companies were different. We began to see that a wider, united action was needed: an umbrella organization to fight these corporations.

THE NORTHERN PLAINS RESOURCE COUNCIL

While trying to save our land from mining in those days, things just seemed to happen. And so it was with the founding of the Northern Plains Resource Council (NPRC). The big event on the Bull Mountain Landowners Association (BMLA) agenda was to participate in the first coal symposium to be held in Billings which supposedly would present all sides in the coal controversy. We knew that the "front men" had been working eastern Montana even before they hit the Bulls, and they were getting some Xes on their dotted lines. We felt the need to get together with these other landowners to share fears and strategies. They undoubtedly would come to this gathering, so we'd have a chance to meet and talk with them.

In the meantime, we heard from Billie Hicks, a member of the Audubon Society who was on the planning board, that the "environmentalist" on the panel was from North Dakota's Knife River Coal Company, and that all the panelists would be industry men. We told her we'd get our own environmentalist, and she could assure that he got on the panel.

Cecil Garland, founder of the Montana Wilderness Society, accepted our invitation to be our environmentalist. But we were informed that the panel was full, and that it would be unfair to those giving up their valuable time to come to Billings to add anyone else.

When I told Cecil that they would not let him on the panel, he said not to worry. He'd come anyway, a day early, and if I'd gather a few interested people together, we could plot our strategy. About eleven of us met that evening, and we plotted and discussed. The need for an umbrella organization kept coming up, and finally, Cecil said, "Why don't you just form one?"

"How?"

"All you need is a name, officers, membership dues and a letterhead."

After much discussion, Mrs. Pfister came up with the name Northern Plains Resource Council. She said the Northern Plains would be our territory, and if we called ourselves a resource council, we would not limit ourselves to just coal. She indeed had an eye for the future. We elected officers and each of us paid the five dollars dues to become the charter members.

The following day, the symposium began with formal introductions, but soon our strategy was clear: we were going to have our say and challenge every word spoken by the panel members. The panel members were constantly interrupted, challenged and argued with, not only by our group, but by the entire gathering. There were few passive listeners. Nothing was accomplished, but it generated a lot of righteous indignation.

After the meeting, we signed up lots of new members from all over eastern Montana and Wyoming for our Northern Plains Resource Council. We were becoming a community. This casual beginning was a far cry from the accusations made by the big eastern potentates that subversive outsiders, probably communists, had come in to organize and finance us.

The problems of individuals became the concern of all of us. We began to grow beyond ourselves and became strong in the doing. As we grew, we took on many issues relating to land, air, water and people. More local groups became affiliated, each with its own "ox being gored," as Bob Tully put it.

Each affiliate was responsible for its own issues, and reported on them and their actions to the board. Each affiliate was assigned a staff member, who helped with organizing, research and coordination. The staff people worked hard at keeping the members working.

Members were responsible for speaking out at public meetings, before the legislature, and on radio or TV. Affiliates could pursue issues under their own organization, but if it was to become official NPRC policy, it had to be approved by the board, and by the membership at the annual meeting.

NPRC has become very sophisticated compared with the early impetuous days and learned many tricks of the trade from the companies we have dealt with, including that of having "moles." One time we learned of a major policy change made by Montana Power Company a day before it was to be made public. It happened that we were meeting with some of the company's representatives on the same day. Yet, when we confronted them with this information, they shamelessly denied it. One thing we did not assimilate was the corporate penchant for outright lying. We had nothing to hide. Our cards were on the table.

One writer, Stan Steiner, observed: "The ranchers are dumbfounded by the morality of the power companies. They feel greatly handicapped for valuing credibility, trust and honesty. They have difficulty dealing with corporate tactics. They make the mistake of treating corporations as people. These old-fashioned ranchers feel powerless."

Maybe he was right — momentarily. But he was wrong in the long run. We learned quickly, and we gained power. We were strengthened by knowing that we were fighting not only for our rights as individuals, but for the preservation of our values and the land. Hopefully, generations to come will thank us.

We used this power to persuade representatives of those dehumanized corporations to recognize our right to defend our business, ranching, as vigorously as the corporations represent their business. There are rare moments when we feel some progress is being made.

Our early efforts were haphazard when compared to our more sophisticated, knowledgeable work force of the 1980s and 90s, but they were not without results.

Dick Colberg, our first chairman, was present at the founding of NPRC, lived in Billings and agreed to act as interim chairman for six months.

Our first contact with Dick was when he and a partner came out to our Bull Mountain ranch and asked permission to cut wood. We recognized them as being trustworthy, and true environmentalists when they said they would use a mule instead of a motorized vehicle to haul the wood out. Unfortunately, the mule got loose dragging a chain and they were unable to catch it or see where it went.

Some days later, our sons Joe and Tommy, each riding a colt they were breaking, spotted the mule on the other side of the mountain, still dragging the chain. In their efforts to capture or haze him back to home territory, the mule went wild. So did the colts. One unloaded his rider and took off saddled and bridled.

The two boys, one afoot and the other on horseback, finally managed the seven miles back to the home corrals with the mule more or less under control. Once the mule was securely penned, the boys wrangled fresh horses and headed out looking for the horse that had run away.

Dick came to get his mule with a small one-horse trailer. It took him the best part of the day to load that animal. Boyd sat and watched and guffawed at the ornery animal's antics. Boyd withheld help, as he thought Dick should experience just how much misery a mule could deal a person.

Dick attended a meeting in Roundup of ranchers organized by the Bull Mountain Landowners Association to discuss the mining situation and its impact. At the end of the meeting he said, "I just have to tell you that listening to this group all day, I sense you have a deep caring for one another." He also commented that he was impressed with the fact that there was no high-pressure salesmanship, that each participant's views were respected, and that a friend was not thought any the less of if he did not choose to join our infant organization.

Dick, as first chairman of NPRC was well aware of the issues, especially in the Sarpy Creek area, which was another strip-mining battleground and the home of his grandmother. The floor of Dick's house became our first office. Our first attempt at a news bulletin was called *Battle Tactics*. It contained exchanges of experiences and advice gleaned from all the coal-impacted areas of eastern Montana and into Wyoming.

Dick took a giant step from his lowly position on that "office" floor in his house to a seat in the House of the Montana Legislature. By nature, he was an artist, potter, builder, creator and teacher, not a politician. But he had a job to do, and he asked people to vote for him so he could do it.

Some time after his six months as NPRC chairman was up, Dick attended a meeting at Eastern Montana College where Montana Senator Lee Metcalf was holding hearings. I was to testify for NPRC. During an intermission, Dick was talking to a friend, who told him he'd been hired for $2,000 to take moving pictures of industry men making good environmental statements. One of the company men, seeing Dick as a friend of their PR guy, joined them and urged this man to get good footage before those f***ing environmentalists began to speak.

Dick noted that when we did speak no one seemed to care or even to listen. This made him both sad and mad, and he felt a terrible urge to do *something* to make our cause an issue. But how to get heard? The only ones anyone was listening to seemed to be in politics. Could that be the way to go? If one ran for office, one could choose one's issue and espouse it to the high heavens.

He won his seat in the Montana House of Representatives in 1972 to serve in the 1973 assembly. Bob Tully remembers that during this session, "in the proverbial smoke-filled room, Ellen Pfister, Kit Muller, Dick Colberg and I believe, Pat Sweeney spent almost all night writing the strip-mine reclamation bill (HB555) to be carried by Dick". HB555 was defeated in the House chiefly because there was a bill in the Senate sponsored by Senator Bill Bertsche of Great Falls, which seemed to be the bill that would be passed. Our busy lobbyists were successful in introducing enormous amounts of language practically verbatim from HB555 into Senator Bertsche's bill, which became Montana's strip-mine law.

So Dick became involved in much of the early strip mine legislation, including our earliest effort, which was to remove strip-mining coal from the list of public uses which brought it under eminent domain.

As the pressures mounted and the mud slinging began, Dick realized that, in the political game, you become ruthless and dehumanized, much as in the heat of battle in war time. He found himself playing the political game, and that was not the self he wanted, so he gave up his seat before the end of his term.

Ellen Pfister became our next chairman, and soon had things whipped into orderly shape. We rented an office in downtown Billings, one bare room in the somewhat run-down Stapleton Building. The first job for the staff was to sand down floors, clean, and paint. Then they hustled around to find tables, chairs, desks, other donated items, and second-hand equipment.

The early staff was made up of rancher's sons and daughters, but soon included young, educated, idealistic people from both Montana and out of state.

Most of the staff lived communally at one time or another in "Bozo Villa," an older two-story house within walking distance of the office. The beginning salaries were $200 a month, supplemented slightly by generous donations of meat and garden produce from her introduced species.

Bob died in 1989. The vital part he played in the formation of NPRC and the directions it took remain an integral part of NPRC's history and will not be forgotten. We who knew him will miss Bob the most at our annual meetings, where the crazy, hilarious banter between Bob and Wally McRae was what we looked forward to the most.

SMOKESTACKS ON THE PRAIRIE

Boyd and I first encountered Wally McRae at rodeos. Boyd had a string of bucking horses which rodeo stock contractor Dale Small used in his shows and Wally was the announcer. To us, Wally's lingo and the performances of the horses took precedent over the contestants, although we knew many of them and we rooted for the riders, including our sons Joe and Tom.

Wally had a way with words and not only knew the rodeo routine, but usually something interesting about every contestant and horse. As rodeos and coal activities started overlapping, Boyd told Wally after a rodeo in Forsyth that he should go to Washington, D.C. Wally's reply was that if he went to D.C., it would be at taxpayer expense. This led us to believe that maybe he had political ambitions, but nothing could have been further from the truth. He was more diplomat than politician, and his heart was in his ranch and developing his poetry.

Wally went from entertaining the NPRC crowd at our annual meetings to becoming an amateur actor and one of the most famous of the cowboy poets. Many of his early poems deal with the emotions of those days fighting for survival against the coal companies.

His group, the Rosebud Protective Association (RPA) was in existence even before the BMLA, so Wally was familiar with the battle but he was called into full action when the Colstrip power plants became NPRC's main issue. He did end up testifying in Washington, but not at taxpayer expense.

While NPRC members were speaking out, the staff, too, was working away creating small but effective miracles. One of the earliest and most notable was a booklet showing the extent of coal leasing in eastern Montana. By painstakingly going to every court house in eastern Montana, these ranchers' sons documented federal, state and private leases, where they were, who held the leases, and the terms of each. These were tabulated and all put on maps, with different colors showing the different types of lease. This type of study had never been done before, and the net result showed that instead of the accepted figure of some 300,000 acres under lease in eastern Montana, there was ten times as much land under lease.

Industry men like John G. McLean, chairman of Continental Oil were urging the government to promote western coal development, thus forcing the whole lease situation into the foreground. A General Accounting Office report suggested that the government was not getting a fair price for its federal coal. And a later report noted that speculators, with no intention of mining, were buying up cheap coal leases and holding them until they could sell at profit on a rising market.

Reclamation and environmental regulations were not required on the older leases and were not being enforced on more recent ones. In 1972, the U.S. Senate passed a resolution calling for a moratorium for one year, or until the Senate could act on strip-mining legislation, on any further leasing of federal coal lands in Montana. Secretary of the Interior Rogers Morton refused to uphold it. Senators Mike Mansfield and Lee Metcalf of Montana, and Frank E. Moss of Utah wrote

Morton, calling his actions "unconscionable" and "indicative of the arrogance of the executive branch." They challenged his statement that the Interior Department could, or would, guarantee "environmentally acceptable mining."

A MONSTROUS PLAN FOR THE PLAINS

In 1971, in the midst of this controversy, Ellen Pfister discovered a bombshell. Daughter of Bull Mountain ranchers Bill and Louise Pfister, she had earned a law degree in Mississippi. Her father felt a lawyer was needed in the family to ranch in modern times. Ellen was working for a title company in Jackson, Mississippi, when a friend called her, asking if she had seen the article in the paper about the "North Central Power Study" being distributed by the U.S. Bureau of Land Management in Billings, Montana. Ellen located the Associated Press article and immediately rang up her mother in Billings. Her mother had not seen the study or read about it in the Billings newspaper. Louise Pfister made a beeline to the BLM office and requested a copy. After a few hems and haws from the clerks she was given one copy. It didn't take more than a casual glance for her to realize she was holding a live bombshell.

"I'd like a few more copies," she asked.

"Only one to a customer," was the reply. "We don't have very many."

"Well, you'd better order a lot more and quickly," Louise advised.

It soon became a best seller, and the BLM was hard-pressed to keep up with the demand. Why?

The study was a fantasy for the future in the West written by some 35 major public and private electric power suppliers in 15 states from Illinois to Oregon, along with the U.S. Bureau of Reclamation, at the instigation of the Assistant Secretary of Interior for Power and Water Development, James R. Smith. The plan would not only rival the industrialized Ruhr Valley of Germany, but it would out-produce it. Within the year, the study was dead meat, but not before it had done both harm and good.

Even though the study was too graphic, too large, and completely unattainable financially, the government had rationalized that an all-encompassing plan for developing the West as the U.S.'s energy supply source would assure a regulated, orderly development. But it had just the opposite effect. Each coal company, consortium or partnership interpreted the mining laws and regulations based on their own sense of need, and ignored the laws accordingly.

Luckily, the magnitude of the plan horrified most Montanans. This was not how they pictured their state's future. They for once put aside their characteristic complacency and moved into action. As Boyd put it, "It scared the shit out of them."

Most of us had no idea that the coal reserves of the Fort Union Formation in the Powder River Basin of Wyoming and Montana and in the western part of the Williston Basin in Montana and the Dakotas is the richest known deposit of coal in the world. The 1.5 trillion tons of coal is within 6,000 feet of the surface. One hundred billion tons are in seams 20 to 250 feet thick, and are close enough to the surface to strip-mine. This formation makes up 20% of the world's known coal reserves and 40% of the U.S coal reserves. At the 1970 consumption rate, this coal would supply our needs for 450 to 600 years.

Boyd Charter

ABOVE, LEFT: The Northern Plains Resource Council's logo.

ABOVE, RIGHT: Ellen Cotton put this cowhide sign on her ranch near Birney, Montana, in 1977. Terrence Moore photograph.

BELOW, RIGHT: Montana Governor Ted Schwinden signs legislation giving farmers new borrower's rights to keep them on the land through a farm crisis. In the back row, left to right, NPRC leaders and staff: Robbie Green, Meg Nelson, Jeanne Charter, State Representative Cecil Weeding (the bill's author), Dorothea Schultz, Jack Heyneman, and Russ Brown.

BELOW, LEFT: Wally McRae, left, Bob Tully, right, and Tom Tully, back, entertain at a NPRC annual meeting.

CENTER, LEFT: In addition to coal mining, NPRC has long been active in reforming hard rock mining policies at the state and national levels. Jean Clark is the spokesperson at this 1993 rally for modernizing the 1872 Mining Law.

In addition to the coal supply, coal gasification plants would be built at the mine mouth, as this was the best and most efficient way to utilize the coal, eliciting no transportation problems. The pollution would not be a problem because no one lived there, at least not anyone of importance.

Seven generating plants were to be built in the area of Colstrip (population 266). This would be the largest power project in the world. This was to be just a small part of what was envisioned by the North Central Power Study, but even then, it had the potential of poisoning the sky with more ash, more acid rain, more chemicals and other pollutants than all the emissions from the cities of Los Angeles, New York, London and Moscow put together. While some saw Colstrip becoming a city of 25,000, others thought it an exaggeration. The rumor mills were rolling. What would happen to those of us who lived here, the ones of "no importance"?

"Ranchers will vanish like the Indians," quotes author Stan Steiner. "We are the new vanishing race."

Poet and rancher Wally McRae said, "I have become, for all practical purposes, an Indian. Like the Indian I am standing in the way of progress, because I live and work above part of the world's largest known reserves of fossil fuel. But I resist."

Walking Bear, attending the first annual meeting of NPRC, came up with a solution for us: "The government will have to create a reservation to put all you ranchers and environmentalists on."

On the maps of the North Central Power Study were located forty-two power plants. Twenty-one alone clustered between Colstrip, Montana, and Gillette, Wyoming, an area just 70 by 30 miles. Nothing like keeping the pollution centralized! Perhaps it would go straight up? I don't think we knew much about the hole in the ozone at that time. Thirteen of the projected plants would generate 10,000 megawatts each, 14 times more than the infamous Four Corners plant near the Navajo Nation in Utah, Arizona and New Mexico. Even then, Four Corners was famous for being one of the world's worst polluters.

They also planned a huge diversion of water from all rivers of the Yellowstone Basin, requiring dams, storage reservoirs, pumping heads and pipeline — a fine project for the Bureau of Reclamation to get into. But what about fish? Irrigation? Drinking water? How about the loss of downstream water on the bigger rivers?

During the thirty-five year life of the project, the land surface, equal to half the size of Rhode Island, would be destroyed. The right-of-way for transmission lines would about cover the state of Connecticut and there would be a possible population increase of between 500,000 and a million people.

Wally McRae summed it up this way: "In the language of my neighbors, the Cheyenne Indians, the name for white man is the same as that for spider — *veho*. As I see the 'webs' of the high voltage lines, the 'webs' of railroads and strip mines, the poisons we exude from our activities, the rivers sucked dry of their life-giving juices, I am reminded of the wisdom the Indian exhibited with his prophetic name for us. Truly, we exhibit all the characteristics of a veho."

There were those who saw things in a different light. As in, "Anne Charter is a very nice lady but..." I overheard these words just as the engine started up with a roar on the small plane I was taking back to Billings after another round of testifying at the state capital. I had quietly taken a seat right behind two of my opponents on the strip-mining issue. We had been testifying before a committee dealing with strip-mine reclamation laws or eminent domain or any one of the mining issues which kept drawing us to Helena during the heat of the fight to protect our land. I can't remember what was under discussion that day, but I do remember that I wanted to tap them on the shoulder and ask, what was the end of the sentence?

Only members spoke in public or on radio or TV. The easiest target for the staff was the current chair. Once, during my term as chair, when I reprimanded my son Tom for some misdeed, he just looked at me with a dead pan expression and said, "Ma, when we want to hear from you, we'll turn on the TV."

Within the first six months of its inception, NPRC initiated a lawsuit against the Montana Power Company (MPC) seeking to prohibit continuation of construction on Colstrip generating plants 1 & 2 until the requirements for a permit had been met. MPC stated they were acting within the law while constructing the plant "as long as they weren't getting to the major portion of the polluting device (the burner and boiler)." But the court ruled against us, yet another example of what Senator Mansfield called "executive arrogance."

Wally McRae predicted that power-company dollars would win, regardless of the impact on the environment or the incompetence of the agencies upholding the law. He allowed that Montana Power Company's legal stunts made a mockery of the Board of Health, the Legislature and the people of Montana. And Fletcher Newby, director of the Environmental Quality Council, charged the state health department with relying on incomplete information provided solely by the power company.

Electricity generated at the Colstrip mine-mouth would be sent east and west over 765 kilovolt transmission lines (T-lines). The intended use of these super high-voltage lines resulted in a nationwide controversy. They not only disrupted farming, ranching, mountain valleys and scenic views, but the potential damage to the terrain, livestock and humans from electromagnetic-field emissions was not known. Russia had published some pretty scary reports of the harm that occurred to those who worked on the lines over an extended period.

On the television program "60 Minutes," we heard of a group in upstate New York involved in the power line controvesy. The program put us in contact with them. Later, again on TV, we saw farmers from a small Minnesota town protesting that their fields were being bisected by T-lines. We called the town telephone operator to find out whom to contact there.

Boyd introduced himself by saying, "Have Gun, Will Travel," the name of a current TV serial. Later, groups from all over the country with T-line problems met in Minnesota seeking some solutions. It was a peaceful, serious-minded group, but we learned that helicopters had flown over our meeting place, expecting heaven-knows what kind of trouble.

When Montana Power Company (MPC) wanted to string their electricity from Colstrip to the coast, our family had our own lawsuit against them. From the

155

start, we opposed the concept of creating the electricity in our back yard then sending it to the coast. We opposed industry mascot "Reddy Kilowatt" promoting the use of more electricity to create a market for more mining and more generating, and we weren't about to let them cross our land and ruin our view without a struggle. Our view was important. Our ranch is located in Hoskin's Basin, outlined by a semi-circle of sandstone rims. The opening scene of the movie, "The Little Big Man," starring Dustin Hoffman, was shot on this location, a view unobstructed by any evidences of modern civilization.

For a long time there was a gap in the transmission line where it was to cross our land. The ranchers and wheat farmers along the line were apparently convinced that they couldn't win a lawsuit, or else the money must have looked good to them. Instead of giving in, we went to court. The court allowed the rest of the line to go through. However, MPC did have to pay our attorney fees and court costs, and we received enough compensation to drill an artesian well providing water for our cattle on the south end of the ranch. Until then, reservoirs were our only water source and often they went dry.

In 1983, Wally McRae pointed out that the loss of our court battle over the permitting of the Colstrip units was, in reality, a kind of victory. The company learned the expensive way that it's not such a good idea to locate coal-fired power plants in a rural area when the plants are not needed. Trying to sell unwanted electricity to faraway places is not good business. McRae noted there was a pervading theory that NPRC had tried to prolong and delay the permitting of Colstrip units 3 and 4. "It's not true. We tried to stop those power plants plum cold, dead in their tracks." They were not only not needed, and built in the wrong place, but the cost of $1.8 billion was exorbitant and MPC had no justification in asking for a rate increase of 55% to help pay for their share. NPRC intervened in a rate case later before the Montana Public Service Commission for that very reason, charging that "ratepayers should not have to subsidize the faulty decisions made by energy companies."

Proving correct about Colstrip helped NPRC. We provided good copy for the media, and became recognized as a hard-hitting outfit with a history of being right. "We weren't negative, we weren't punitive, we weren't short-sighted. We were right!" said Wally. "And what's more, if we had stopped them, it would have saved everybody grief, embarrassment and lots of money."

The controversy which surrounded the permitting of Colstrip 3 & 4 only added insult to injury after the siting of Plants 1 & 2 and NPRC understood that MPC would never be able to justify the cost to the ratepayers. Though they tried to get Governor Tom Judge to take a stand, he kept insisting he had to be neutral, as it was up to the Board of Natural Resources to make the decision.

THE SUNDANCE KID RIDES AGAIN

During this time, we were planning our most ambitious money-raising event yet; a reception in Billings to honor Robert Redford, followed by a showing of his 1969 movie, "Butch Cassidy and the Sundance Kid." Redford was to make an appearance and make a few remarks after the movie. We invited many state officials and political allies to this event including Governor Judge. Then, just a few days before our big reception, Governor Judge openly came out in favor of granting the permits to build Colstrip 3 and 4.

The day of our big reception arrived, as did Redford with his two children. NPRC staffers Pat Sweeney, Bill Mitchell and I met them at the airport and ushered them quietly into an empty hangar for a short briefing before the press conference scheduled at Eastern Montana College. The kids loved it, and Redford caught on quickly.

Redford preferred to stay in a house, so Pat Sweeney offered his parent's home. The reception proved to be a festive success, with everyone reacting well to Redford's friendliness and boyish charm. Then, Governor Judge appeared, accompanied by his wife, Carol and an aide. During his term of office, Judge had tried to induce more producers to come to Montana to film their Westerns. He apparently thought it might help to have his picture taken with Robert Redford.

During the hush when Judge arrived, someone hastily whispered to Redford not to get his picture taken with the Governor. He took the advice.

When someone told Boyd that Judge had come, he said, "Keep me away from that bastard," only to turn around and come face to face with him. So Boyd put his arm around Judge's shoulder (a typical Boyd gesture) and said, "I want to be able to tell my kids that I put my arm around the biggest chicken-shit, son-of-a-bitch in the state of Montana."

Boyd had greeted Redford by saying, "I thought you were supposed to be good looking." They were fast becoming friends, especially when Redford, who was doing research for a documentary on the Outlaw Trail at the time, found that Boyd's dad had been a member of the Hole-in-the-Wall Gang. When the time came to leave for the movie, Boyd announced he'd be damned if he'd sit through that movie. Redford felt the same, so the two of them talked Cassidy-gang episodes until it was time for me to introduce Redford on stage after the movie.

As NPRC grew out of the Bull Mountain Landowners Association, so the Western Organizaton of Resource Councils (WORC) developed from NPRC. Both serve as "umbrellas" NPRC for local affiliates in Montana; WORC for resource councils in six western states. On both levels, working together prevents neighbor from being played against neighbor or state organization against state organization in our ongoing tussle with big business and government bureaucracy.

NPRC has been accused of erecting fences to keep people out of Montana, and of being against everything: against progress, industry, jobs, subdivisions, against plowing up the range for wheat and against having absentee land owners instead of family farms. But there is an ancient Chinese proverb that well reveals the true attitude of NPRC members: "The best fertilizer for the land is the footprints of its owner."

A cartoonist once depicted NPRC holding secret, middle of the night meetings with "environmentalists," and "building a fence around Montana." So Chairperson Helen Waller, responding to such negative press, explained exactly who those "nocturnal, environmental fence builders" were: "Our members are primarily farmers and ranchers and no one knows better than a rancher the purpose of a fence. In the west, a fence marks the boundary line between one man's property and his neighbor's. It's existence does not imply that no one is allowed from one side to the other. The code of the West simply requires that when one does cross over that boundary, there are certain requirements of conduct."

We at Northern Plains put all our cards on the table and we stand by our principles. Our weapons of choice are homework, education, persuasion and, hopefully, setting a good example. We entered the political arena and were heard. We proved that a bunch of rugged individuals acting in unison can prevail.

MAGPIES AND RANCH FRIENDS

Even with much of our lives focused on saving our land from strip-mining and trying to put into effect overdue environmental laws, ordinary life went on at a slower pace. By 1968, we had sold our cow-calf herd, and we'd even stopped pasturing yearlings, which Boyd liked to buy in the spring and sell in the fall. His health was not good enough to do even this anymore, so we were just renting out our pasture.

But Boyd still liked to go to the cattle sales. Seeing two young dry heifers worth the money go through the ring, he bought them to butcher. One proved to be with calf. Of course, he couldn't have her butchered, so the alternative was to keep her, in spite of the fact we would be dealing with a first-time mother.

Fall came and we were alone at the cabin taking it easy, as Boyd had angina and couldn't do much. I wandered out to the corral to see how our heifer was doing, and found her stretched out trying to calve. Later in the day, I checked on her again, only to find she had made no progress. When I reported this to Boyd, he allowed as how he'd better get the calf pulling chain and we'd drive out in the Jeep.

We had pulled many a calf in the early days by roping the cow to a corral post, attaching a chain from the calf's legs to the Jeep. Boyd supervised the withdrawal by issuing orders, I'd back up the Jeep very, very, slowly, ready to stop on command.

This heifer was far from a corral post, however, so we decided our best option was to try and pull it out by ourselves. Boyd attached the chain to each foot and each of us took hold of it. We pulled in unison. It took a considerable amount of effort, and with one final, back-breaking tug, the calf finally slid out. Boyd had an angina attack and I heard my back crack!

Boyd couldn't move and neither could I, but the heifer who apparently had been saving her energy, jumped up and was on the fight! Rolling over on my stomach and getting on all fours, I found I could get up, which I did as quickly as possible, taking off my jacket to wave in her face. She backed off enough so I could help Boyd up and back to the Jeep. He had put his "TNT" (nitroglycerin) pill under his tongue and had slipped the chain off the calf's legs. We left mother and child alone to get acquainted, and the next day I was off to the chiropractor.

Though Boyd and I were often alone up at the cabin, we had our usual gathering of creatures nearby, including some feathered friends, our magpies. Magpies are not the most popular of birds; they are considered a great nuisance by many. However, when a young one falls from a nest and is rescued and cared for, it does make a great pet. It was in the fire of 1959 that our first magpie came to us. Our boys cut down a smoldering tree, which unbeknownst to them, had a magpie nest in it. Of its three baby birds, one was dead, one injured and one unharmed. He was named Isador.

He became a friend that would land on the head of an unsuspecting visitor, as well as on the heads of the family. Isador stayed mostly outside and one would never know when he'd come swooping down for a visit. He was never kept in the cabin and never became very tame. As the years passed, if a magpie would loiter around the cabin awhile, we always thought it was probably Isador. But we never could know for sure.

Gatemouth, our second magpie pet, was found on the Nilson farm when Kit and Hank were living there. Kasey, age five, brought it out to the cabin with her when she came to visit. We never confined Gatemouth, but fed it and talked to it a lot. It would fly in and out of the cabin, perch on heads, shoulders and arms, cock its head knowingly when addressed, and make loud magpie squawks when hungry. Gatemouth stayed around all summer and reappeared the following spring when we moved into the cabin. Gatemouth finally left us to join a magpie colony, and probably raise a family, one way or another. We never did know whether it was a male or female.

Although we missed out on the nuptials of the magpies, we helped celebrate a ranch wedding of our own when son Steve, then running the neighboring Brown ranch, and Jeanne Hjermstad were married. It seems history keeps repeating itself.

Jeanne was raised in Chicago and graduated Phi Beta Kappa from Wellesley with a B.A. in Greek and earned a masters in environmental education from the University of Michigan. She came to Helena, Montana, to work for Bill Bryan, also a Michigan graduate, who was helping environmental groups raise money. While lobbying the legislature in Helena, we became acquainted. Jeanne, wanting to be where the action was, soon joined the Northern Plains staff in Billings and married son Steve.

Their wedding brought ranchers and conservationist from all over Montana. They set up a teepee on the lawn of the Brown Ranch and many of the younger guests spent the night, either in the teepee or rolled out on the lawn in sleeping bags. The next morning groom Steve cooked sourdough pancakes for the gang.

The ceremony was held in a hollow by a meandering stream. Guests parked their vehicles in the meadow by the road then walked down to a slope where they could sit and overlook the ceremony. A sheer rock cliff was background for this woodland site, and I subsequently named it Cathedral Rocks. The acoustics were so clear that every word spoken was heard, even by those quite a distance away. I wonder if similar acoustics made possible Jesus' Sermon on the Mount?

Following the ceremony an outdoor feast featured rocky mountain oysters deep-fried on pitch forks in huge cauldrons of oil, and plenty of music and dancing.

Many toasts were exchanged at the family dinner held on the eve of the wedding at the Spur Bar's Chuck Wagon Cafe in Billings. Jeanne's Dad, Hans, made a joke about his daughter marrying into such a wealthy family. One that owned so many "Charter" airlines and "Charter" buses. All of Jeannie's Norwegian relatives had come from Minnesota. But, just as my parents had been uncertain as to what my future would be, hers wondered if their beautiful and talented daughter would spend the rest of her life following the hind end of a cow.

I began to see history repeating itself. Both Jeanne and I were city-bred and college-educated; each of us married a cowboy without a ranch. My children, then two sets of grandchildren swam in the ranch water holes, climbed up rock

Boyd visits with Ellen Cotton at the wedding.

Boyd, Anne, and Tommy

faces and hunted for secret hiding places in caves. They walked the trails and rode in the hills, playing Indian.

For most ranch families in the summertime, the secret to surviving is never to sit down. What kept things interesting is that you never knew who was going to drop in or when, as guests usually came unannounced. They'd just be "stopping by," even if they'd come from miles away. We've done the same, and when asked if we'd eaten, we'd assure them we had. But then the kids would usually chime in and say how hungry they were.

After our last ranch dog had died and Boyd had retired from active duty, son Tom presented us with the last blue heeler puppy raised from the original Australian strain. She had the sharpest puppy teeth and the longest puppy claws, and used them both to her advantage. Boyd named her Claws-Jaws. The last thing we needed at that time was a puppy, but we lived through her puppyhood and she attached herself to me when working, trailing or gathering cattle. I didn't know much about working a cow dog, but we got along okay.

When Boyd found that cancer, which had been arrested ten years before by lip surgery, had reasserted itself in his jaw and that extensive surgery would be necessary, he said, "No thank you," and that was the last time he saw a doctor. His doctor was kind enough to keep him supplied with pain pills, increasing the strength as needed, so that toward the end Boyd was in a daze a great deal of the time. But he was living out his last days in our cabin in the Bulls, in the country he loved and had fought to protect. That summer of 1978 was one of the best we had ever experienced; the grass was stirrup-high and emerald-green all summer long. Although Boyd stayed in bed most of the time, whenever visitors came he would rally and almost seem his old self — and all that summer there was a heart-warming procession of visitors. Many of his old friends from Jackson, Wyoming, came to have one more memory-lane gab fest with this teller of many tales. The last to come was Stan Steiner, author of *The Ranchers* and the one to immortalize Boyd's words: "When we die, America dies."

Daughter Kit had been staying with us at the cabin those last few days. I think Boyd wanted her to be home with her kids when they started back to school. He died in early fall 1978, just before school began.

LIFE WITHOUT BOYD AND TOMMY

It takes a year, as common wisdom goes, to get back to living again after the death of a spouse. I spent as long as I could at the cabin, returning to the house in Billings when winter set in.

I partially reverted to the city side of me: time for involvement in my church, for going to college reunions and religious retreats, for visiting friends and relatives in St. Louis and my sister, Louise, in Sea Island, Georgia.

It was during a visit with Louise that I learned that my son, Tommy, had been in an accident. He and a friend had been calving out a large herd of two-year-old, first-calf heifers, a taxing undertaking to say the least. It was a twenty-four-hour job and it meant many sleepless nights. When the last heifer had been calved out, they decided they needed some rest and recreation.

One of their rancher friends had just bought some team-roping and bulldogging steer calves, so all his rodeo-minded friends decided to congregate at his ranch for a little practice. All went well until Tommy went to leap off his horse to bulldog a calf. The calf ducked under his horse, causing the horse to stumble, catapulting Tommy, who landed on his head.

I was wakened in the night with the news. When I heard what had happened I didn't know whether to pray for him to live or to die. He remained in a coma for almost two years.

The doctors gave us no hope of his coming out of it. But we had to have hope. He had no visible injuries and had been in perfect physical condition. We'd heard of miracle recoveries from comas, and a friend whose son had come out of a coma partially handicapped after months of therapy, told me what they had done to help their son.

The therapy included a variety of sensory stimulations including playing tapes, talking to him and generally making a great deal of noise. While still in the hospital, Tommy's friends made a tape giving an account of the latest rodeo they had participated in. They even came to visit, with much bantering and fanfare, to celebrate his thirty-third birthday.

Later, when he had been transferred to a small, friendly nursing home, this same crew stopped by at eleven one night on their way home from a rodeo. The nurse on duty, knowing them from previous calls, let them in for their nocturnal visit. We all clung to the hope that even though Tommy was in a deep coma, our presence or words would get through to him.

He was the pet of the nursing home and many of my church friends came in to pray and help with the massage therapy I gave him every day. We wanted to keep him limber in case he came out of the coma, and we wanted him to know that we cared. The lady across the hall, in her nineties and in a wheelchair, would sometimes wheel over to Tommy's room to massage his feet.

For a long time I prayed for Tommy to come out of the coma, even if it meant he might not be his previous self. But finally I realized those were my wishes and probably not what Tommy would have wanted. I just put him in God's hands and found the answer to my prayers in the love and devotion of the people who sur-rounded Tommy and me.

One day, just after returning home from seeing him, I received a phone call that he had died. God in His mercy had released him.

During the time I was ministering to Tommy I lived in town with my son Joe's family, and had the joy of teaching little Mike nursery rhymes and helping with the new baby named Boyd. But living in a city full-time was not for me. I need the land, the animals, the wildlife and the C.M. Russell views from my window as the light plays on the grasslands and distant mountains. It is food for my soul, a constant reminder of my creator. I wanted to live on the ranch again.

DUGOUT AND FIRE

On the advice of our accountant, and from the desire to be back in real ranching, Charter Ranch, Inc. (me, Kit, Joe, Steve and families) decided to start a cow/calf herd. As we would be running a year-round operation, we would need a ranch headquarters with a house and barn and corrals on the lower ranch. Steve would run the ranch. So Steve and Jeanne and I decided to build a passive solar house together.

We knew what we wanted, having done much research through our NPRC spinoff, Alternative Energy Resource Organization, but we needed an architect to design a structure with a dirt roof that could withstand the pressure of being earth-bermed. We discovered Jim Coons, who had built an active solar home to live in, but was also up on passive solar.

We all worked together on the plans, and as far as we could see the layout was just what we wanted. What layman can visualize the end result from a set of plans?

Before its construction we were calling our house the Little House Under the Prairie. After construction, the Not So Little House. Now, we call it the Dugout, a suggestion made by one of Boyd's friends, who said Boyd always vowed dugouts made the best places to live: warm in winter, cool in summer.

It had seemed a bit pretentious at first, with its tower-like entrance, but we grew to fit it, or it us, and it does blend into the surroundings.

The north walls are earth-bermed, the south side is all windows. There are high clerestory windows which bring light into the windowless dining room and kitchen. The walls are reinforced pink scoria block raised by a contractor. The rest of the house was built by son-in-law Hank Nilson, with his laborers, Steve and Jeanne. We estimated it would take three months to build. It took us a year.

Everything had to be cut to fit, as the west end faced slightly west, and the east end slightly east, so as to get maximum sunlight. The front (south) rooms are three steps lower than the back (north) rooms. All pipe fittings are below the cement floor, as well as air vents that bring air into the house at earth temperatures and serve as our air conditioner in summer.

The high clerestory windows when opened, suck the hot air out and let the cool air from the vents in. The cement floors are colored and stamped to look like tile. They absorb heat from the sun, as do the walls.

We put insulating shades or curtains on the windows to keep the heat in and the cold out at night. One soapstone wood stove in the living room is our backup heat for those sunless days. Mornings can be a bit chilly here, and grandma, that's me, has been granted a few concessions. My Indian name became Two Robes, and I am allowed a small electric heater in my room.

The house was finished just in time for the arrival of baby boy Ressa, named after our good friend Ressa Clute. Steve had been named after his Dad's best friend and Boyd after his Dad's best friend, so a tradition was carried on. We keep track of the age of the house by Ressa's birthdays.

I moved into my own spacious room which welcomes the rays of both the rising and the setting sun. I look out over Hoskin's Basin, where this lower ranch is located. The basin is a half circle of sagebrush grass lands, surrounded by rims. On top of the rims, to the southwest, are wheat fields. In the "olden days," with springs coming out of the rimrock walls, this basin was a haven for the cattle herds on the drive north from Texas.

The ranch south of the headquarters is treeless except for a lonesome pine standing about half a mile from the house, west along the fenceline. It is a destination for a walk, a solitary, high outcropping of rock with the pine growing from the middle. As of now there are new small pines growing up between the rocks.

To our extreme north is Cedar Ridge. Because of its higher elevation it supports cedars and pines and has been the source of many arrowheads and other Indian artifacts. There is, or was, a rock face of Indian pictographs which fortunately was photographed and recorded because we haven't been able to find them for a number of years. They were not protected, as in a cave, so nature may have changed the face of the cliff.

As the years alter the appearance of our faces, so do they alter the face of the land. In most cases this is gradual, but as trauma or illness can turn hair white overnight, so can the excesses of nature. Fire, flood, tornado, or hurricane can cause instant radical changes to the land. A fire did this to our land.

BLACK SEPTEMBER

In the fall of 1984, while we still had our summer cattle on the mountain, the great fire started. Manageable fires are one thing, but the Bull Mountain fire of 1984 was something else. That year our governor was quoted as saying, "All Montana is on fire," and so it seemed. The countryside was tinder dry and the winds raged at gale force. Just a spark would start a major fire. Ours started not over a mile from our cabin and fence line, but the prevailing wind took it away from us. Of course everyone turned out to try to keep it under control, but with little success.

Attempts were made to create a back fire. Son Joe witnessed the gas tank carried by Doug Spaith exploding, setting him on fire. Doug was terribly burned and subsequently died in a burn treatment center. He was a friend, liked by all and the only fire casualty experienced in these parts. His death was hard to accept.

More than ranches were endangered by the fire of '84, as it burned in an area inhabited by "mini-farmers" with houses or trailers located in scenic settings on small tracts that were heavily forested. Government fire fighters tried to save houses by spraying a green detergent on the roofs. Some were spared. The fire spread so fast and the winds were so erratic, a crazy pattern emerged with one house burned, the next one left standing.

Were houses saved by wind or by prayer? It was hard to tell. A neighbor could hardly say I prayed for my house, but forgot to pray for yours.

Most of the fire-fighting efforts were in vain and the inferno swept through the pine hills for four days. Then another fire started, origin unknown. It crossed the highway some ten miles west of our ranch and headed in our direction. Joe and Steve were alerted on the fire line and took off for the ranch to open gates, so the cattle would not be trapped. The boys saw the fire following the ridgeline, headed for Railroad Creek, and tried to outrun it. This turned out to be a race for their lives.

As the boys came off the mountain, the fire came boiling over the ridge trapping the cattle where they stood. Joe and Steve drove ahead of the fire until they got out of our ranch and could head in another direction. The cattle weren't so lucky. Seventy head of yearlings were trapped and suffocated, or their feet were so badly burned they had to be shot.

There were two huge fires which roared into each other in the Bull Mountains south of Roundup. The fire jumped the highway and destroyed dozens of homes on small acreages and burned 145,000 acres of grass and timber.

As with all disasters, good and bad came out of it. The worst was the looting which was unimaginable to most of us. The best, of course, was neighbor helping neighbor and strangers helping victims.

We received offers for cheap feed to replace our burned grass and the following summer a crew of young Mennonites came from Kansas and Mississippi to rebuild fences all summer for us and our neighbors. The Mennonites only let us provide lunch on the fenceline. An older couple accompanying them rented a house in Roundup, and provided the young men with lodging, board and laundry service.

167

These young men were great to work with and to have as friends. When the work was done and it was time for them to go back to their own farms, all the ranchers put on a great feast for the boys at Sue Mikkelson's guest house. We presented them with T-shirts with a Bull Mountain logo to remember us by and they sang for us *a cappella.* We'll never forget their concert nor their friendship and what they did for us.

Johnny Brown, longtime neighbor on the southeast border of the home ranch, made the crowning remark. A neighbor, with whom he had been feuding, joined the crew trying to save Johnny's house, and Johnny was heard to say, "With enemies like this, who needs friends?"

The fire also spared our view. The trees on the near ridge remain green. But even the burn has its beauty. When the sun shines on burnt pine needles, they glow orange. After a rain, a child might think pine trees come in either green or orange.

Though the "40" was still my favorite short walk, one that I had made a jillion times, after the fire I could miss a turn, be unable to find familiar paths and feel confused or disoriented. But it was still a special place, and I would still walk along the edge of the rim rocks to get a panoramic view of the land.

Behind the rims the land sloped down into a miniature valley, surrounded with pines and rock formations that spread out like fingers. Before the fire, the effect was quite magical, almost a fairy land.

On the walk back, you pass by the face of a large rock filled with holes which we call "the mail boxes." We've often left notes stuffed in them or a small rock with something scratched on it.

Beneath the ledge under the exposed coal vein was a cave big enough for a playhouse and there were all sorts of tunnels through the rocks that the small and agile could climb through up to the top. When children or grandchildren were big enough, they would come here to play. They built numerous forts and tree houses in the pines nearby which they called their "hide-outs."

It was here we scattered Boyd's ashes from the top of the rimrocks over the country he loved. We scattered Tommy's ashes there too, and somewhere on the face of the cliff are Boyd's and Tom's names and dates chiseled into the rock. I hope my ashes can be scattered from the same spot and that these ashes will never mingle with the dust from coal being mined.

GRASS AFTER FIRE

After a fire, grass often comes in more lush and vigorous than before and so it was on the mountain, although the cattle had to perform some fancy footwork to get to it through the fallen timber. It showed up the grass on the lower ranch, which is more arid, with less fertile soil. The lower ranch didn't look like the prairies of endless grass described when the buffalo roamed the land.

Steve and Jeanne began questioning their grazing practices as they continued to take care of the cattle. Allan Savory came into their lives bringing the Savory Grazing Method from the semi-arid lands of South Africa. His method is based on observations that large herds of wild animals graze without damaging the vegetation, because they are constantly on the move. Grass needs time to grow after it has been grazed down.

Steve and Jeanne, through NPRC, helped Allan form a non-profit organization which became The Holistic Resource Management (HRM) Center. With a handful of friends who ranched in diverse but not too distant areas, they formed an HRM group which met regularly at each other's ranches. They learned how each place operated, exchanged experiences, and tried to figure out the best ranching plan for each operation. This continued for several years until these ranches grew comfortable with the new grazing concept and had adapted it to their own individual needs.

The advent of electric fence made smaller pasture divisions possible. By grazing these smaller pastures or "cells," then moving the cattle onto new pasture, the grass was given time to recover and grow tall again. Over several years, Steve and Jeanne worked out a plan for the entire ranch, including water holes for each small "cell."

By now, I was no longer active in the cattle part of our operation. When I went on a cattle drive, it was to pilot the pickup which accompanied our horse drawn chuck wagon. My role was baby sitter and caterer.

As I described in a letter to my sister during the long, hot summer of 1989:

I'm back in bed in the trailer having taken Annika, who sleeps with me (we get along fine), to the cabin for breakfast. I have my coffee and am looking out at a fairly rainy looking cloud that is muttering and rumbling. At least it will be a cool day and I don't feel the compulsion to get into my garden early to water and putter. What a garden year and how I have enjoyed it—everything is coming on now—snowy white cauliflower, broccoli, first ears of corn, first ripe tomatoes, cucumbers, zucchini, peas—all picked small and tender—buttercrunch lettuce that stays crisp and delicious—enormous red cabbage plants along the edge of asparagus bed, an artistic delight—and finally after years of effort, an asparagus bed that would be up to Dad's standards.

This has been a timely year for the garden to produce for we seem to have had constant company (nothing new to you). After trailing cattle to the mountain, we settled in and were soon joined by two male seniors from Vassar looking for a ranch experience and sent to us by rancher friends(?) who didn't have room for them. We lodged them in the teepee in the pines above the cabin, fed them well and got quite a bit of work out of them. Steve has a knack of putting the young and restless to work and having them think it fun.

Early in the summer of 1989 two unique guests showed up. Ressa came running in saying two hippies were coming up our ranch road on motorcycles. They wore holey jeans, had long hair and sported trail dust. One turned out to be my great nephew, Whitney Linman; the other was Holgar Schulz from Germany, on tour of the country. The two met at a campsite in Yellowstone Park and decided to travel together to our ranch, so Holgar could see what a working ranch was. They put their camping equipment up on the roof, and an all summer odyssey began.

Holgar took to cowboying like a fish to water. Whitney had visited us before so he knew the ropes. Holgar was a carpenter studying architecture. He was also a great fixer-upper and with Whitney as his assistant, they managed to shape up everything that needed fixing when not cowboying. As a parting gift, Holgar made us two beds with drawers underneath, the head and foot boards made of gnarled juniper.

The highlight for our two summer helpers was when we trailed the cows and calves up to their summer range in the Bulls. One could easily say the most enjoyable part of ranching is the cattle drive. Brandings, too, are a great social event, but they are more commonplace, and there is a lot of hustle, work, sweat and dust. Trail drives are pure pleasure and take you back in time. You ride all day and the chuck wagon is waiting at the camp site. You feast on beef, beans and dutch-oven biscuits and lots of coffee laced to taste for the imbibers. Then come singing, swapping of tall tales, and if you're lucky someone has included a guitar with his bedroll. It can't always be planned, but a full moon adds to the romance. Cowboys have always been aware of the vastness of the universe around them. You become aware of it too, as you curl up in your bedroll. The plaintive cowboy songs linger in your consciousness as you doze off to dreams of Texas cattle herds heading for Montana.

It was a drive such as this that Whitney and Holgar participated in. Arriving at the campsite they were the roustabouts who put up the teepee and the tent for Ress Clute's chuck wagon. The heavy cast iron stove was unloaded and set it up in the tent. Outside, fires were built for the dutch oven cooking and for the camaraderie. Friends and neighbors not riding on the drive were invited to come pot luck and join us for campsite activities.

Cowboys raced after calves headed back to where they had sucked last, while others chased down the mothers in a sometimes futile attempt to get them to mother-up; small children rushed here and there evading their mothers; the Frisbee games at first played on the ground got very lively when those on horseback joined in.

THE BIG DRIVE

Not many people have the privilege of participating in cowboy activities any more, and Holger documented the entire event on our camcorder, taking a copy with him back to Germany.

The spirit of cattle drives both past and present must have been in the minds of cowboy cartoonists Stan Lynde and Barry McWilliams as they doodled in the dust on the hood of a pickup truck. They were searching for an idea big enough to celebrate one hundred years of Montana's statehood. They envisioned ten thousand cattle, two hundred wagons and five thousand riders trailing from the banks of the Musselshell River to the rims overlooking the Yellowstone.

When they presented this idea, Montanans split into two groups: the scoffers and the lets-do-it crowd. The optimists were headed by Jim Wempner, who joined Stan and Barry in selling the idea, eventually forming the Latigo Corporation to spearhead the Drive. Heads were scratched for a way to come up with the finances and figure the logistics for this enormous event. Perhaps an outside expert, a planner of such events, should be brought in? But this proved to be disastrous, and the cattle drive almost collapsed. Montanans, however, can be a stubborn bunch. They were determined to do it themselves and they pulled it off.

The 2,700 head of mixed-breed cattle, plus 112 longhorns, served as well as ten thousand. The herd of 3,500 horses could be rivaled in size only by those gathered by the Indians at the Battle of the Little Big Horn in June 1876. Herding were 105 experienced drovers. Trailing behind were 2,400 riders and 200 wagons.

Jay Stovall, trail boss, went on his first cattle drive at age nine. Lynn Taylor was chief horse wrangler. Each person was responsible for taking care of and feeding his own horses. Picketing corrals and feed and water were the responsibility of the wranglers. Lynn, a veteran of wild-horse roundups, was confident in his experienced wranglers. The wagon master was Gwen McKittrick, who started his wagon train off with the traditional, "Wagons Ho."

This once-in-a-lifetime event happened thanks to endless donated hours, miles driven and meetings attended by countless volunteers. The national and international success of the drive was only surpassed by the enthusiasm of the participants who came from Montana, and from all over the U.S. and other countries.

Traveling about ten miles a day, the drive crossed our land, camping on the north end one night and the south end the next. The south-end camp was the last night of the drive, and we couldn't believe the solid line of headlights stretching from Billings to our ranch for this enormous final celebration held in circus tents with live music and dancing.

Headlines in the paper the next day read "Charters happy with concert despite damage." The article stated that the owners of the Charter Ranch were glad everyone had a good time, but that they had certainly not expected such a crowd. We were quoted as saying that the cattle and wagons didn't really do any damage, but that vehicle traffic does tear up a pasture. Although everyone was great individually, 20,000 great individuals were a bit overwhelming. The article conveyed our appreciation for the riders who stopped by to say thanks for letting them pass through the ranch.

Our own celebration happened the evening before. We invited the press, both national and international, to a deep-pit barbecue. Our visiting relatives Bud and Sally Schleicher helped us get the house and grounds in order, as Steve was a drover on the drive and unavailable to help. NPRC staff came to our rescue, cutting up old fenceposts for firewood and staying up all night stoking the fire until the pit was filled with glowing coals. Three, forty-pound, richly seasoned beef roasts, sealed in foil and wrapped in wet burlap, were placed on the coals; the pit was covered, then sealed with dirt so that no oxygen could get in.

We set up long tables in the garage for pies, cakes, breads and beans brought by NPRC members from all over Montana. By five o'clock more than a hundred people had assembled. Our purpose was to launch a campaign to break up the monopoly of the meat-packing industry by a few giant companies. Straw bales were scattered outside where people could sit while Steve and Jeanne each gave a short, to-the-point explanation of the problem. Some other folks talked and Senator Max Baucus, who rode on the drive, signed the anti-monopoly petition.

Then the feast. The pit was opened, the meat unwrapped and transferred to platters with the juices it was cooked in. If there is a more delicious way to cook a roast, you'll have to show me (I'm from Missouri, the "Show Me" state).

Members of the press from several foreign countries attended. The two we got to know best were Russians we labeled "Gestapo" and "P.R." But, of course, once we got to know them, they were just two interesting people. When they went through the meat line the first time, they said, "Just a little bit, please." They came through the line two more times! It was the same with the rocky mountain oysters. These are tender testicles taken at branding time when the male calves are castrated. We had frozen our "oysters" and saved them for this occasion. Joyce Lamphere, the wife of our Methodist Church minister, deep-fried them. Though she had never heard of these delicacies before, they disappeared as fast as she could cook them. So did the 300 dutch-oven biscuits cooked over the coals by Don Golder, Champion Campfire Biscuit Maker of the Bull Mountains. When the festivities were over the Russians asked if they could record an interview.

Jeanne Charter and Ellen Pfister met them in the NPRC conference room in Billings. It was equipped with a plain wooden table and a few mix-and-matched chairs. The Russians greatest interest was in our concept that the best fertilizer for the land is the owner's footsteps. They discussed at length how Russian peasants and farmers produced more on land that was theirs to cultivate, rather than on communal land. They heartily endorsed our effort to save the family farm. And they could not help being impressed by the fact that we worked out of the simplest of headquarters. We truly were "grass roots."

The cattle drive cannot be dismissed without addressing its counterpart, the Great Montana Centennial Sheep Drive. It was probably the greatest and most enjoyed spoof in Montana's one hundred years of statehood. Reedpoint resident and businessman Russ Schievert headed up the "Let-er-Go Unincorporation." He was well qualified as the self-proclaimed black sheep of his family. In addition, he had owned several bum lambs, visited numerous 4H Fairs, and his wardrobe included a sheepskin coat and several wool sweaters.

The Montana Highway Patrol estimated that three to five thousand vehicles turned off Interstate 90 into Reedpoint during the "Drive." There were as many as 11,000 spectators. The entire town of Reedpoint was involved, all ninety-six residents. There was a dyed-in-the-wool red, white and blue patriotic sheep. There were numerous Little BoPeep shepherdesses. Sheep wagons paraded along with the bands in the traditional manner. One wagon sported a sign: Have you hugged a Norwegian sheepherder lately? The parade was only to be six blocks long, but it was suggested, as in the good old movie tradition, if they went around the blocks enough times the sheep could outnumber the cattle in the cattle drive.

On a more serious side, while the Latigo Corporation had designated any profits from the cattle drive to go to a scholarship fund for deserving ranch children, the sheep drive raised funds for the Reedpoint library. They raised $10,800— twice the expected amount. The Reedpoint girl's basketball team raised money for its jerseys and trips to tournaments by selling hamburgers and soft drinks. The Spanish Club raised enough money for a trip to Mexico. The Reedpoint Sheep Drive became a successful annual money raiser as well as a tourist attraction.

OILCLOTH MEMORIES

We had one more visitor that fall of 1989. My sixty-six year old cousin, John McDonell Augustine, brother of Mary, flew in piloting his ultra-light airplane. John not only built his plane, but had logged some 8,000 miles traveling coast to coast and to both north and south borders of the United States. Shy and reserved by nature, he came to life when he relived for us his adventures.

Cousin John landed at the Roundup airstrip and telephoned us from there. After seeing the layout of the ranch, John decided he could land here, so I drove him all the way back to Roundup. The next day, early in the morning before the wind came up, he appeared, flying up our ranch road and landed by the corrals. He hitched his plane to a corral post and came in for a visit. His tales were not just of the adventure, hardships (which he didn't consider as such) and the fascination of scenery viewed from such a low elevation, but also of the people, their kindness, help in times of need and the interest in his unusual mode of travel. He had found shelter on many farms and ranches and made many lasting friendships.

John's saga came to an end that fall in Iran, Texas, when an unexpected violent downdraft caused his ultra-light plane to crash shortly after takeoff. This was a tragedy for those who loved John, but John's dreams were his adventures, and it was probably the most appropriate way for him to go. All of us would like just one more chance, just one more day, just one more...but when the time comes, as it inevitably will, isn't it perfect timing to be living out one's dreams?

Each of us has his own dream, and must carry it out in his individual way. Siblings especially seem to strive for separation from each other in their attempt to feel secure as independent individuals. The old English tradition of leaving the estate to the eldest son must have been partially based on this understanding. The family that can work together through successive generations is unique. A side benefit of the English edict is that the benefactor is exonerated from any prejudices.

So, as in most cases where the property is left to more than one individual, the time came for the ranch to be divided between the three remaining heirs. Both the mountain ranch and the lower ranch were split into thirds.

During the summer months, Steve and Jeanne operate their cow-calf herd out of Railroad Creek on the south side of the mountain from a teepee, modern sheep wagon and a set of corrals. They trail through the Pfister ranch, making the trailing more authentic as they no longer have to go up the old highway through the mini-farms.

Joe and Kit run their two-thirds together, taking in cattle on summer pasture only. Joe and the boys use the mountain cabin as camp headquarters when they ride through the cattle or have maintenance work to do. The rest of the time I am there alone in the summer with my garden and cats.

My gardening takes on a slower pace and it is a bit lonesome without the children. I have stools scattered at convenient places for more and more frequent rests and for thoughts of the past that come with my mellowing years.

I have implied that gardening is in my genes, although my approach is somewhat different than the rest of my family. While their gardens in St. Louis and the east are lush and productive, mine, here in the arid West, tends to be sparse and unpredictable. Soil, climate, length of season and available water all contribute to these results. The challenge was my motivation, and my main efforts were to improve the soil through composting and adding manure.

My children's gifts to me were often garden-oriented. Son-in-law Hank Nilson tilled my garden for me every spring, and saved his grass clippings; son Steve transported manure from the "Dugout" corrals to the mountain garden.

Growing flowers and lawn at the cabin took time. The perennials that could survive were poppies, columbine and purple iris with a few bulbs that would show up in early spring before the grass got too high. If I was late getting out to the cabin in the spring, the horses would have to do the initial mowing of the lawn and I'd follow later with my hand-pushed mower. Some summers the horses did all the mowing. In addition to my hardy perennials, I've managed to get one bright red rose bush to survive out there. It is planted by the front gate, and grew one single rose at a time. Every time I passed it I would quote the lines, "I think that seldom blooms the rose so red, as where a dying Caesar bled." I feel that out of necessity I have acquired the Japanese talent for seeing beauty in a single flower or rock or trickle of water.

In addition to gardening I have a "thing" for rocks. Son Joe shares the obsession with me.

The first rocks I collected were used to outline a planned flower bed along the far side of our first ranch house. I had just finished gathering all the stones I needed when the well that supplied water for the corrals went dry and had to be redrilled. The well driller came out, consulted with Boyd, and went to work. I continued my work in the house paying no attention to what was going on outside. A few days later I took the wheelbarrow into the corral for some nice rich soil for my new flower bed. When I wheeled around to the side of the house, there was no flower bed—all my rocks were gone. They had been tossed down the well to make the redrilling easier.

Summers at the cabin on the mountain ranch, I have become fascinated with the infinite variety of colors displayed in the lichen-covered rocks. I made many trips up the mountain trails to find special rocks to bring home. The best ones always seemed to be the farthest away or highest up.

One day while walking on a hillside near the cabin, in a place I had walked many times before, I came upon some colorful stones that equaled any I had gone so far afield to find. As the Bible urges us to have "eyes that see," I discovered I need not have gone all the way to the mountain top to find a closeness with my creator. I found the eyes to see in my own backyard.

The garden is not the only place for meditation and remembering. The cabin, so full of memories, is still my favorite place to be. And my favorite place to sit is outside on the patio or at the old wooden table in the kitchen. The table came with the cabin. Its round top is of rough boards shaped and nailed together, its legs are slightly tapered two-by-fours. Its place is under a hook for a gasoline lantern.

Anne Goddard Charter

Steve and Jeanne Charter continue the ranching heritage outside of Billings, Montana. Photograph by John Gayusky.

Anne and Steve Charter. Photograph by Darlene Joyce.

Charter family celebrates Christmas at the ranch in 1997. Left to right, BACK, Jeanne, Ress, Boyd, Donna, Joe, Bert Nilson, Steve, and Mike. FRONT, Anne, Hank Nilson, Kasey Nilson, Kit Nilson, Annika, and Jill.

When the Steve Charter family and I were living there summers, we substituted an extendable table for the old one which was put outside to be used when we barbecued.

Beginning with our first summer in the cabin, I bought a new oilcloth table cover every summer, leaving the old ones on as padding for its rough surface. The table began to take on a character of its own. The table was where everyone automatically gathered, people from all walks of life, some strangers on arrival, some kin, some visitors from far away places, some the opposition. We remembered them all by the table cloths they set their coffee cups on. When trying to remember when something happened, we would flip through the many colored, many-patterned oilcloths and memory would be refreshed. "Oh yes. That was the year when... "

When Steve's family was no longer living there, the good furniture had to be taken out lest it be stolen, a not uncommon occurrence. Old Round was brought back in, alas devoid of its coverings which had been sacrificed to the ravages of nature. But it's a new day and I'm starting again with plastic.

While peeling through the tablecloths of memory an article from a Sydney Harris syndicated column came to mind. He was addressing the debate between the environment and the economy at the time that nuclear reactors were being built. The construction was being delayed by "environmentalists" who said that water temperatures would be raised to a degree where fish couldn't survive. The industry spokesman said that he liked people more and fish less. Harris pointed out that "it is not a question of liking fish more or people more, but one of recognizing that the balance of nature calls for cooperation, not conflict, for cultivation not eradication, for reverence, not ruthlessness; for respecting the basic fragility of the ecosystem by making no changes that might have irreversible consequences." Of people involved in decision making he says, "It is not enough to be brilliant; that brilliance must be allied with vision, humility and humanness. Without these," he continues, "we destroy the very structure we are so ambitious to create."

Wendell Berry, speaking at the 1994 NPRC annual meeting, said: "Now, we must begin to confront the probability that human intelligence is not competent to control the problems of working on the scale to which we have been tempted by our technological abilities. These are people who see nothing odd or difficult in a world of unlimited economic growth and unlimited consumption in a limited world."

Wendell Berry encourages us to start with the people in our communities. Who exactly are we and can we make a difference?

Ranchers, who depend on grass for a livelihood, know grazing must be managed in a way that allows the roots of the grass to go deep into the nourishing soil, down to where the moisture is. When we refer to people as "grass roots," we are saying they are rooted deeply in the place where they live. Their base of action is their community, their concern is its welfare, their strength is derived from this rooting.

Such "rootings" are being developed with astounding successes in many varied cultures in this country; from inner-city neighborhoods and schools to the efforts to save the family farm. When the holistic resource organization began teaching a new grazing method, area groups of ranchers and farmers met together to improve their operations. This sharing gave them their sense of community.

Steve and Jeanne Charter are working on a new way to market cattle that is beneficial to the producer, as well as to the consumer in the community. As Wendell Berry put it: "What we have before us, if we want our communities to survive, is the building of an adversary economy, a system of local or community economics within, to protect against the would-be global economy."

In order to do this he points out, "We must be people who take a generous and neighborly view of self preservation, who do not believe that they can survive and flourish by the rule of dog-eat-dog."

So it is up to us, those of us rooted in place. Grassroots people need to change the way we live on this planet. How many seasons, how many stories, how many new table cloths will it take?

Words of wisdom are expected from those who survive four score and a few extra. For mine, I must borrow from Andrew Young, in his book "A Way Out of No Way." He says he does not pray for his children and grandchildren to be spared the struggles of life but rather he prays "that they come to know the presence and the power of God in the midst of the turmoil and challenge of their lives. And that they continue the struggle against evils and injustices of their times, whatever and wherever they may be."

To that I say Amen.

THE END

EPILOGUE:

THE ULTIMATE UMBRELLA

I have called our organizations "umbrella groups" and they work well as such. But I have found they work even better under God's Ultimate Umbrella. As I look back on my life and spiritual journey, I marvel at the Grace I received while under this protective umbrella of love and how gently one grows in Grace when surrounded by others gathered under this protection.

Once, when intent on praying for my children and their families, one at a time, I saw us all gathered in a meadow seated on the ground listening to Christ who was seated in front of us. When He had finished his message, He started walking toward a gap in the mountain and we all got up to follow Him.

The first time I saw the Camp on the Boulder during a retreat, I thought that this could be my meadow. Often now, when I pray for my family, I call them into the meadow, and once Boyd and Tommy, whom I had not thought to see among the living, were there also. Another time I envisioned Boyd and myself sitting with our arms around each other. This was unusual, for due to our upbringing, both of us were uncomfortable with public shows of affection. After his death, I regretted having missed the little hugs of affection and kisses at greetings and departure.

APPENDIX ONE:

THE GODDARDS AND THE CARTERS

Family trees as such fail to inspire me. In fact I found it humbling to see my heritage reduced to names and dates and myself as just another statistic about to be hung out on a limb.

These dry bones of the past, however, can come to life again if by chance a story has been handed down along the generations. There are white hats and black hats (in Western mythology the heroes or good guys wore white hats, the villains black ones) and skeletons (those long hidden from public scrutiny) in most every family closet. They have only to be searched out, dusted off and brought to light.

The Goddard and Carter branches, (I wonder if Carter is just Charter with the h(ell) knocked out) have born much fruit in the guise of documented history. Unfortunately, the other branches, the Augustines and Brushes on my side, the Magors and Charters on Boyd's leave most of their earlier history to conjecture. Hopefully some of you who read this will be better sleuths than I and will be able to add new leaves to the branches of our past.

Drawings of the original Goddard house in Brookline, Massachusetts.

Goddard Coat of Arms

ARMS: Gules a chevron vair between three crescents argent
CREST: A stag's head couped at the neck and affronted gules attired
MOTTO: Cervus Non Servus, "A Stag not enslaved"
SYMBOLIC: The shield is red - red in heraldry means fortitude, or blood, or a burning desire to spill blood for his God or country. The chevron represents the rafter of a roof. Symbolically it means that a man may hold high and responsible office and his reputation and character are above reproach and the country and the people under his administration feel safe, secure, and sheltered under a roof.

The vair is a fur and is always shown blue and silver, unless mentioned otherwise. The French say it originates from the time when one of their great kings, Charles Martell, fought a glorious and victorious battle with the Saracens (8th Century) and, among the spoils were found in large numbers, certain kinds of furs, and their bounty pleased him so that he presented a number of them to his noble leaders. In the year 726 AD, he created an order of the vair which the family and their descendants use as part of their armorial ensign. The crescents in the arms seem to verify this, as the crescent was the emblem of the Saracens and therefore is often used in memory of the taking of the trophy away from them in open battle.

The stag is a docile animal, but his antlers denote strength, while his exceeding quickness of hearing and his swiftness of foot make it a principal bearing in armorial bearings.

The Goddards

English history has been revitalized through many a contemporary novel. In England ancestors can quite easily be traced back to the time when they didn't know how to spell their own names. Goddard, for instance, comes from the Saxon and could be Goddart, Godard, Godred, or Godderts, signifying goodly or well disposed. Apart from these discrepancies in spelling, things haven't changed that much. Wills in the 1400's were deemed important enough to be recorded, giving us information, not so much about the person as his worldly possessions. They have proved, however, invaluable for ancestor search. People's importance through the years has been chiefly identified by material wealth, the biblical warnings about moths, rust and robbers found in Matthew 4:19, mostly unheeded.

The earliest branch of the Goddard family tree that I know of was John Godard of Poulton whose will was recorded in 1454. He was followed by so many Johns, I couldn't keep them straight. My goal being to establish the direct line from John Godard of Poulton to my family, I have numbered each generation to the present (1996): sixteen in all, encompassing 500 years.

John(1)'s Will of 1454 named the lands he owned, but also of interest is how they were acquired. During the reign of Henry the VIIIth a Godard must have done the king a favor, and the Church must have done him a disfavor for the lands of North Udmouth, County of Grants were taken from the Abbey of Bradenstork, and the adwowson, the right to name the holder of a church benefice, of Clyffe (Cleve) Pypard was taken from the monastery of Lacock, in order to be granted to the Godards.

The recipient of this Will, John(2) had changed the spelling to Goddard, and thus it has remained. John(2)'s property went to his son John(3) Goddard Vicor of Upham in Aldbaurne, as he was the only male descendent of the Goddards of Clyffe Pypard. At that time, the name Godard had descended from father to son for 370 years. He married Elizabeth Beringer, and so the direct line continued as follows to William Goddard, the first of this family to emigrate to America.

Vicor John(3)'s Will dated 1557 left Clyffe Pypard to his oldest son John(4) and Swindon to son Thomas. The direct line of the Swindon family became extinct with Ambrose Goddard of Rudloe in 1774.

John(4)'s heir, Edward(5) was born in 1584. He went to Oxford and married Priscilla D'Oyley. The D'Oyley family had an arrangement with the Crown whereby they presented annually to the King a tablecloth worth three shillings, in exchange for their right to the estate of Pus Hall (Pushill). Conjecture is that this was the origin of the word doily.

Edward(5) was politically active, as was his brother, Thomas of Upham, Squire of Swindon. The only difference being that Edward represented Wiltshire County as a member of the Parliament, whereas Thomas was a Royalist. This proved to be to their advantage, for as with ongoing civil wars, the party in power would vary. Each brother, when his party was in power, helped the other to avoid the fines and the other disabilities he would be subjected to as an enemy of those in power. Quite different from what happened to families on opposing sides during our Civil War.

Edward(5) died intestate in 1647 having lost his properties during the wars in spite of his brother's help. His son John(6) was granted the letters of administration. He became a member of the Worshipful Company of Grocers, a guild. (Two hundred years later his descendent, Joseph Warren Goddard, founded the Goddard Grocery Co., in St. Louis, Missouri.) John(6) became a citizen of London in 1691.

His son, William(7) was baptized in 1627 and in due time married Elizabeth Miles, and this became a factor in his sailing for America. William(7) had been able to acquire property, but had also suffered losses, as many of his business ventures involved cargoes on ships sailing the world's high risk shipping routes. And it seems he had a penchant for high living, especially when a ship came in. How much of this he shared with his wife and family, I don't know, but his mother-in-law must have approved of him, or had great concern for her daughter and grandchildren. Mrs. Foote, as she had become, had loaned her brother 100 pounds at one point, the collateral being a mortgage on his house and property in America. When her brother died with the debt unpaid, Mrs. Foote told her son-in-law that if he could collect on this debt, the property was his. With this tantalizing prospect he decided to sail for America moving his wife and children in with her mother no doubt, as he put all of his furniture and possessions in storage.

He sailed in 1665. On arriving in America he took possession of his property and moved in.

Soon after he left England, a fire destroyed the property he had left in storage and the dreaded plague was spreading through London. It was also conjectured that had he been following his father's political leanings and associations, he would have been at odds with the royal government then in power.

All things considered, on hearing the news of the fire and plague, he made up his mind to stay in New England and promptly sent for his wife and three surviving children. They lived in Watertown, Mass. where he became a freeman in 1677. It was necessary to be a church member before you could become a freeman. Like so many of the early settlers, he made his living as a farmer and teacher, no previous experience needed.

William(7)'s son Joseph(8) had been born in London about 1655. He died in 1728. He was almost a teenager when he arrived in his new country. When he married Deborah Treadway in 1680, they settled in Muddy River, later to become Brookline, Mass. His holdings consisted of about 72 acres which included a house, orchards, and meadows. The property was located on what is now Goddard Avenue and thus the line of Brookline Goddards was established.

He also had a land-grant in Deerfield, Massachusetts, dated about 1687. Deerfield comes again into family history through the Carters when they were victims of the Deerfield Massacres of 1756 (61)?.

Joseph(8) deeded his properties to his son John(9), born in 1699-(died 1785). In 1725 he married Lucy Seaver who died. In 1729 he married Hannah (Jennison) a widow, the mother of their son John(10) born in 1730. John(9), however, opted to stay in Worcester, Massachusetts where he had made his home and raised his family, so he deeded the Brookline properties to his son John(10) in 1753. Thus John(10) became the tenth descendent from John Godard of Poulton-a matter of about 300 years.

John(10), who became known as John the Wagon Master, was able to add another 34 acres to the 72 he received from his father, the original Goddard farm. His first wife died, in childbirth. His second wife Hannah Seaver bore him 12 sons and 3 daughters, of these 10 grew to adulthood.

If we thought some of the English ancestors were politically active, they couldn't hold a candle to the Wagon Master. Between 1763 and 1770 he held about every job the county had to offer: constable, Surveyor of Highways, Selectman, Assessor and Collector of the town of Brookline and for several years thereafter he acted as moderator of the annual town meeting. From here he became a Representative in the State Legislature, but declined to run for Governor or the U.S. Senate.

By 1770 confrontations with the British were growing. John(10) was a witness to British soldiers firing on the townspeople in State Street in Brookline, and he witnessed to such at their trial. In 1772 he was on a committee concerned with "violation of the rights of the Province" by the British and helped with the Bill of Rights drawn up by the citizens of Brookline. As the inevitability of outright war approached, he was selected in 1774 to be on a committee of 5 to assess the readiness of the town in case of an unexpected attack by the British. At the same time he and one other representative of Brookline were sent to the Provincial Congress in Concord. They reported the support of the Brookline residents if Independence was declared.

This same year John(10) received his appointment as Wagon Master for the Army, his job, to see that supplies were transported as directed by the Commissary General. It was up to him to hire the Wagoners, but this proved no easy task as they already had all the work they could handle hauling people's private possessions as they attemped to get out of Boston. The farmers were in the midst of harvest, so their wagons were also unavailable. Seeing no solution for this, he handed in his resignation, not wanting to waste the taxpayer's money or his time. The council passed a resolution that wagoners could be conscripted by Impress by the authority of the Justices of Peace and Selectmen, but this didn't work either. The Teamsters still refused to haul supplies, consequences be damned.

This all changed, however, when in July 1775, Washington's troops surrounded the beleaguered town of Boston. The British had marched right through Brookline, and there had been no fighting from the town's fort, with six mounted cannons. Located on the Muddy River, which runs into the Charles, this part of the town was later incorporated into Boston, but at the time it provided Brookline with a seaport.

Boston was held by the British forces under General Howe, and was inhabited by Tory sympathizers and those who had been unable to get out ahead of the occupation.

General Washington appointed John(10) Goddard, Wagon Master, under his command in July of '75, as he was preparing for the siege of Boston.

This story of March 4th, 1776 was told by John(10)'s son Joseph(11), who was just 14 at the time of this historical event. Although not his exact words, this is the story as he might have told it to his children and grandchildren over and over again.

> Although I was just 14, I was already a good farmer and had driven
> oxen ever since I could remember, so when I begged my father to let me
> help haul the army supplies, he let me join the ranks. For weeks we hauled
> army supplies secretly at night right past Howe's troops, collecting them
> for the attack on Boston. They were being stored right on our farm and I
> must say these were exciting if scary times.

184

The powder and shot were hidden in a square, hip-roofed house with a central chimney and the cannon were hidden under the hay in the barn. In another small building several hundred pounds of gun powder were stored in the loft while a garrison of soldiers was housed underneath. If that gun powder had gone off, it would have been the end of every building on our farm and of all of us too.

What made the situation even more precarious was that a Tory family lived just a few fields away. They often entertained British officers and their wives, and on occasion these officers would ride through the woods surrounding us looking for anything suspicious. Luckily, there were no give away signs and they didn't ride at night. The officer's wives and the Tory sympathizers who lived in Boston with their high falutin' ways made quite a contrast to our hardworking mothers. They dressed in brocaded satin, and wore high, powdered wigs, while our mother's dressed in homespun linsey-woolsey. Our mother's clothes were made from scratch; producing their own wool, they spun it, wove it into cloth, then dyed it with butternuts. Perhaps secrecy was possible because the glamour of "fine ladies" distracted the officers from closer scrutiny of their duty. In contrast, our mothers were involved in our efforts every step of the way.

We were gathering supplies in preparation for the fortification which was to be built on Dorchester Heights all in one night. On the moonlit night of March the 4th, 1776, 300 yoke of oxen moved soundlessly over the rutted track and I drove one of them. When we prepared our wagons we wrapped the wheels in hay so that they wouldn't make any noise. Our orders were: no cracking of whips, no shouts to the oxen. We were to guide the oxen with just a touch of the goad.

The night before, we had cut small slender trees from the woods of Dorchester and Milton. Long bundles of these sticks were tied together making what we called fascines. These too were hauled to the site of the fort, along with the cannons, the cannon balls and powder kegs, and bullets for the long flintlock guns all hidden under hay, of course.

Once there, the fascines were piled lengthwise in rows with hay in between. The whole was then covered with dirt. Behind this barricade the cannon, guns and ammunition were positioned. What a thrill it was to hear that General Howe was awakened the next morning by our cannon fire. We were also told that he had said we Americans had accomplished more in one night than his soldiers could have done in six weeks. Of course, many of his troops were Hessians, conscripted to fight, and their hearts weren't in it the way ours were. We will always remember March 17th, St. Patrick's Day, for that is when General Howe evacuated his troops from Boston.

General Washington urged Dad to continue his service, but he declined, after all he had his farm to run and all us boys to raise.

An undated newspaper clipping from some 120 years later, stated that "Mr. Abijah Warren Goddard will be 95 in March 1898," so it was probably printed shortly before that date. The clipping adds this story to my text:

> Several hundred pounds of gun powder were still stored in the loft of a shed opposite the house, and a sentinel was kept on the place to guard the premises, but after a time it was thought best to remove the stores to Concord, and Mr. John Goddard himself drove one of the teams the whole distance, and the powder was used at the battle of Lexington. He was an eye witness to that battle and on that day loaned his fowling piece to a Brookline man, who was anxious to fight, and had no gun. In some way, the gun was lost during the action. Years after, when Mr. Goddard was on his way to Sherborn, he stopped for refreshment at the Wayside Inn. There, over the wide chimney piece, he saw a gun, which upon examining, he found it to be the one lost on the memorable 19th of April. The landlord gave it up to it's owner who brought it home and kept it until his grandson was old enough to use it. It is still in the Goddard family, though not in Brookline. General Washington highly appreciated the service of Mr. Goddard, and urged him to accompany the army to New York, but he declined, as he thought his duty was to his family.

His son's grew into men who lived diverse and interesting lives, carrying on a proud heritage.

Son, Sam, married Mehitable Dawes. Her father, William Dawes and Paul Revere rode through Boston and Brookline the night of April 18, 1775 to warn the countryside that the British were on their way to try and capture the military supplies stored in Concord. Sam and Mehitable eventually moved to London and their correspondence with the folks back home has provided much of that day's family history.

Son, John, went to Oxford planning to become a minister. Apparently, only those preparing for the ministry had to go to college at that time; doctors learned from doctors, lawyers from lawyers etc. and anyone willing, could be a school teacher. He changed his mind, however, and would have liked to have been a doctor, but his health was not the best and he felt he would not be able to endure the long hours and trips that would be expected of him. So, John found a partner to go in the apothecary business with him and to set up shop in Portsmouth, N.H. But because of the war, he had a problem, there were no drugs available in America. They could be purchased in Spain, however, so off he sailed to that port. Unfortunately, the ship he was on was captured by the British and he was taken prisoner. He was so starved on the prison ship, that he was able to escape through a porthole and to swim to an American ship. However, that ship too was captured, and he remained a prisoner until his father was able to buy his freedom in an exchange. After being released, it took him a long time to make his way home. When he knocked on his door, he was so emaciated that his own mother didn't recognize him. Not expecting him, she thought he was a stranger. He didn't give up his dream, however, and was eventually able to open an Apothecary as planned.

Son, Ben, born about 1773, was a farmer and merchant and the stories we heard as children in the early 1900's must have been about him, although we were told little of the history or background. We had heard from our parents tales of the Goddard house which had a widow's walk, where wives could look for the return of their ships, and a secret room where possibly someone could have hidden from Indians or the British.

I have since learned that many houses built in those days had a trap door in the ceiling to get to the second story. A house belonging to the Gardner family and later bought by Benjamin Goddard, actually did have a secret room. The Goddards found a hidden, sliding panel in the ceiling which hadn't been opened in over a 100 years. All that was in it was an old sword, but it had the Gardner family crest on it.

We also liked to hear about the ships that sailed to all those exotic ports to take American products overseas, and bring back their priceless cargoes. We were led to believe that the variety of porcelain vases that lined some of the closet shelves of our childhood home in St. Louis, Mo. were part of those cargoes and of great value. When our home was sold however, and many antiques disposed of, it was discovered they were mostly replicas, not originals.

Well, Ben, although brought up a farmer, got into the shipping business like his forefather, William(7), only he began trading in the opposite direction, America to England. He underwent the usual successes and losses, until one of his ship's cargo arrived intact, and turned out to be so valuable that he was able to retire at age 46. He made enough to buy the estate which included the house where Sam's wife, Mahitable Dawes, lived as a child. Ben's father and mother lived out their days in the smaller house on the property. His father, John the Wagon Master died in 1816, age 86. His mother died in 1821 also at the age of 86.

A book titled Nathaniel Goddard, A Boston Merchant, 1767-1853, was printed in 1906 at the Riverside Press for Private Distribution. Nathaniel was the 4th son of John(10) the Wagon Master and the one who had the most trouble with his Dad while growing up. He didn't like any part of farming and from an early age had his heart set on being a merchant. John(10) considered this an unrealistic, youthful dream and deemed he knew best which career his son should follow since he refused to farm. He forced him into numerous painful, unsuccessful apprenticeships, refusing to give him the 100 pounds ($333.33) he had given to each of his older brothers to help them start their careers. Nathaniel finally was apprenticed to his brother John, who had the apothecary in Portsmouth, N.H. In those days, as now a drug store was not limited to drugs, for it carried about everything needed by the townspeople from wine and groceries to ironware. Nathaniel learned some doctoring and the retail trade, but his heart was still set on being a merchant. Finally realizing this, his father agreed to help. He raised 120 pounds in loans and gave him the same 100 pounds in value he had given each of the brothers. Thus, with a capital of about $566.60, Nathaniel was able to sail to Passauraquoddy Bay, to set up a store, selling to disbanded British troops, Tory refugees, roving Indians, and English convicts. It was a rough, dangerous, lonely life, but in the first year he increased his capital to $1000. He stayed with it for seven years, then turned the management of his store over to Colonel Trescott, whom he characterized as "part of the noblest work of God, an honest man". He was now free to go to Boston, get married and become wealthy, owning many ships which carried his cargoes to all the known ports of trade.

During the lean years, (he had been his mother's favorite) his mother always stood up for him and tried to encourage him. She once said, "Don't worry, something will turn up."

His reply, "Perhaps so, Ma'am, but not unless I turn it up."

Son Joseph(11), who told the story of the night of March 4th, inherited the family estate, the reason being that he had no career as his other brothers had, and because he had always stuck by his father when he needed him on the farm. It was valued at 500 pounds and after deductions, he was to repay this sum to his brothers.

Joseph(11) was born in 1761. He married Mary Aspinwall, had eleven children by her, was widowed at age 69, and then married Mrs. Snelling of Boston, a widow age 45. In a family discussion about this upcoming event, brother Nathaniel said, "The paper may say 'Married, Mr. Joseph Goddard of Brookline, age 70 to Mrs. Snelling of Boston, age 45; may this youthful couple be happy in wedlock another century.'"

"Uncle Joe" according to Nathaniel, predicted that he would die at age 86, saying his father and grandfather had died at that age and that it would be disrespectful of him to live longer. He died in 1846, age 85.

Joseph(11) lived on the family estate all his life and left it to his son, Abijiah Warren(12) Goddard in 1831.

From undated newspaper article:

> Another son of Captain Joseph Goddard is Mr. Abijah Warren Goddard, who lives in Goddard Ave in the house next to the old one, which was built in order to have more modern conveniences than the other afforded. He was born in 1803 and will be 95 in March of 1898. He distinctly remembers seeing, from Goddard Heights, the Chesapeake sail down Boston Harbor, June 1, 1813 to fight the Shannon. Mr. Goddard had always been active in business and has represented the town in the state legislature. His daughter, Mrs. Watson, (Miss Eliza Goddard), and her daughter, Miss Watson, reside with Mr. Goddard, making seven generations of the Goddard family born on this historic farm.

The name Warren was introduced into the family when a son was born to John(10) Wagon Master, shortly after the Battle of Bunker Hill. He was so dedicated to the cause that he carried his son to the site, sword by his side, and had him christened Warren, in honor of General Joseph Warren.

In the newspaper clipping was pictured two charming colonial farm houses, the second showing the date, 1767 on the chimney. The house was built by John, the Wagon Master for his growing family.

> The old Goddard house, still standing has it's date, 1767, painted on the chimney, but it took the place of one far more ancient which stood nearby. The Goddard family may well be proud of it's genealogy, for from the retirement of this secluded farm have gone forth men who have become a power, both in Europe and America in various walks of life, and men whose patriotism has brought them to the front in every emergency when their adopted country needed them.

Abijiah's son, Joseph Warren(13) is my grandfather. Warren Goddard(14) is my father, and Joseph Warren Charter, my son.

It has been 500 years, 14 generations from John Goddard of Poulton to Warren Goddard of St. Louis. My brother George(15) and his son, John(16) continue this line of descent.

The genealogy of the Goddard family reveals that through the years Goddard men have lived up to the symbolic interpretations of their crest: they have defended their country and their towns; provided leadership; displayed character and gained reputations beyond reproach. It is a heritage to be proud of-and to live up to!

The Carters

Samuel Carter's life was a success story, but one fraught with tragedy. His father, also Samuel Carter, lived in London, England where son Sam was born in 1665. For reason unknown, he emigrated to America at age 12, landing in Boston,

Charter

Mass. There are many stories of young boys emigrating to America in this part of our history, but the details of Samuel's journey are unknown so we are left wondering if he went as a cabin boy, or in steerage with friends. Did he have any contacts in the new world or did he have to wander the streets in search of a job. Whatever the case might be, he must have been very enterprising, for by the age of 21, in 1686, he had settled in Deerfield, Mass., had begun to acquire property and become involved in community affairs, and was soon elected to office. By age 25 he married Mercy Brook and four years later was able to build a house for her and his growing family. The house was located within the fort opposite the old meeting house and was still standing in 1882, some 200 years later.

By 1704, married for 14 years, they had seven children probably ranging from around 2 to 13. On the fateful day of February 29th, he'd left home for some business in neighboring towns, on returning, he saw smoke and flames rising up in the distance from the town of Deerfield. Suspecting the worst, he gathered with men from neighboring towns, about 40 strong, to go to the rescue of the townspeople and his family. Undoubtedly, he was armed as I don't imagine they ever left home without their guns in those days. It was indeed an Indian attack and massacre. They were able to drive the Indians out of the town and finished the battle in a nearby field, but when he returned to his house he found his whole family had been captured and spirited away. His only trophy from this battle was a blanket which was listed along with all the plunder from the battlefield, so that all could be sold for the benefit of the town.

He eventually learned that his wife and four youngest children had died or been killed on the long trek into Canada. The three older children were indentured. After three years of trying to get his children back, he was able only to redeem the youngest of the three, Ebenezer, and to bring him to his new home in Norfolk, Connecticut, where he had moved, being unable to face living alone in the ravaged town of Deerfield, even though his house had escaped damage.

Ebenezer, apparently unharmed by his experience, grew up to marry Hannah St. John in 1721, when he was 24. They homesteaded on Clapboard Hills in Newark, being among its earliest settlers. Making the most of this, he was able to acquire large tracks of land on both sides of the highway which eventually became Carter Street in New Canaan. Following in his father's footsteps, he was instrumental in establishing this new town and its first church. He had been living there for 10 years when he joined a group called "Pioneers" who petitioned the Assembly at Hartford to form a society called Canaan Parish. This was granted them in May 1731 as recorded in the Colonial Record, Vol. 7, p. 329.

When the church was officially established in 1733, Ebenezer and Hannah had their membership transferred by letter from the family's church in Norfolk. Their names were the first on this new church's roles.

This same year Ebenezer Carter was commissioned by Gov. Talcott as Lieutenant of the Train Band, and became its captain four years later. All males over 16 were organized to protect the towns. The men were not paid but were led and trained by professionals and were always ready for a call of duty. Captain Ebenezer lived to be 78, dying in 1775.

John was Ebenezer and Hannah's only son who lived to manhood. He was born on Feb. 22, 1730, and in 1753 at age 23, he married Hannah Benedict, daughter of Thomas Benedict, Jr. of Norfolk, an old friend of the families, no doubt. They had seven daughters and two sons who survived and grew up to marry. But, in spite of the fact that Hannah must have been constantly pregnant or caring for a small baby, she was able to help her husband in his military and civic careers by opening her home for meetings and gatherings and supplying the military with meals and overnight lodging.

The story goes that on a September evening in 1780 Hannah entertained a company of thirty mounted soldiers who came to their house to stay overnight.

The next morning she cooked breakfast for them and then watched from her front steps as they rode away. Shortly after this, she was overcome by a congestive chill and died a few hours later.

The "Notes on the Ancestry of Anne Carter (Brush), (Great Grandmother Nana- to me), conclude: "She was devotedly loved by her family; her memory cherished and honored by all who knew her; and her name perpetuated by her descendants; each of her nine children named a daughter Hannah Benedict, after her, and great-great grandchildren and nieces in the present generations also bear that name.

"And this name of our 'patriotic fore Mother' has been chosen to designate the Chapter of the Daughters of the American Revolution, which her descendants in this generation have joined in forming; desiring this to perpetuate her name, and honor and cherish her memory."

Captain John, as he was known, not only built his house across the street from his father's, but he carried on the proud traditions of his family; military, civic and religious, sometimes being referred to as Deacon Carter.

According to Norfolk Records, the Continental Congress at Philadelphia, on Sept. 5, 1774 recommended that he be appointed on a committee to the several towns of the Colony of Connecticut and of course he became a soldier in the Revolutionary War, being commissioned 2nd Lieutenant on Colonel Swift's battalion, raised for service in the vicinity of Teconderoga under General Gates. He was transferred from this command to serve under Captain David Benedict in the 9th Co., 9th Regiment of the Militia in New York, City, 1776 which was under General Wooster's command. When Captain Benedict was captured by the enemy and died in their hands, Lt. Carter was in charge, and received the commission of Captain on May 13, 1777.

In addition to the above command, he was in charge of a Company of Minute Men who had to guard the coast of Long Island Sound, and be ready at all times to repel hostile invaders.

His most notorious deed was undoubtedly the midnight raid he made in conjunction with Captain Dockwood of Stanford, Connecticut. It was on a bitter cold January night when the two captains joined their parties to make a midnight attack on the forces of Colonel Hatfield. It had been so well planned and carried out that they were able to capture the Colonel, a Lieutenant, and Quarter Master and eleven privates.

John's son Samuel Carter was the 4th to be so named. He was born on April 22, 1768 and was 12 when his mother died so suddenly. He married Sarah Hanford on July 14th, 1789 and having to follow his father's brilliant career, the best he could do for history was to produce five children, the one we date back to being Charles Carter. His birth date is unknown, but we do know he married Maria Westerfield, and born to them in New Caanen, Conn. was Anne Elizabeth Westerfield Carter, my great grandmother, known to all as Nana Brush and the sixth generation of Carters since Samuel emigrated to America.

NOTES